LEFT-HANDED LAW

LEFT-HANDED LAW

Charles M. Martin

GUNSMOKE

First published in the UK by Nicholson and Watson
under the title *Gun Law*

This hardback edition 2009
by BBC Audiobooks Ltd
by arrangement with
Golden West Literary Agency

ISBN 978 1 405 68243 5

British Library Cataloguing in Publication Data available.

Printed and bound in Great Britain by
CPI Antony Rowe, Chippenham, Wiltshire

DEDICATION

I DEDICATE THIS BOOK WITH LOVE TO JUNE MARTIN, MY LITTLE GIRL-CHIP WHO HAS JUST REACHED THE RIPE OLD AGE OF EIGHTEEN. MEBBE HER DAD WAS THINKING OF JUNE WHEN HE WROTE ABOUT MARY JANE BOWIE. NOHOW, HAPPY BIRTHDAYS, DAUGHTER, AND FOR ONE TIME I GET IN THE LAST WORD.

Like always,

"CHUCK"

CONTENTS

GUN LAW

Chapter I

GUN-FIGHTERS ALL

ALAMO BOWIE came out of the scrub-oak thicket first. A tall grey man on a big red horse. One gun of the famous "twins" thonged low on his right leg, with the handle tilted out for a fast draw. The second gun of the deadly pair was absent from his left leg, and the reason for this omission was noticeable in the way Alamo Bowie carried his left arm. Like the broken pinion of an eagle that has been wounded in battle.

A second rider followed him into the quiet glade down by the river-bank. Tall and blond with Irish blue eyes, and the wedge-shaped torso of a saddle athlete. Worship and carefully veiled affection in those wide blue eyes for the old gun-fighter who had fathered him through the formative years. Sitting saddle straight up and proud, with Alamo Bowie's second gun riding in the hand-moulded holster on his right leg.

"Me and my Snapper hoss is getting along in years, you might say," Alamo Bowie remarked quietly, and with just a suggestion of regret for the passing years. "You mind what I told you coming down through the timber, Buddy?"

Buddy Bowie nodded his head soberly. Serious and thoughtful beyond the weight of his nineteen years while his palm rubbed the handle of his six-gun. Cow country from high Stetson to high heels, with the marks of rope and branding fire on his scarred rigging.

9

"Either shoot or give up the gun," he recited softly. "You figger Black Bart will bring it up here to us?"

Alamo Bowie smiled without mirth while his hand caressed the worn walnut handle of his forty-five. Wood that had been worn smooth and satiny by years of constant practice. While a studied reminiscent expression creased the weathered face to turn back the years.

"It was ten years ago," he answered slowly, with the drawl of Texas in his deep voice. "Ten years don't mean much to a gun-fighter, son. Ten years or forty are the same to a jigger like that. But I made a promise to Nellie the day we were married."

Buddy Bowie stared steadily with understanding reflected in his eyes. "I remember," he almost whispered. "You and Nellie adopted me and Mary Jane while you were still in the hospital. The doctors wanted to cut off yore left arm where Three-Finger Jack found you with his last bullet!"

"My last gun-fight," Alamo Bowie sighed. "Three-Finger was the fastest I ever faced for a draw-and-shoot. He's been dead just ten years, but I have never forgotten him," and the long fingers of his right hand gently rubbed the useless muscles of his left arm.

"I was only a button, then," the tall cowboy answered softly. "I remember you back there in Tombstone with a bullet through yore left arm. Black Bart sent you word that he was the fastest, but the law caught him and sent him to prison over in California. Mother Nellie was mighty happy to hear the news."

"He escaped three years ago," Alamo Bowie said quietly. "It might take him quite a while, but Black Bart would head for the Mimbres Valley as soon as he could. The years would mean nothing to him, nor the lawmen riding his trail. He will come, son."

"He promised to kill you," and Buddy Bowie hunched his powerful young shoulders forward. "According to the code," and the young blue eyes began to glow.

"He ain't the kind who would ever forget once he passed his spoken word."

The grey gun-fighter closed his eyes and fought his silent battle. Ridges of ropy muscle made a frame around his stubborn mouth while the little veins stood out and throbbed on his high forehead. The long fingers of his right hand twitched with eagerness to feel the kick of a bucking gun. A soft groan escaped from his lips when he shook his head.

"I promised Nellie," he whispered. "But a gun-fighter can't change his blood, Buddy."

Both men swung down from the saddles and faced each other there on the grassy bank of the river. Alamo Bowie tall and straight like a great grey Eagle. Buddy an inch taller and wider of shoulders. Blue eyes changing to smoky grey when he gripped his foster-father by the shoulders. Choked back a sob when the useless left arm dangled limply in his grasp.

"I didn't make any promise," and his deep young voice was edgy. "You said Black Bart was fast?"

Alamo Bowie shrugged the strong hands away while hell leaped to his narrowed grey eyes. His face was like a chiselled rock of craggy granite, and he bit off his words as though they cut his tightly pressed lips.

"You can't change a gun-fighter once he gets the salt of powder-smoke in his blood. You ain't never killed a man, feller. I'm telling you not to start!"

The tall cowboy stepped back a pace and set his strong jaw stubbornly. "Yo're ten years older than you were when they sent Black Bart to prison," he reminded grimly. "And so am I!"

Alamo Bowie smiled grimly. "I'm forty years old, and you think I'm an old man, eh?" he asked bitingly. "You think I've slowed up to a whisper just because I made Nellie a promise?"

"Ten years without working at yore trade," Buddy muttered. "It would be like me getting away from cattle for ten years. A rope wouldn't feel natural in my hands until the burns healed over and turned to tough hide. And a bucking hoss would spill me shore as sin."

Alamo Bowie stared without smiling. "You figger I've lost the feel?" he whispered huskily.

"Up there," and Buddy Bowie pointed at two dots circling high above Cooks Peak. "See those two buzzards floating lazy-like?"

Instinctive action loosed the muscles in Alamo Bowie's right arm and sent his hand down and up with the speed of light. Black powder smoke snuffed out the muzzle-bloom that tipped the long-barrelled gun just as one of the circling dots dissolved in a fluff of floating feathers. The tall grey gun-fighter stared high overhead when the second bird disintegrated beside its mate.

He turned his head slowly with the roar of his gun echoing in his ears. He was sure that there had been only one shot fired, but Buddy Bowie was cradling a smoking iron in his big right hand. Both men jerked out spent shells in unison, and reloaded before pouching their weapons. Alamo spoke first with an expression of wonder on his weathered face.

"I didn't hear yore gun speak," and shook his head slowly. "How did you know which one I would take?"

"Like always," the tall cowboy answered promptly. "You took the one on yore own side."

Alamo Bowie continued to shake his head. "Yo're fast, son. Too fast to get you anything but grief."

Buddy Bowie shook his head. Then: "Black Bart. I taken up where you laid them down!"

Alamo Bowie changed; changed fast. His thin lips trapped open to show strong white teeth. The strength of two arms rippled down through his muscles, and into the hand that gripped Buddy by the arm. His deep voice was raspy with a passion beyond his control. A vibrant penetrating anger that etched indelibly into the brain of young Buddy.

"I marked Black Bart for my cutter ten years ago, feller. Made a promise not to take it to him, but I told 'Nellie that if he ever came to me with gun-talk, I'd spell him the answer through powder-smoke. Hear me plain, Buddy. It's between me and Black Bart, and I'll hold it personal against the man who cuts in on the play!"

Buddy Bowie bore the pain of those vicing fingers without flinching. His blue eyes held steady to match the slitted grey of his foster-father. Curly blond head nodding to emphasize each point until Alamo Bowie had finished his talk and stepped back with a shamed expression on his bronzed face. He had talked long for him; had bared the secret of a gun-fighter's heart.

"Like you said, Alamo," Buddy murmured softly. "You packed the twins on yore legs for years. Black Bart answers to yore cutter, but he answers to mine if he whittles yore notch!"

Alamo Bowie smiled grimly and remembered the years when he had carried the law as special Agent for Wells Fargo. He had matched guns with the fastest in the south-west; outlaws who rode the owl-hoot trails in the far reaches of the badlands. Men who had lived only to challenge his speed . . . and had died for the same reason.

"It's a disease you don't want to get, Buddy," he said gravely. "You won't ever stop once the salt of powder-smoke gets into yore blood. Yore heart pumps faster and yore fingers tingle every time you hear that some fast gun-hawk is heading yore way. You know you have him beat, but you just can't take any rest until the day when you face him for a show-down according to the Code of old Judge Colt!"

The deep voice buzzed like the distant drone of bees

while the tall gun-fighter leaned forward with hand shadowing his gun. Forgetful of everything except the trade he had followed for so many years, and of the men who had challenged his supremacy.

Buddy Bowie stretched to his six-feet-and-a-bit. Feathers from the dead buzzards floated down and flattened out on the ground. His blue eyes studied them abstractedly while his calloused palm went instinctively to his gun and rubbed slowly. The gun Alamo Bowie had carried on his left leg for so many law-riding years.

"Gun Law," he murmured softly. "You don't know where it starts, and sometimes you don't know you've rocked hammer until the gun bucks up in yore hand to ease the pain in yore fingers."

The grey gun-fighter jerked around with a startled look in his narrowed eyes. "You've felt that?" he whispered hoarsely. "You've knowed the pain of hell in yore hand when some fast gun-slammer passed you by in the street?"

Buddy Bowie nodded without looking up from the feathers. "You taught me all I know about a six-gun, Alamo," he answered quietly. "That's how you've kept in practice, and I heard Joe Grant tell about you meeting One-Shot Brady and Three-Finger Jack. Those two are dead, but I can't hardly get my breath when the talk gets around to Black Bart!"

Alamo Bowie reached out and swung his adopted son around slowly. Searched the blue eyes and probed deep into the very heart of the youth. Then the grey gun-fighter nodded his head slowly and tapped the arching chest with a stiff forefinger.

"His name, son. And tell it straight."

"Huh? You mean Black Bart?" Buddy asked slowly.

Alamo Bowie stared steadily and shook his head. "You made talk about gun-fighter's pain in yore hand when some fast hombre passed you in the street," he corrected sternly. "You ain't never laid eyes on Black Bart. We both know that, but there is somebody else you never mentioned!"

Buddy Bowie lowered his eyes and dug a little hole with the toe of his boot. "Didn't know I was talking so much with my mouth," he muttered.

"You wasn't," Bowie agreed. "But I can read the sign, Buddy. Mebbe you better spell it out, and get it off yore chest. It might help some right now, and save a lot of trouble later."

The tall cowboy shrugged uneasily and raised his head when the sound of pounding hooves rattled down from the mesa trail. Alamo Bowie also turned to stare at a pair of horses coming out of the timber. A pretty girl of about twenty followed by a tall slender youth perhaps a year older than Buddy.

"Daddy," the girl shouted. "I want you to meet our new neighbour. I brought him over to see you and Buddy."

"Mary Jane is bringing company, son," Alamo Bowie murmured softly, and then his face changed when he caught the look in the eyes of the tall cowboy. "Remember yore manners, feller," he whispered sternly. "Mary Jane is yore sister!"

The girl reined her horse to a stop and swung down like a cowboy. Hair the colour of ripe corn-silk, and blue eyes that were much like Buddy's. Dimples in her cheeks when she smiled, and she ground-tied her horse and turned to Alamo Bowie.

The dark stranger dismounted and swept off his black Stetson to show curly black hair. Black eyes, and the wisp of a moustache on his upper lip. Black bullhides and polished hand-made boots, and he also turned to Alamo Bowie when the girl made the introductions.

"Mister Leslie, this is my father, Alamo Bowie.

Buddy is my only brother, and he is tophand with everything on the B Bar G."

The dark stranger turned to Buddy and raised his eyes. "Tophand with everything?" he murmured softly.

"Mister Leslie has bought the old Lasky place," the girl interrupted quickly. "He's registered his brand as the Circle L."

Buddy Bowie ignored the interruption and answered the stranger as though his sister had not spoken. "Yeah, with everything," he grated harshly. "Glad to know yore name, Leslie!"

"Yuma Leslie is the handle," and the stranger smiled. "Over on the forks of the Colorado and the Gila, I rated tophand."

"There's a difference between mountain cattle and desert stock," Alamo Bowie cut in slowly. "But a real cowhand learns quick, no matter where you put him," he added thoughtfully. "Double-rig or single-cinch; tie-fast or take yore dallies. It all depends on the kind of country you work."

"If the gent happens to be a real cowhand," Buddy added bluntly, and stared at the stranger.

Yuma Leslie smiled with his eyes. "I'll be twenty-one next month, and the Circle L is bought and paid for," he answered softly. "The money was earned raising cattle, if that tells you anything."

"I'd tell a man," Buddy growled. "Some folks shore work fast at whatever they do."

Alamo Bowie had stepped to the side where he could study both cowboys. He could tell from the hang of the stranger's gun that Yuma Leslie was fast. Everything about the slender waddy spoke of speed, and the grey gun-fighter caught his breath when his eyes swept down to the black forty-five Colt thonged low on the right leg. The ebony handle was pitched out rustler-style for a speedy draw.

Alamo Bowie forgot personalities while he tallied his findings. A few faint scratches told him that the trigger-dog had been filed away. Seven-inch barrel and balanced by a master. Hand-moulded scabbard cut away, with the bottom open. Swivel holster?

Wise grey eyes searched for a bolt and found none. Long-fingered hands hooked in the gunbelt, and Alamo Bowie shook his head one time while some vague figment of memory tormented him. Somewhere he had seen a face that resembled the features of the dark stranger. Somewhere he had seen a gun tilted in just that same manner. But where?

Buckskin Frank Leslie? The grey gun-fighter slowly shook his head. Buckskin Frank was in Yuma prison, and had no relatives as far as anyone knew. Yuma prison and Yuma Leslie. Strange coincidence there, if a man could make sense of it. Alamo Bowie shrugged his shoulders and stiffened when the stranger interrupted his racing thoughts.

"Yeah, I work fast," Leslie answered Buddy Bowie. "I notice you've been shooting off yore iron recent. Mary Jane and me heard the shots when we was coming down through the timber yonder."

Buddy Bowie dropped his hand down and stopped the move abruptly. "Shot a buzzard," he grunted. "I don't like buzzards none to speak of."

Yuma Leslie shrugged his shoulders and grinned to show even white teeth. "And you had to take two shots to do the job?" he chuckled.

The Irish temper in Buddy Bowie leaped to his blue eyes and flamed briefly. He caught the mockery in the tones of Leslie, and his deep voice was under control when he answered slowly:

"There were two buzzards, and I used a hand-gun. Yonder's the feathers."

"Nice shooting for both of you," Leslie answered swiftly, and dropped his eyes to stare at the gun in Alamo

Bowie's holster. "Of course everybody knows that Alamo Bowie is fast with his tools."

Again that fugitive something that was familiar to plague the memory of the tall grey gun-fighter. No one but another gun-fighter would use such a phrase, *fast with his tools*. Yuma Leslie belonged to the fraternity, and by his own admission he was a top-hand in the desert country.

"Sheriff Joe Grant introduced me to Mister Leslie," and Mary Jane tried to change the subject. "Uncle Joe said that we needed more settlers here in the Mimbres Valley. He said there have always been too many of the wrong kind, and not enough of the kind that makes a country grow."

"He ought to know," Buddy growled.

Alamo Bowie was watching Buddy. The tall blond cowboy was staring at Yuma Leslie with right hand rubbing the grip of his gun. Fingers trembling in a way the old gun-fighter knew from long years of experience. Gun-fighter's pain that nothing could take away except the bucking kick of exploding powder and speeding lead. An ache that throbbed and tormented like rheumatic misery.

Buddy Bowie turned away and caught his breath with a little moan scarcely heard above the whisper of wind in the pines. His hand flashed down and up to set the horses boogering when his gun roared. A little sigh of satisfaction breathed across his lips when the echoes died away, and the gun was back in leather when Yuma Leslie stared at the top of the bank across the little river.

A headless snake was writhing and twisting in a death convulsion where the grass stopped on the bank. A fat diamond-back as thick as a man's wrist, and four feet long.

"Not bad," Yuma Leslie murmured, and his own right hand swept down to the tilted handle on his thigh. Two shots ripped out and blended like one, and Buddy Bowie set his teeth when he saw another whipping body tilt down over the bank.

"Usually, you will find two where you see one rattler," Leslie murmured.

Alamo Bowie was watching closely with eyes narrowed to slits. He saw the second snake stop suddenly and strike with its headless body. Saw the supple wrist swivel when Yuma Leslie seated the smoking gun back in holster leather without looking down. While Mary Jane caught her breath and stepped close to her brother with a pleading look in her wide blue eyes.

Buddy Bowie jerked under her touch like a small body determined to have the last word. Then he checked himself abruptly and stared at the smiling face of Leslie.

"I hate buzzards, and I don't like snakes," and his eyes were frosty with challenge.

"That's what Mary Jane was telling me," the slender cowboy answered with a smile. "You've had a good teacher, cowboy."

Buddy Bowie shrugged. "That goes for you, too," he answered quietly. "Like as not, I'd know him by his handle if you was to mention his name."

Yuma Leslie shrugged carelessly. "I watched them all," he answered lightly. "Wyat Earp, the Clantons, and Buckskin Frank. Just picked up my own style as I went along."

Alamo Bowie leaned forward to listen. None of the three named had a style like this yearling stranger. Grey eyes studied the tilted handle with head shaking negatively.

"There was one gent packed his cutter something like the way you wear yores," he said slowly. "But he's been dead nearly ten years."

Yuma Leslie turned swiftly. "This *muerte hombre?*" he rapped sharply, and waited for the answer.

"Three-Finger Jack," and the voice of Alamo Bowie

was flinty. "But there is only one man alive who pitches 'em the way you do when yore iron clears leather!"

Yuma Leslie tried to smile while he studied the hard face. He knew he was under scrutiny, and he glanced from Buddy Bowie to the high-breasted girl at his left.

"I'd admire to know," he murmured softly. "You mind telling a man about this other *buscadero*?"

Alamo Bowie stared for a long moment. "Long-coupled jigger who writes poetry every time he sticks up a stage or does him a killing," he answered plainly. "On the Wanted Posters they label him 'Black Bart'. He throws down like you do!"

Yuma Leslie shrugged lightly with a little smile in his dark eyes. "I've heard of him," he admitted. "Fast as chain lightning, and he did a lot of time in prison over on the coast. The law caught up with him back about ten years like you said."

Buddy Bowie turned slowly and stared at Alamo. The gaunt grey gun-fighter was watching the face of Yuma Leslie intently. With head craned forward and eyes glittering with suppressed excitement. While his right hand reached up and rubbed the withered muscles of the left arm hanging at his side.

"Black Bart made a get-away," Alamo Bowie stated quietly. "He'd be forty-odd now. Fairly rapid with his tools, but like as not he's all stove up by now!"

His face showed disappointment for a brief instant when the dark stranger agreed with him. "Like as not," Yuma Leslie murmured. "A gent can't stay young all his life."

"You wouldn't know," Bowie grunted sharply. "You have never been anything but young!"

"That's right," the dark cowboy agreed quickly. "A gent ain't young but once. You mind if I ride over to the B Bar G to see Mary Jane once in a while?"

Alamo Bowie loosed his muscles then and stood at ease. He glanced at the flushed face of his adopted daughter. Mary Jane was tall for a girl, with a rounded full-breasted figure. Strong arms and shoulders from roping and riding, and now her blue eyes darted to Alamo's face and tried to read his thoughts.

"Mary Jane is her own man," Bowie said softly, but the change in his deep voice told of his affection for the pretty girl. "Reckon you will have to ask her, Leslie."

"Might be better for you to wait until folks know you better," Buddy cut in gruffly. "Being my only sister, I kinda ride herd on Mary Jane!"

"Buddy," the girl pleaded softly. "Please!"

"He's right," Yuma Leslie interrupted. "I'd feel the same way about it myself. No hard feelings, cowboy."

He stepped up and offered his hand with a friendly smile. Buddy Bowie caught his breath and stared at the strong slender fingers. Then he reached out and gripped . . . with his left hand.

"I'd kill a man who hurt Mary Jane," he muttered thickly.

Yuma Leslie jerked his right hand away and substituted his left. "Same here," he purred between clenched teeth. "That's one thing you and me agree on, cowboy!"

Buddy released his hand and stepped toward his horse. "It's going to keep you busy getting yore new outfit started," he growled. "You won't be having much time to visit around for a spell of time."

"You said folks ought to know me better," Leslie answered coldly. "That's one of the reasons I invited myself over to yore place. I ain't hard on the eyes, and I can get along fairly well when I'm treated like a white man."

"You and Buddy is both right according to yore own lights," Alamo Bowie interrupted smoothly.

"But it's going to take you some little time to get the Circle L running smooth."

"Not so very long," Leslie answered. "I brought eight men over with me from Arizona, and right now they are out working the brakes," and he turned to Mary Jane. "There's a dance in Deming Saturday night. Can I take you?"

Buddy Bowie had one foot in the stirrup and dropped it to the ground. He turned in time to see Mary Jane nod her head, and he bit his lip when Yuma Leslie smiled across at him. While Alamo Bowie watched them both and waited.

"It's a date then," the dark cowboy told the girl happily. "I'll ride over about·sun-down to get you."

"Steady, son," Alamo Bowie warned Buddy softly. "Don't go to fighting yore head like a Pilgrim."

The blond cowboy clicked his teeth and watched Yuma Leslie hit his saddle with one leaping jump. Mary Jane was also watching the young Circle L owner with a smile on her pretty face, until she caught the expression in the blue eyes of her tall brother. Then she whirled and faced him with a glint changing the blue in her own.

"You mind your own business, Buddy Bowie," she said sharply. "I will listen to Daddy Alamo, and you stop rubbing the handle of your gun that way!"

Buddy glared at her and swung up to the saddle. Then he swallowed silently and rode his spurs down the trail without glancing back. While the fingers of his right hand ached with misery. Only now he knew what caused the pain.

Chapter II

OUTLAW SIGN

MARY JANE came to Alamo Bowie when her brother had disappeared around a bend in the river trail. Her light blue eyes were misted and troubled, and the grey gun-fighter patted her shoulder gently when she leaned against his broad chest.

"I'm afraid, Daddy Bowie," she whispered. "Did you see the look in Buddy's eyes?"

Alamo Bowie nodded soberly. "I noticed it," he murmured. "I saw the same look once before when Buddy was about nine years old. It was in the old hotel at Tombstone, when the doctor wanted to cut off my left arm. I told him I was either going to get well all in one piece, or be planted the same way, and he argued strong against it."

The girl shuddered. "I remember," and her throaty voice was low and strained. "Buddy held one of your guns in his two hands and threatened to kill the doctor. The same one he carries on his right leg right now."

"He'd have done it, too," Bowie answered with a note of pride. "Loyal to his pards, Buddy is."

"But he is just a boy," the girl murmured. "Tries to boss me like I was a little girl with pig-tails."

"This new feller," and Alamo Bowie came right to the point. "You don't know anything about him, Mary Jane. Being my partner in the B Bar G, as well as sheriff of Luna County, Joe Grant told me about this new Circle L spread. Seems to me that Leslie tried to make trouble with Buddy."

"Yuma Leslie is only a boy like Buddy," the girl defended. "I think it is wonderful because he has already made a success of the cattle business."

"If he did," Bowie answered, and his hard face showed the doubt he felt. "It takes brains to make that much money in four or five years, even in a country where boys grow fast. If you asked me, I'd say that Yuma Leslie didn't show much savvy when he picked on our Buddy for a ruckus."

"Guns!" the girl sighed. "And you taught Buddy," she accused.

Alamo Bowie stiffened. "I've lived by my guns," he answered gruffly. "I carried gun-law up to the time I met Nellie."

"But you have been so different since then," the girl answered. "Except those times when you were teaching Buddy."

"He ought to know," Bowie grunted. "With trouble riding in to meet us most any time now, and I'm not forgetting you and Nellie, and the sheriff's gal."

"Nellie has been like a mother to both Buddy and me," the girl said softly. "And now she is worried about Buddy."

"Worried about Buddy?" he echoed with surprise.

Mary Jane nodded. "She says it's a disease. She saw you and Buddy practising; heard you telling him about famous gun-fighters you knew in the old days. Men like Clay Allison and Bat Masterson."

Alamo Bowie stroked a scar on his chin. "I figgered Buddy was old enough to know," he answered slowly. "He couldn't be more like me if he was my own flesh and blood. I know just how he feels when his fingers get to aching for the grip of a gun-handle. But we better be heading for home now."

He stalked to his horse and mounted awkwardly because of his left arm. Mary Jane jumped her horse like a cowboy, and rode down the trail to rub stirrups with him, and she knew that his thoughts were far away on the law trails he had followed for Wells Fargo. Trails that had led from El Paso to Yuma, and far to the north.

Only the chatter of squirrels and blue jays to break the stillness of mid-morning while they followed the river where the lush grass grew knee high. Alamo Bowie had found peace in the high New Mexico country, and the B Bar G had prospered. And then she noticed a sudden change come over the tall man at her side.

Alamo Bowie had stopped his big red horse and was leaning forward in the saddle. Staring at the broad back of a man in the trail not more than twenty yards away. The stranger seemed alone until a jerking movement turned him sideways, and Mary Jane caught her breath when she saw a young girl trying to escape from the long powerful arms.

Alamo Bowie stepped down from the saddle and straddled the narrow trail with shoulders hunching forward. Grey eyes slitted and hard when his raspy voice split the straight line of his lips.

"Tie her loose, hombre!"

The stranger was well over six feet tall, and muscled like a bull. A heavy red stubble covered his face, and his thick lips skinned back over broken yellow teeth when the sharp command jerked him around with both hands shadowing the two heavy guns thonged low on his bullhide chaps. So sudden were his movements that the girl spilled from his arms, and tumbled to the grass before she could catch her balance.

The red-whiskered stranger stomped his left boot to stop his turn and slapped down with both hands. Alamo Bowie stood quiet in the trail; left arm limp at his side. Then his right hand moved swiftly down and up with thumb earing back the filed hammer when metal flashed in the morning sun. His shot roared away like the boom of a cannon before red-beard had cleared leather, and the grey gun-fighter caught his bucking gun on the recoil for a follow-up.

Mary Jane hung in the saddle with eyes staring at the stranger. The big man was leaning forward with a stricken beaten look in his staring eyes. The colour of his dirty grey shirt changed swiftly on the left side. Both big hands opened slowly and dropped the half-drawn guns back in moulded holster leather. The huge bulk leaned farther and crashed down like a rotten tree across the trail. Then the rattle of rusty boots muffling the gun-shot echoed from the rocks in the canyon.

Alamo Bowie stalked forward and stared down at the bearded gunman. He holstered his gun automatically and reached down to help the fallen girl to her feet. She clung to him for a long moment before she could speak, and the tall gun-fighter nodded his head slowly and gently soothed her with his right hand.

"That was Red Malone," he tallied slowly to himself. "Wanted by every man-hunting sheriff along the Border." Then he tightened his arm about the tiny girl and turned her slowly. "Buck up, Bonnie," he said softly. "How come you to meet up with him?"

Bonnie Grant shuddered and hid her face against his vest. "I stopped at the B Bar G to see Mary Jane," she whispered shakily, and her voice was muffled. "Aunt Nellie told me that you all had come over this way, so I jumped my horse and rode over to meet you."

"Yore Dad is sheriff of Luna County, Bonnie," Bowie said soberly. "I remember him telling you not to ride these hills alone."

Mary Jane slipped from the saddle and ran forward to put her arms around the trembling girl. Bonnie Grant was tiny and dark, and just past seventeen. Her brown eyes filled with tears when she glanced down at the dead man, and Mary Jane held her close and waited for the sobs to stop.

"I knew you and Buddy were down here by the river," Bonnie Grant whispered. "It was such a pretty morning, and then I met that man blocking the trail. He pulled me from my horse before I could turn."

Alamo Bowie was watching the brush for some sign of movement. "Was he alone?" he asked harshly.

Bonnie Grant nodded her curly brown head. "I didn't see anyone else," she murmured shakily. "He tried to kiss me, and I nearly fainted. I tried to get away, and then you and Mary Jane came."

Alamo Bowie was rubbing the scar on his chin thoughtfully. Red Malone was an outlaw and rustler; a desperate killer with a long list of crimes to his credit. Sheriff Joe Grant would want to know about the outlaw's death, and the grey gun-fighter knew that the peace of Mimbres Valley had been destroyed. The outlaw pards of Red Malone could not be very far away.

"Mary Jane," he said sharply. "Take Bonnie back to the B Bar G while I ride to town to make medicine with Joe Grant. And after this both you girls stay close to the home spread."

Mary Jane glanced up quickly and stared at the craggy look on his lean face. "You think he had a gang?" she whispered.

Alamo Bowie nodded. "Sure of it. Now mebbe you can understand why I taught yore brother Buddy all I knew about Gun Law. We're going to need some of it here in the valley unless I mis-read the sign."

"Him," and the girl pointed at the dead man.

Alamo Bowie shrugged. "I'm like Buddy that away," he clipped shortly. "I always did hate buzzards!"

"He was going to kill Buddy," Bonnie Grant interrupted shakily. "When I said that Buddy was up on the mesa."

Alamo Bowie came forward slowly and leaned to

stare at the frightened girl. "He knew Buddy? Malone talked to you?"

Bonnie Grant nodded her curly head emphatically. "He knew you too," she whispered. "He laughed out loud and said that one of his pards would be glad to know that you were so close, and still able to be about."

Alamo Bowie stared at her without knowing it. "He mention the name of this pard of his?" he asked very softly.

Bonnie Grant tried to think and then clapped a little hand to her lips. "Bart," she whispered. "He said that Black Bart would be glad to know!"

"Black Bart!"

Alamo Bowie echoed the name while a far-away expression crept into his hard grey eyes. Then a smile of happiness and anticipation started at his mouth and spread across his face. While the fingers of his right hand slipped down to rub the blackened walnut handle of his old six-gun.

"Ten years," he said in a hoarse whisper. "I wonder what ten years have done to him? He was fast before they sent him . . . away," and he shook his head. "Long enough to break the strongest man down."

Mary Jane stared at him while a look of growing fear swept across her pretty tanned face. "Daddy Alamo," she pleaded. "You promised Mother Nellie!"

The smile faded to change Alamo Bowie into a man of ice. His jaw jutted out, and ridged up with ropy muscle. Sharp lines cut down each side of his long straight nose while the grey eyes glittered through the slits of narrowed lids. Even his softdrawling voice changed when he pointed to the horses and barked a sharp command.

"Hit saddles, you two. Line out for the B Bar G, and don't stop until you reach the house. I'm lighting a shuck for Deming to see Sheriff Joe Grant about business that won't wait. High-tail!"

Mary Jane and Bonnie climbed their saddles with fear clutching at their hearts. They had heard the stories about this tall grey gun-fighter before he had married Nellie Gray. Alamo Bowie had never left a trail once he had set his Snapper horse on outlaw sign. He had never refused a challenge until the day Black Bart had sent his message to Tombstone. And that day Alamo Bowie had been close to death from the bullet of Three-Finger Jack.

Mary Jane glanced at the helpless left arm and shuddered. "You promised Mother Nellie," she reminded again desperately. "I can see it in your eyes, Daddy Alamo!"

"I promised not to trigger a gun unless Black Bart brought it to me," the grey gun-fighter corrected harshly. "I'll keep that promise," he added more softly. "I'll even do more than that. I'll give the law first chance to round him up!"

Bonnie Grant caught her breath sharply. "You mean, Daddy?" she whispered in a faint voice.

"Joe Grant is the sheriff," Bowie answered steadily. "And a braver man than Joe never lived or carried the star. I remember the time . . ."

"I remember it, too," Bonnie sobbed shakily. "Daddy was wounded by One-Shot Brady not far from here. And you met Brady up there in the mountains and killed him!"

Alamo Bowie nodded his head and mounted his big red horse. "You girls git," he ordered sternly. "Tell Nellie I will be back from town after dinner, and not to worry. I'll remember my promise to her."

He hit his Snapper horse with the hooks, and roared through the brush with square shoulders braced back. Filled his lungs with the high mountain air while the old familiar tingle coursed through his veins and sang a song in his fighting heart. Gun-fighter's song, that is heard only by those who carry the salty tang of powder-smoke in their blood.

Eyes alert and eager when he came to the short-cut across Black Mountain and swung into the trail leading to Deming. Sheriff Joe Grant would want to know, and his old partner might want some help. Now there were two Bowies to give that help if it were needed.

Down the winding Main street with the red horse stepping high while curious eyes stared, and heads nodded knowingly. Alamo Bowie rode straight up the street like a man with a purpose until he passed the Drovers saloon down by the loading tracks. He reined to a stop when he saw a tall black gelding tied to the rack, Branded B Bar G on the left shoulder, and Alamo Bowie ground-tied Snapper and swung down with a question in his eyes.

A line-back dun was tied close to the gelding, and Bowie squared his shoulders and twitched his gun against hang. He knew those two horses and their riders. With the hot blood of youth driving them into something that might be avoided.

He shouldered through the swinging batwings and side-stepped against the wall until his eyes had shed the light. Then he walked slowly to the near end of the bar when he saw Buddy standing in front of a small glass of beer farther down.

The beer was untasted, but the tall blond cowboy was staring into the mirror of the back bar. Watching Yuma Leslie a few feet away while the Circle L owner poured a drink and downed it neat. Neither of the two saw Alamo Bowie, and the bar-tender slid a bottle of whisky down the mahogany.

Alamo Bowie tilted the bottle and filled two glasses to the brim. Whisky straight with a chaser of the same, and he wiped his lips with the back of his hand after making the customary pair of passes. His grey eyes wandered down the bar and stopped when they came to the hand of Buddy. The tall cowboy was flexing his fingers unconsciously. Gun-fighter's habit.

Yuma Leslie placed his thin glass on the bar and turned slowly. "You looking for me, Bowie?" he asked softly, and his dark eyes held steady on the face of Buddy Bowie. "You follow me in here to get something off yore chest?"

Buddy Bowie nodded, and came straight to the point. "I followed you," he answered in his deep voice. "Might as well say it now. You stay away from the B Bar G until yo're known better!"

Yuma Leslie set his teeth while the angry colour mounted to his high cheek bones. "Are you the boss of the B Bar G?" he asked thickly.

"What you might call straw boss," Buddy grunted. "And I don't care a straw for some of the folks who have rode into the valley lately."

"Speaking of straws, I'll draw a pair with you," Yuma Leslie answered very softly, but his dark eyes lighted up eagerly while he searched the face of Buddy Bowie for some sign of impending stampede.

Alamo Bowie saw it coming, and cleared his throat loudly. Pushed away from the bar when the two cowboys jerked around to face him. He ignored the scowl on Buddy's face when he walked down the room and nodded to Yuma Leslie.

"I'm still boss on the B Bar G," he said quietly. "Something you wanted to see me about?"

Yuma Leslie was crouching forward with no indication of fear on his dark face. He glanced at Alamo Bowie and raised his eyes swiftly to include Buddy. It was evident that he was restraining his anger with difficulty, and that he resented the older man's intrusion into what he considered a private quarrel.

"I asked yore permission to come to the B Bar G," he said hoarsely. "Then this salty yearlin' goes on the prod and tries to ride me out of the herd. Might be as well for him to know I don't booger easy!"

Alamo Bowie turned his head slowly and studied both

boys. "Offhand, I'd say that neither one of you chips would high-tail and holler for help," he answered slowly. "Of course, I know Buddy better than I do you."

Buddy Bowie slid in front of Alamo and tightened his lean jaw. "Asking you not to buy chips, Alamo," he growled softly, but with a note of respect in his deep voice. "Mary Jane is my sister, and I don't cotton none to this Arizona jigger!"

Alamo Bowie reached out his right hand and swung the big youngster aside without effort. "I'm telling you to stop fighting yore head," he answered evenly, but his grey eyes were watching the face of Yuma Leslie. "Just wanted to tell you that it's come like we figgered this morning."

Buddy gave back a step, and his eyes narrowed to points. "You mean . . .?"

Alamo Bowie nodded. "Gent by the name of Red Malone tried to man-handle Bonnie out on the river trail right after you rode away. Malone is dead!"

His eyes widened a trifle when Yuma Leslie repressed a sudden start. The dark eyes changed colour for a moment; gleamed with a red light that winked out as quickly as it had come. Buddy Bowie forgot Leslie for a moment in his eagerness for details.

"You smoke him down?"

Alamo Bowie nodded his head with a little emphatic jerk. "Yeah; he lost time trying to make a double draw. Red Malone always ran with a pack, Buddy. The rest won't be far off."

A tall wide-shouldered man came through the swinging doors and high-heeled it straight for Alamo Bowie. Grey at the temples to put his age at forty-odd. Five-pointed star on the left side of his vest; one forty-five six-gun thonged low on his right leg. Ruddy cheeks weathered by wind and sun, with the steady unwinking light of authority in his blue eyes.

"Howdy, sheriff," Alamo Bowie grunted. "Just rode in to see you."

Joe Grant nodded. "Howdy, Alamo; Buddy. I see you gents have met Yuma Leslie, new owner of the Circle L."

"Met him twice," Buddy growled. "And I don't like him no better than I did the first time."

"Sho, now, Buddy," the sheriff reproved. "That ain't no way to make a feller welcome. What you got yore hackles up about?"

Alamo Bowie took the play and changed the subject. "You ever hear of a gent by the name of Red Malone?" he asked quickly.

"Malone? That outlaw is wanted bad in five States," the sheriff answered. "I'd tell a man I know him!"

"He's dead," Alamo Bowie said softly. "I had it to do, Joe."

Joe Grant stiffened and pushed back his Stetson. "Sorry you forced gun-play, pard," he answered slowly. "The law can handle his kind without a draw-and-shoot."

"Mebbe, mebbe," Bowie murmured. "But he was packing crossed gun-belts, Joe. When I came across him in the river trail, he was man-handling a girl."

Joe Grant frowned. "That don't call for a killing," he growled. "It's the old gunpowder in yore blood, Alamo."

"All depends on whose leg is broke as to how bad it hurts," Bowie answered softly. "You'd have done the same in my place," and he hesitated to break the news he knew would bring killer-light to the sheriff's eyes.

Chapter III

HOT BLOOD

YUMA LESLIE was forgotten for the time while the sheriff rubbed his chin and stared at Alamo Bowie, trying to read all the grey gun-fighter implied in his slowly spoken words. An outlaw had been killed, all of which proved nothing to Joe Grant except that Alamo Bowie had lost little of his speed and accuracy.

"You could have brought Red Malone in," he said at last. "Ten years ago you would have done it."

"Ten years ago the chances are I would," Bowie answered thoughtfully. "But I don't carry the law any more like you know," and Alamo Bowie continued to stare down at his boots. "On top of that, I think a heap of the little filly he was holding in his arms and trying to kiss in spite of her struggles."

"That's yore range up there," the sheriff said slowly. "Mary Jane?"

Alamo Bowie shook his head slowly, and glanced at the dark face of Yuma Leslie. The cowboy was leaning forward as though waiting for the answer he already knew, and wanted to hear repeated.

"*Our* range," Bowie corrected quietly. "The B Bar G stands for Bowie and Grant."

Joe Grant expelled his breath forcibly and stared at his partner hard. "Our range," he repeated, and his eyes changed quickly. "You telling me it was . . . Bonnie?"

"Yeah; Bonnie. But Malone slapped for his cutters without making any talk. Two-gun man," he sneered softly. "I left him back there on the river trail, so you

34

better send the Coroner out to establish the cause of
his demise!"

Joe Grant clenched his big hands and tried to control
the anger that swept over him like a spring flood. "The
dirty unwashed son," he growled hoarsely. "You
done right not letting him clear leather, Bowie!"

Buddy Bowie crowded up and stared at his adopted
father. "You didn't tell all of it the first time," he
muttered. "He hurt Bonnie any before you broke
him loose?"

"Not any, Buddy. Like you said, I didn't get a
chance to tell it all," and he glanced again at Yuma
Leslie.

The sheriff was fighting his anger down, and Bowie
touched him lightly on the arm. "You better ride
out that way, Joe," he suggested. "This feller done
some talking to Bonnie before me and Mary Jane rode
him down."

"Yeah? He said '. . .?"

"Said Black Bart was riding gun-sign on both me
and Buddy. Thought I'd give the law first chance."

"You did that?" Joe Grant asked softly. "After
what he said about you ten years ago?"

Bowie shook his grey head. "Because of what I
said ten years ago when Nellie and me were married,"
and Alamo Bowie set his lips grimly. "I promised
not to trigger a slug again a man unless he brought
it to me."

"I remember," the sheriff grunted. "Glad you
broke over when you saw him and Bonnie."

"Figgered he'd brought it to me," Alamo Bowie
excused himself. "He was on B Bar G range."

"I didn't make any promise," Buddy interrupted
harshly. "You say he mentioned my name. What
kind of a looking hombre is this Black Bart?"

Alamo Bowie was watching the face of Yuma Leslie.
The young Circle L owner was leaning against the

bar filling his glass. He glanced up carelessly and raised the drink to his lips without apparent interest. Bowie hesitated a moment and then turned to Buddy.

"You made me a promise," he reminded softly. "But you ought to know the brand and ear-markings just in case you cut his sign. Tell him, Joe."

"Black Bart is a tall lanky gun-slammer with coal-black hair and eyes," the sheriff recited descriptively. "Like Leslie yonder, only older. Bandit and rustler, and rapid with his tools. Has a habit of writing poetry after he makes a stick-up or a killing. Must be all of forty-five by now, and rumour had it that he spent a lot of time in Arizona after he made his break from prison."

"Like Leslie, eh?" Buddy repeated softly, and swept the Circle L owner with contemptuous eyes.

Yuma Leslie came forward like a cat. "Meaning what?" he purred throatily. "Tell it scary, cow-boy!"

Buddy Bowie shrugged. "Meaning that this here outlaw has black hair and eyes like yores," he answered steadily, but his right hand shadowed the grip of his gun. "You heard what the sheriff said when he was tallying off the points of Black Bart."

"Figgered you'd put it something like that," Leslie sneered, but the light of battle burned strongly in his eyes.

Joe Grant frowned and growled low in his throat. "Being the Law here in Luna County, it's my duty to warn you yearlings," he muttered. "I'll arrest the one of you that makes the first pass for his hardware," and he stared into the angry blue eyes of Buddy Bowie. "That goes for you, too, Leslie," he added, to take out the sting.

"I don't look for trouble," the Circle L owner answered carelessly. "But I always meet it halfway when it faunches up to cut my sign."

"I've been knowed to meet it that far and step over the line some to give the other feller a chance," Buddy boasted hotly. "Any time, Leslie! Any time!"

"Any time . . . you call it," Leslie answered softly, and locked glances until the sheriff broke the deadlock.

"We got to get together on this," he announced sharply. "Running a spread of yore own back there in the brakes, you stand to lose a heap of stock when this outlaw gang gets to work, Leslie."

Yuma Leslie shrugged. "I can take care of my end," he answered lightly. "I've got eight good hands riding on the payroll, and every one of them rides fully dres ed. Right now we're running about two thousand head all told, but I aim to buy more feeders and she-stuff and build up my herds."

Alamo Bowie nodded approvingly. "That's cow-savvy, Leslie," he agreed. "But rustlers don't care whose beef they cut out."

"She's open season on wolves," the sheriff remarked. "If Red Malone was aiming to operate up here, it's a cinch his two pards were with him, or somewhere close by. I mean Tucson Bailey and Torio Feliz."

"I know Tucson," Leslie answered slowly. "He's fairly fast with a hand-gun, and his Mex side-kicks throws a knife so fast you can hear it whistle. Looks like the Bowies are going to be some busy for a spell of time."

Alamo Bowie raised his head. "How come?" he demanded.

"Them two was pards of Red Malone like the sheriff mentioned," Leslie answered carelessly. "They will bring it to you shore as sin."

"Reckon they will," the grey gun-fighter agreed, and then leaned forward. "But how come you figger them to let yore stuff alone?"

"Gun Law," Leslie grunted. "I can put nine gun-hands against them, and none of my boys has learned to throw off his shots."

Alamo Bowie curled his lip into a hard smile, and then frowned when Leslie downed his drink and filled up again. Joe Grant followed his gaze and spoke to Leslie.

"You drink pretty hard for a yearling, Yuma. That stuff don't mix too good with raising cattle."

"I'll attend to both in my own way," the cowboy answered shortly. "Up to now I've done right well for a yearling."

"Yeah; up to now," Buddy Bowie cut in nastily.

Alamo Bowie came up in front of Buddy and spoke softly to the Circle L owner. "I haven't interfered before, Leslie. But mebbe you better stay away from the B Bar G until we know you better. I reckon you know what I mean, and all my folks are sticking close to the spread until this other business is settled."

Yuma Leslie pushed away from the bar and cuffed the black Stetson down over his glowing eyes. "Meaning Saturday night?" he asked softly.

"Meaning that, and every night," Alamo Bowie answered steadily. "I got nothing personal against you, but don't come riding until you learn to control yore appetite for liquor."

"All of which sounds personal to me," the cowboy rapped angrily.

Alamo Bowie stepped back and measured him with cool grey eyes. Then he shook his head and spoke softly.

"Speed, yes," he murmured. "But the difference in experience would be too much handicap. Think it over, cowboy. You got too many good points to lose it all just because you lost yore head."

The young cowboy glared at him with hell leaping high in his dark eyes. "You figger I'm afraid?" he growled.

Alamo Bowie shook his head again. "You ain't afraid, Yuma," he said quietly. "She's just the other way around with both you and Buddy. You both got too much of what it takes . . . for yore own good."

The change in pace broke the resistance of the dark youngster. The lambent flame left his eyes and changed them to thoughtful pools of doubt. Then he saw Buddy Bowie watching him with a sneer curling the lips of his mouth. He deliberately filled his glass and tossed it off while his eyes glared at the grey gun-fighter.

"Be seeing you," and he slapped the glass on the bar and waved his left hand. Then he tugged his hat low and stomped from the room without a backward glance.

"Got the makings of a man, Yuma has," Alamo Bowie said quietly. "He ain't afraid of all hell, and something happened lately to throw him off his stride."

"Yeah," Buddy growled. "And I aim to see that it don't go any farther. He was hot to meet me until he made a date for Saturday night!"

Alamo Bowie turned and regarded Buddy sternly. "Yo're in a bar-room, now, son," he reminded. "And a gent never mentions the name of a good woman in a place like this."

Buddy coloured up and lowered his eyes. "You should have slapped me to sleep with the barrel of yore gun," he growled. "I just forgot everything when he grinned at me out on the trail."

"And you followed him down here?" Joe Grant asked softly.

Buddy Bowie nodded. "I followed him, Joe. Just wanted to have a talk with him."

"Gun talk?" the sheriff persisted.

"You give it a handle," Buddy grunted. "I ain't much of a liar!"

Alamo Bowie was watching Buddy, and he nodded his head like a man who knows. "Reckon yo're right, son," he agreed slowly. "But you want to learn to hold yore head until a man brings it to you. Joe Grant will tell you the same."

"That's Gun Law," the sheriff agreed calmly, and then his eyes began to glitter again. "You better finish telling me about Bonnie," he grated harshly.

"Safe as can be," Alamo Bowie answered quickly. "I sent her to the B Bar G with Mary Jane. Knew you'd want it that away, and you better leave her with us until we do what has to be done."

"I'll ride out with you," and Joe Grant shouldered between the two Bowies and started for the swinging doors. "She's all I got now, Alamo."

The tall gun-fighter did not answer until they were mounted and headed toward the B Bar G. A little man in a grey suit was leaning over the body of Red Malone when they reached the scene of the killing. Joe Grant swung down and clipped his words.

"Howdy, Doc. You ready to fill out the papers?"

The little Coroner grinned when he turned his eyes on Alamo Bowie. "Like old times," he chuckled. "Red Malone got it dead centre, and he came to his death while committing felonious assault on the person of a minor child. Justifiable homicide, and looks like he won't be the last, from what I heard."

"That minor child was my Bonnie gal," the sheriff answered huskily. "You take care of the body, Doc. Was me, I'd forget my office and leave his carcass for the buzzards!"

"Stranger high-tailed through here just a few minutes ago," the Coroner spoke up hastily. "Didn't say much, but acted like he knew the deceased."

Joe Grant turned swiftly. "You know who this stranger was?"

The coroner shook his head. "Tall dark youngster on a line-back dun," he described. "Good-looking feller with black hair and eyes."

"Yuma Leslie," Buddy said harshly. "You mind he said he knew Tucson Bailey and the Mex?"

"Just a minute, Buddy," Alamo Bowie interrupted. "Leslie had to pass here on his way to the Circle L. He knowed the corpse was here, and I figger it was only natural for him to light down and have a look."

"Shore," Buddy answered with a sneer. "And on top of that, he was sure that the rustlers wouldn't touch his stuff. Yeah; he's got a lot of good points, that jigger!"

A rifle barked sharply from a distant ridge, and snatched the hat from the sheriff's head before he could answer. Alamo Bowie whirled with hand reaching down, but he stopped the move when he saw a ring of powder-smoke float lazily above the brush across a wide deep canyon.

"That was just a warning," the grey gun-fighter said confidently. "And damn good shooting if you ask me."

Joe Grant picked up his hat and stuck a finger through the bullet hole. "Can't run him down," he muttered. "All of three mile around the trail to that hide-away."

"Yeah," Buddy Bowie repeated softly. "He's got a lot of good points."

Alamo Bowie came up and touched the cowboy on the arm. Waited until Buddy turned to face him. Then he shook his head and stared until the cowboy dropped his eyes.

"That ain't cutting it square, Buddy," Alamo Bowie murmured. "When the other feller ain't on hand to talk for himself."

"Seems to me he talked plenty loud," and Buddy pointed across the canyon. "Gun talk if you ask me."

"Which nobody did," Alamo Bowie snapped. "You don't like him. All right. But what about Tucson Bailey?"

Buddy raised his honest blue eyes. "Saying I was mebbe wrong," he muttered. "Yuma Leslie ain't the sort of jigger to dry-gulch a man, as much as I hate his innards."

"Spoke like a man, Buddy," Bowie praised quietly. "And he would say the same about you. But that ain't figgering this here puzzle."

The little Coroner coughed softly and stared at the trail-side brush. The three men turned and followed his glance. Yuma Leslie was sitting his horse easily with a grim smile on his dark face. Staring at Buddy Bowie while the fingers of his right hand hooked in the heavy belt above his gun.

Alamo Bowie caught his flipping hand and grunted softly. "'Tain't safe to cat-foot around that way on my range right now," he said coldly.

"Safe enough the way I done it," Leslie answered as coldly. "If I was what the button said I was, I could have cut you all down and nobody the wiser."

"Reckon you heard the whole confab," Buddy Bowie took him up. "So what you aim to do about it?"

Yuma Leslie ignored him while he flipped something to the sheriff from his left hand. "Take a look through these," he murmured, and waited for Joe Grant to cup the field glasses to his squinting eyes.

The sheriff was staring intently across the canyon. "Two hoss-backers," he muttered swiftly. "And one of them is a Mex!"

"Yeah," Leslie murmured. "I was sitting my hoss back there aways when I heard the shot," and he stared at Buddy all the time he was talking.

"You heard me say I was wrong," Buddy growled sourly. "But that don't change things a bit with me."

"It changes them considerable with me, Leslie," Alamo Bowie cut in. "Glad to know you're a square-shooter."

"Looks like you know me some better now," the dark cowboy answered softly. "I'm no angel, but I don't stand for a feller to call me out of my name."

"We'll be seeing you after this rustler business has been cleared up," Buddy interrupted grimly. "Not before."

"Listen, Button," Leslie answered hotly. "The sheriff ruled us out for now with six-guns. You want to step down out of that henskin and try yore luck like a man?"

Buddy Bowie slid to the ground and unbuckled his belt. Alamo Bowie jerked his head at Joe Grant when the sheriff acted as though he would interfere.

"Let 'em go," the gun-fighter muttered. "Mostly hot blood, and it might do some good if they work some of it off."

Yuma Leslie stepped down and hung his belt on the saddle-horn. Lighter by ten pounds than Buddy, but he moved with the lithe grace of a jungle cat when he stepped forward with hands knotted into rocky fists.

"Win or lose, it will be worth it," he told the blond cowboy and danced in with left fist jabbing like the flick of a snake's tongue.

Buddy Bowie gave ground and spat salty blood from his bruised lips. Then he started a swift attack that bore Yuma Leslie back with knuckles breaking through his guard to start his nose bleeding. After which they circled each other warily until Leslie came in fast to jab Buddy off balance. His right whistled over and caught the blond cowboy on the point of the chin, and Buddy buckled his knees and began to sag.

Alamo Bowie caught his breath and waited with an ache in his chest. Yuma Leslie saw his advantage and followed up with both hands swinging. Buddy reached out and fell into a clinch to pin those hammering fists down, and he snorted loudly while Leslie tried to break free.

Buddy Bowie gathered his strength and threw the dark cowboy back and to the side. Then he caught his own balance and waited with both hands in front of his swelling chest. Blue eyes blazing to match the glitter in the dark ones opposite, and Yuma Leslie brought the fight to him.

He danced in lightly and jabbed with his left. Buddy took both blows without batting an eye. Yuma Leslie set himself and crossed with a beautifully-timed right, and so intent was he that he failed to see the haymaker starting from Buddy's belt.

The blow beat him to the punch and thudded against his jaw solidly. He shivered like a tree while his eyes lost expression and began to glaze. Then he buckled his knees and pitched to the ground on his face, and Buddy Bowie watched him for a long moment and blew on his skinned knuckles.

"You feel better?" Alamo Bowie asked quietly.

Buddy raised his head and widened his eyes. "How'd you know?" he whispered.

Joe Grant smiled. "That beats gun-play," he said softly. "It ain't like you to let him lay without offering to help, Buddy."

Buddy Bowie picked up his own hat and ran to the river bank. Filled it to the brim and came back slow. Poured the cold water slowly in Yuma Leslie's face, and he was standing by his horse fastening his belt buckle when the dark cowboy stirred and came up fighting.

"Steady, Yuma," the sheriff called sharply. "You went fast asleep, and the fight is over."

Yuma Leslie staggered to his feet and weaved like a drunken man. "Where is he?" he growled savagely.

"Right here," Buddy answered. "Ain't you had enough for one day?"

Yuma Leslie shook himself like a dog coming out of water. He was breathing regularly when he turned and stared at his opponent with lips curled at the corners.

"Not enough for to-day or any other day," he stated icily. "You want to try yore luck some more?"

Buddy Bowie frowned and then shook his head regretfully. "Wouldn't be a fair shake, Leslie," he answered. "I out-weigh you by ten pounds, and that was what whipped you. Saying I'm sorry I said what I did when that shot was fired."

"You go to hell," Leslie shouted, and bit his full lips while he turned his head and winked his eyes. "And I'll give you the ten pounds and bring it to you the next time I see you!"

He swung on his heel and almost ran to his horse. Kept his back turned while he buckled his gun-belt, and then he vaulted to the saddle without touching the stirrups and scratched with both feet. While Buddy Bowie watched him with a grim smile on his tanned face.

Alamo Bowie glanced at the tall cowboy and leaned forward to watch. The fingers of Buddy's right hand were flexing rapidly while he stared at the straight back racing through the trees. When Yuma Leslie had rounded a bend and was lost to sight, the grey gun-fighter spoke his mind.

"You never met him before to-day, Buddy. You can't feel thataway."

Buddy turned swiftly. "Saw him in town twice before to-day," he contradicted. "Felt thataway the first time I laid eyes on him. Won't ever be no different!"

"You mean to say you aim to carry this thing farther?" Joe Grant demanded gruffly. "After whipping him with yore maulies?"

Buddy Bowie faced around stubbornly. "He ain't whipped," he grunted. "They ain't nothing going to make that salty yearling stay whipped until he quits doing what he's doing."

"And you aim to make him quit?" Joe Grant asked softly.

Buddy glanced at Alamo and set his jaw. "I'd tell uh man," he growled.

"You mind what I told you back there in Deming," the sheriff said sternly. "Yore father and me is pards, and I do my duty as I see it. Just remember that when you go edging up to that Circle L waddy!"

"About this corpse," and the little Coroner spoke for the first time since the fight had begun. "If you gents will give me a hand to rope him on his hoss, I'll take him back before the sun gets any higher."

Buddy Bowie mounted his horse and rounded up the tall sorrel grazing on a high shelf. Led the animal back and blind-folded it with his neckerchief while Alamo and the sheriff raised the body and laid it face-down across the worn saddle. Handed the bridle-reins to the Coroner, and Alamo Bowie sighed when the little doctor disappeared down the trail.

"Let's get back to the B Bar G," he grunted. "I sent word to Nellie that I would be back right after dinner, but we can always get a bait of grub."

Joe Grant jumped his saddle with a muttered curse. "Forgot about Bonnie there for a spell," he muttered irritably. "Thanking you for doing what you did, Alamo."

Chapter IV

THE ANGEL OF TOMBSTONE

MARY JANE BOWIE and Bonnie Grant clattered through the big yard of the B Bar G with eyes watching the tall woman on the wide front porch. Nellie Bowie nodded approvingly when both girls dismounted at the holding corral and stripped the riding gear from the sweating horses before turning them into the pen.

"Buck up, Bonnie," Mary Jane whispered. "We don't want her to think we are afraid."

Nellie Bowie was in her middle thirties, and the silver in her hair added to her mature loveliness. Before she had married Alamo Bowie, men and women alike had called her . . . "The Angel of Tombstone." Some fugitive memory of the past brought an expression of apprehension to her fine brown eyes, and she nodded thoughtfully when the two girls came up on the porch. She studied the sheriff's daughter for a moment and slowly shook her head.

"Bonnie," she began softly. "You have been in trouble, child."

Bonnie Grant bit her full lips and moved her head just a trifle before she could speak. "It's Daddy," she barely whispered. "Mister Bowie made a promise. He said the law would have first chance at those terrible outlaws!"

Nellie Bowie closed her eyes and drew a deep breath. It had come at last, just as she had known it would come some day. After ten years of comparative peace Alamo Bowie would again become the man-hunter.

47

She had seen it in his eyes that very morning when
he had headed for the river trail with Buddy. Always
thoughtful of others, her hands stroked Bonnie Grant's
curly hair while she held the tiny girl close to her
motherly heart.

"Tell me, child," she encouraged softly. "About
these outlaws."

"Black Bart is here," Mary Jane interrupted breathlessly. "One of his men caught Bonnie down by the
river. His name was Red Malone!"

"*Was?*" and Nellie Bowie felt a spasm of pain clutch
at her heart.

"Daddy Alamo beat him to the draw," Mary Jane
whispered. "He killed him. And Buddy . . ."

Nellie Bowie stared silently for a long moment.
Then: "Buddy," she said steadily. "Did he kill a
man?"

Mary Jane came close and caught the older woman's
hand in a firm grip. "Not yet," she answered slowly.
"But he wasn't a bit nice to Yuma Leslie of the Circle L."

Nellie Bowie drew the two girls to a seat on the steps
and pieced out the story. Bonnie Grant was thinking
of her father . . . and of young Buddy Bowie. Mary
Jane gazed dreamily toward the serrated rim of the
Black Range and pictured the dark handsome youth
who had made a success of the cattle business before he
was man-grown. While Nellie Bowie peopled her mind
with the men who rode for the law . . . and carried
the curse of powder-smoke in their blood.

At last the story was finished with each of the three
women seeing the events in a different light. To the
girls the situation meant romance and high adventure.
To Nellie Bowie it meant the Drama of Life . . . and
the Tragedy of Death. Men would die that other
men might live. Such was the judgment of Gun Law.

Two horses came up fast through the cottonwood
lane and headed straight for the porch. Alamo Bowie

swung down and came to Nellie before he spoke to the girls. His right arm went around her shoulders and held her close while he looked steadily into the deep brown pools of her moody eyes. The only woman he had ever loved in all his gun-chequered career.

"It's come at last, Nellie," he said soberly. "But I remembered my promise to you. He brought it to me, and he went for his guns first. I thought you would want to know."

Nellie Bowie nodded her head. "I do know, Alamo," she answered steadily. "Mary Jane told me. You did what had to be done."

"Knew you'd understand," the tall grey gun-fighter murmured. "He stood there in the trail . . ." and he turned his head to glance at Bonnie Grant. "Name of Red Malone, and he went for his irons without making talk."

Nellie Bowie turned slowly and placed her two hands on the broad shoulders of Buddy. "Not you, son," and her voice held a prayer. "Your heart will always be restless if you take the first step. I am sure you know that."

Buddy Bowie shifted uneasily and avoided her eyes. "He brought it down to me, mother Nellie. And I didn't like the way he looked at Mary Jane!"

"Sister is older than you," and Nellie Bowie smiled gently. "Have you thought of that, Buddy?"

"But she is a girl," the cowboy growled. "I've always sotter looked after her like you know."

"Yuma Leslie is just a boy like yourself," Nellie answered gently. "There must be much that is good in one so young. Won't you try to find some of that good, Buddy?"

"No'm," and Buddy shook his head angrily. "He bragged that he made enough money raising cattle to buy the Circle L, and him not yet twenty-one. Alamo says the same thing."

Alamo Bowie nodded when Nellie turned to study his craggy face. "I got to Deming in time to stop a gun-ruckus between them two," he said slowly. "Buddy was on the prod and looking for trouble. Young Leslie was in the Drovers saloon filling himself with whisky. They were edging up to each other when I bought chips in what they both figgered was a closed game."

"Buddy," Mary Jane whispered. "You did that?"

"I didn't drink a lot of whisky to get up my fight," the tall cowboy answered hotly.

"Joe Grant came in and warned them both that he would jail the first one who made a gun-pass," Alamo Bowie finished soberly. "And the sheriff meant just what he said."

Mary Jane caught her breath and lowered her eyes. Alamo Bowie was watching her; saw the stricken expression sweep over the light blue eyes to tell of an ideal shattered. His voice was soft and gentle when he spoke to the drooping girl.

"You won't see Yuma Leslie until we know him better, Mary Jane. Trouble is riding up to the B Bar G. Gun trouble."

Bonnie Grant stepped close and touched his arm. "Daddy?" she whispered. "Is he coming?"

Alamo Bowie patted her shoulder and spoke quickly. "Forgot to tell you, Bonnie. Joe is coming right away. Stopped back there by the forks in the trail to read sign before coming here. Sounds like him coming now."

Drumming hooves rattling up the lane turned every head toward a fast-riding cowboy. Range-wise Alamo Bowie was the first to recognize the newcomer, and he grunted under his breath.

"It ain't Joe," he murmured. "Looks like young Jim Golden, nephew to old John of the J Bar G!"

The J Bar G rider was tall and slender. Twenty-three

at the most, but serious and thoughtful beyond his years. He swung down at the rail and took off his battered Stetson while he nodded to the two girls and Nellie Bowie. Then he raised his head and locked glances with Alamo Bowie while he framed words in his mind before speaking.

"Old John is asking for help, Alamo," he stated bluntly. "A gang of wide-looping rustlers ran off about four hundred head of our young steers."

Alamo Bowie avoided the eyes of Nellie and glanced at Buddy. The tall cowboy was staring at Jim Golden with an eager light in his blue eyes. The tall gun-fighter set his lips and turned back to the J Bar G rider.

"You run down the sign?" he asked quietly.

Jim Golden fumbled in a vest pocket and produced a soiled paper. "Found this here in the north paster close to Burro Mountain," he answered. "Old John figgered you would want a look-see."

Alamo Bowie took the paper and scanned it briefly. Written in a bold legible hand easy to decipher, and Bowie nodded and cleared his throat suggestively. Then he read the message aloud in his deep drawling voice. Tonelessly and without excitement.

> *We're giving Mimbres three big cheers,*
> *And taking all your choicest steers ;*
> *When you find this, we'll have a start,*
> *Salud and Adios . . . Black Bart!"*

Nellie Bowie listened and pressed a hand to her mouth. Buddy rubbed the handle of his gun while low rumbling growls whispered from his lips. Bonnie Grant stared with wide brown eyes that held a stricken look of fear for her sheriff father. While Alamo Bowie thought swiftly and nodded his grey head.

"It's a job of work for Joe Grant," he stated bluntly.

"The sheriff will round him up a posse and ride out there to the J Bar G."

Young Jim Golden twisted his Stetson between strong brown fingers. "Yeah," he agreed. "And old John sotter figgered you would ride out with the posse to read the sign. Like you did that time years ago when the Big Four gang raided the J Bar G."

Alamo Bowie glanced at Bonnie Grant and then turned to Nellie with a question in his grey eyes. Nellie Bowie studied his face for a long moment and nodded without speaking. A slow smile curled the corners of the gun-fighter's stern lips when he turned to Buddy and muttered an order.

"Rope out and saddle a pair of fresh hosses, son. You and me will be riding with Joe Grant when he starts with his posse. Yonder's a bunch of hoss-backers heading down across the valley."

"But the sheriff couldn't know yet," Jim Golden cut in. "I figgered to ride down and pass him the word."

"The sheriff knows," Bowie answered quietly. "Some of Black Bart's gang were down here this morning. Get them hosses ready, Buddy."

The sheriff and four men rode into the yard and reined in at the porch. Joe Grant smiled at his daughter and shook his head slightly. Then he turned to Jim Golden and studied the sweating J Bar G horse. Alamo Bowie handed him the message and waited until Grant had softly read it under his breath, but loud enough for all to hear.

"Him," the sheriff muttered. "He meant that poetry for you, pard."

"Me and Buddy will ride with yore posse, Joe," Alamo answered evenly. "It was old John Golden who first brought me up to this country, and it was over there on the J Bar G where you and me first touched skin. I'm not forgetting."

"Looks like history repeats herself," and the sheriff

swung down and went to his daughter. Put his arm around her while he turned her face up and stared deep into her eyes.

"You all right, honey?" he whispered gruffly.

Bonnie Grant circled his neck with her arms and clung tightly. "I'm afraid for you, Daddy," she whispered. "You are all I have now. If something should happen——"

"Sho now," the sheriff muttered. "You got plenty of good friends, Bonnie gal. You stay here with Nellie and Mary Jane, and don't fret yore pretty head none about an old rawhider like me. And don't you be forgetting that I have Alamo and Buddy to side me."

"I do feel better," the girl answered with a little sigh. "Because Alamo and Buddy are riding with you. But do be as careful as you can."

Joe Grant frowned and then grinned. "Like you said, Bonnie," he answered. "Alamo is worth an army like we all know, and Buddy is cut out of the same piece of hide. Like as not we will stay at the J Bar G to-night, and pick up the sign come daylight."

"It cuts back toward Mimbres Valley there in the lavas," young Jim Golden interrupted to explain. "Me and old John figgered that new jigger up on the Circle L might have some news."

"Meaning Yuma Leslie?" the sheriff asked.

"Tall dark gunnie with black bullhides," Golden explained descriptively. "Fast as a cat, and prideful as all outdoors."

"That's Leslie," the sheriff agreed. "You see him recent?"

"Met him pounding the mesa trail when I came in," young Golden answered. "Him and his riders have been working the brakes back yonder for nearly a month, but we only saw them from a distance until to-day."

"We met him a couple hours ago," Alamo Bowie

added. "He told us he brought eight hands over from Arizona, and he aims to buy a lot of feeders and she-stuff to build up his herds. She's hard riding back there in the badlands, but there's plenty of good feed. Bear grass, with plenty of gramm and sacaton."

Sheriff Joe Grant knew that Bowie was talking to take the minds of the women away from the manhunt. Bonnie was watching Buddy Bowie with a look on her face the sheriff had never seen there before. He turned to glance at Mary Jane, and was startled at the resentment he discovered while the girl stared at young Jim Golden.

"You called Yuma Leslie a gunnie, Jim Golden," Mary Jane accused sharply. "You might choose your words more carefully!"

The J Bar G cowboy flushed and shuffled his big boots when he raised startled eyes and saw the anger in her blue eyes. "Reckon yo're right, Mary Jane," he answered quietly. "But I was thinking of the way he sat his saddle, and the tilt of his gun-handle: the way he packs it for a fast draw. You can tell he's been practising with it for years."

"Daddy Alamo practised for years, and so did Buddy," the girl retorted sharply.

"And they call me a gun-fighter," Alamo reminded evenly. "Yuma Leslie has swallowed smoke and felt the jar of a killer's gun in his hand!"

Buddy Bowie led the two horses up in time to hear the last remark. He studied the face of Alamo and swung his eyes for a glance at his sister. Gone was the boyish smile when his lips tightened to etch hard lines down around his mouth.

"And he might feel the bite of lead one of these days," he growled deep in his throat. "I told him the same thing!"

Mary Jane jumped to her feet and faced him angrily. "You might feel it your ownself," she almost screamed.

"You went out of your way to force Yuma Leslie into a fight!"

The tall cowboy stared at her and glanced at Alamo Bowie. Nothing had been said about the fist fight down by the river, and when Alamo shook his head one time, Buddy knew that Mary Jane was referring to the meeting in Deming. Then he went over to his sister and put his hands on her shoulders. Studied her angry eyes for a moment before he spoke.

"You'd want it that away between him and me?" he asked softly.

Mary Jane tried to release herself and then buried her face in his shoulder. "No, no!" she moaned. "I won't ever see him again if you will promise to hang up your gun and stay at home with Mother Nellie and me."

The little group remained silent while they waited for Buddy's answer. Now his blue eyes were wide while he patted the shoulders of his only sister and stared into the distance toward the Black Range. As though he were seeing things over there, and then he shook his head slowly.

"I can't promise you anything like that, Sis," he muttered. "There's something about that jigger I just can't explain. That's the reason why I said it would be better for us to know more about him. I figger it will come out in time. Figgered it would break through before you got interested enough to hurt you much."

Jim Golden forgot himself and allowed an expression of misery to sweep across his bronzed face. Bashful and tongue-tied where women were concerned like most of the stalwarts of the cattle range. And only Nellie Bowie read his secret with a little tug at her understanding heart.

"I don't care anything about him," Mary Jane denied resentfully. "I only met him yesterday through Uncle Joe."

"Buddy is partly right, Mary Jane," the sheriff said quietly. "There is something about young Leslie that neither Alamo nor I can make out. He knows cattle and hosses, and he knows too much about . . . guns!"

Mary Jane raised her head stubbornly. "So does Buddy," she countered. "Because Daddy has taught him all about guns!"

"That there's the point, Mary Jane," Alamo Bowie explained patiently. "Most any gun-passer could tell that I taught Buddy. What puzzles all of us is who taught Yuma Leslie."

"He throws down like Three-Finger Jack used to," the sheriff murmured thoughtfully, and his eyes betrayed the fact that he was lost in the past, and had forgotten the presence of the three women. "And he packs his iron with the handle wide and forward in a way I've never seen before."

"With the trigger filed," Buddy added. "He slips the hammer under his thumb, but he works so fast I couldn't tell whether he used a point shot or centred l.is sights."

"I'm checking some on that feller," Joe Grant volunteered bluntly. "Might be the sheriff over Yuma way could tell us something about him. Sent a letter out on the stage just this morning."

One of the men in the posse shaded his eyes and stared out across the broad valley. "Like I figgered, sheriff," he grunted softly. "We left Jud Leeds back there in the office when we rode out to follow you and Alamo. That's him fanning his hoss down the hind legs and coming hell-for-leather!"

Joe Grant turned to watch the racing rider. Jud Leeds was one of his deputies, and it would take something of importance to make him leave his post in Deming. The horse roared through the lane, and slid to a stop near the little group. Deputy Leeds shouted hoarsely before the spraying gravel had spattered to earth.

"Lordsburg stage was held up, sher'ff. They took the mail sack along with the strong box!"

Joe Grant glanced at Alamo Bowie and back to his deputy. "Find out who it was?" he asked quietly.

"Tall loose-jointed gent dressed in black," the deputy recited breathlessly. "He left a piece of poetry pinned to the boot after he grabbed the loot."

"Black Bart," Alamo Bowie growled softly. "You say he took the mail sack?"

"We found the sack close to town," Leeds answered with a scowl. "Several letters missing, including the one you wrote to the sheriff in Yuma, Joe," he added meaningly.

"That puts a Federal charge against him," Joe Grant stated heavily, and stared at Alamo Bowie. "Reminds me of the time eleven years ago when you carried a commission as a deputy U.S. Marshal."

"Which same I turned in long since," Alamo Bowie growled softly. "She's yore job of work the way I see it, Joe. I'm just going along to help you read the sign. And I don't think you need any outside help from the Federal men."

Joe Grant smiled grimly. "About you just riding out to read sign, Alamo," he grunted. "That's what you think right now."

Nellie Bowie heard him, and covered her trembling lips. "That is what I think, too," she whispered.

"You might as well tell her," Buddy Bowie interrupted. "Tell her what Red Malone told Bonnie down there on the river trail!"

Nellie Bowie stared for a moment and then turned to Bonnie Grant. The girl shrank back with a little sigh and stared down at the toes of her tiny boots. Then she raised her curly head and bit her full lips before she spoke to Nellie Bowie.

"Black Bart is going to kill Alamo and Buddy," she whispered in a little frightened voice. "I didn't want to tell you."

Nellie Bowie stood perfectly still and closed her eyes. Alamo Bowie waited with the ropy ridges of muscle framing his thin straight lips. Nodded his head as though he knew when his wife came to him and looked deep into his hard grey eyes.

"You promised me, Alamo," and her voice was steady and low. "But we left a way out; you and I. So that you would have a chance to live. We love you, Alamo. The children and I. Love you too much to lose you now, after all these years of happiness and peace."

The tall grey gun-fighter nodded his head slowly. "Been like heaven to me, Nellie pard," and his deep voice was husky with an emotion he seldom showed. "I'll take that way we left open if I have it to do."

Nellie Bowie nodded. "I am wishing speed to your hand, Alamo," she said clearly. "If Black Bart brings it to you!"

Alamo Bowie listened like a man in a dream, and then a smile of tenderness broke the rocky grimness of his craggy face. His right hand gripped the hand of his wife man-style, and in that grip was a renewal of the promise he had made on his wedding night ten years ago. Back in Tombstone when the doctors had despaired of his life.

Buddy Bowie came softly behind his adopted mother and circled her with his strong young arms. "Mother Nellie," he murmured huskily in her ear. "A man would go to hell in his bare feet for an angel like you!"

Nellie Bowie smiled then and drew the tall boy into her arms. Studied his smoky blue eyes for a long time while he shifted uneasily under her scrutiny. And waited for her to speak.

"Would you, Buddy?" she surprised him.

Buddy sighed with relief and filled his big chest. "I'd tell uh man I would!" he answered promptly.

"There's Alamo," she continued, and held his eye, with her own. "If something is good enough for him is it good enough for you, son?"

"You just put a name to it and spell it out," Buddy growled softly. "I'll take anything that's good enough for Alamo!"

Nellie Bowie cupped his firm chin in her two hands and nodded slowly. "Say it, then," she urged gently. "Say the words I want most to hear."

Buddy shifted uneasily. "Don't know as I understand what you mean, Angel," he evaded. "You want to tell me?"

"Must I?" she countered, and continued to watch the troubled frown that twisted his tanned face.

"Alamo has first call on that long-riding son," he muttered finally. "I take seconds just in case of!"

"Buddy," she reproved softly. "It isn't like you to evade an issue. You know I didn't mean Black Bart. We were talking about the trouble between you and young Yuma Leslie!"

The tall cowboy jerked back and stiffened his muscles. Growled deep in his throat and turned his head away to avoid her brown eyes. While hard-faced man-hunters looked away and waited for his answer. It came so low that only a murmured whisper was audible to their straining ears.

"It's a promise, Mother Nellie. I won't ride gun-sign on him any more. What's good enough for Alamo suits me down to my boots!"

"Oh, Buddy!" Mary Jane cried happily. "I'm glad you are so much like Alamo !"

Alamo Bowie sighed. He knew what was coming, and he turned his head to shut out the sight of Mary Jane's face when Buddy came out with his reservation.

"I won't hunt him out or clear leather!" he stated harshly. "Unless he brings it to me!"

Nellie Bowie smiled and kissed his cheek. "I knew we could count on you, Buddy," she whispered. "That promise is all I ask."

"And me," a throaty voice echoed behind his broad back. "When this trouble is all settled, I am sure you will change your mind about Yuma Leslie."

Buddy turned slowly to face his sister. "Sorry, Mary Jane," he told her soberly. "But I won't ever change none about that feller. Working with hosses you get to know men, and he's a bad one down underneath."

Bonnie Grant caught his eye and shook her head vigorously. Buddy flushed and dug a little hole with the toe of his boot. Waited for his sister to denounce him, but the girl took a deep breath and turned away. Buddy walked over to Bonnie Grant to cover his embarrassment.

"You stay close to the ranch, Bonnie," he barked. "You and Mary Jane both!"

Joe Grant smiled when his daughter jumped to her feet with dark eyes blazing. "Don't you go ordering me around, Buddy Bowie," she told him through clenched teeth. "Maybe working with horses teaches you something about men, but you don't know any too much about women!"

"I know enough about them to know what happens when they go racking off by their lonesome and get in a tight," he retorted stiffly. "With us men away from the spread, there ain't no telling what might happen."

"Buddy is right," the sheriff seconded. "We might not get back for a day or two, and those outlaws are on the loose like we all know. You girls stay close to home."

Nellie Bowie put an arm around Bonnie and spoke softly to ease the tension. "I will look after the girls, sheriff. Now you men better be starting along if you don't want dark to catch you up before you reach the J Bar G."

She kissed Alamo Bowie before he swung up to the saddle. Buddy and Jim Golden were already riding down the lane to take the lead. The sheriff followed with his posse, and Nellie Bowie turned back to the girls with a hint of tears in her brown eyes.

"I thought we would have peace for the rest of our days," she said sadly. "But I always knew that Alamo would never be any different as long as he lives. They just can't change when it gets into their blood."

"Gun Law," Mary Jane whispered fiercely. "You can see it in their eyes when they get up their mad. They always rub the handle of their guns and stiffen up like a dog on the fight!"

"But they both promised," Nellie reminded with a sigh. "And you wouldn't want to rob Buddy of the chance to defend himself if it meant his life."

"If I only knew Yuma better," the girl whispered. "If I could get him to promise."

Nellie Bowie watched her for a moment and then put an arm around each girl. "Time to get supper," she said calmly. "I am sure everything will come out all right."

Chapter V

ALAMO BOWIE TAKES A PRISONER

TWILIGHT was dipping down toward the north end of Mimbres Valley when the sheriff's posse reached the border of the J Bar G. An old man rode out of the black-jack to meet them. Raised his left hand Indian style and called a hearty greeting when he recognized the two Bowies.

"Howdy, Alamo; Buddy! Knew you'd come a' fogging with yore nose to the ground when you heard the bad news. Mighty glad to see you and the chip."

"Howdy, ol' John," and Alamo Bowie rode close to grip the silver-haired cattleman by the hand. "Looks like you'd stay to home and let the young hands chouse through the brush for yore strays. You want to get all stove up with the rheumatiz?"

John Golden was straight as a tall pine in spite of his seventy years. Long white cowhorns framed his humorous lips, with heavy eyebrows gleaming whitely against the ruddy tint of his weathered cheeks. Steady blue eyes that looked bravely out upon life and found it good. Eyes that now held a steady glow of affection for the man who had saved his life and his fortune more than a decade ago.

"Like before," he answered slowly. "When I get the misery in my joints, I aim to ride herd from the rocking chair on the front porch. Until that time, I aim to sit saddle."

"Young Jim was telling us you lost some stock," Bowie said quietly. "Must have been close by."

"I rode out to mark the place where they rounded up our young stuff and started the drive," the old cattleman answered. "Sotter figgered on giving you a line to start from just to save time."

Sheriff Joe Grant and his men waited and listened while old John Golden pointed out the landmarks. Alamo Bowie nodded from time to time while his keen eyes studied the trampled ground and sighted off into the distance toward the Mimbres Mountains. On the right was Cooks Peak; tail end of the Black Range. With Cooks Canyon running dark and deep into the badlands of the Goodsight Mountains.

Alamo Bowie turned to Joe Grant; spoke slowly and positively. "You better ride to the Circle L in the morning, Joe. Me and Buddy will stay away from there, but Leslie and his men might give you some help. Old John's steers were driven up the canyon toward Leslie's badland range. Working that stretch the last month the way they been doing, chances are they know all the cuts."

His right hand reached up and stroked the long scar on his chin while he turned back to study the trampled sign. Buddy Bowie edged his horse closer and nodded his blond head with silent understanding. Alamo always rubbed the knife-scar when danger was close, and the tall cowboy grinned when the grey gun-fighter spoke casually.

"Better take the boys and ride on with ol' John," he told the sheriff. "Just to make sure, me and Buddy will ride this sign aways there up the canyon. That way we'll know for sure which fork of the trail they took."

John Golden jerked around in the saddle and stared for a long moment.

"You find something the rest of us missed?" he asked sharply.

Alamo Bowie shrugged. "Nothing for sure," he

grunted. "But there's a place up the canyon where the trail forks. One branch cuts over to the Hot Springs, the other leads back into the Goodsights. Save us a lot of time to know just which trail them rustlers took, and it won't need all of us to find out. Me and Buddy will be right along behind you, and mebbe sooner. Tell the Cooky to save us a helping of chuck."

The old cattleman stared for a moment and then nodded his head.

"Like you say," he grunted. "We'll set out a bait of grub for you and the chip."

Joe Grant waved a hand and spoke to his men. "Head for the J Bar G, fellers. All of us go barging after Alamo, we're like to cloud the sign. Be seeing you, pard."

Alamo Bowie expelled his breath with a sigh when the posse rode into the black-jack thicket. Again his hand was rubbing the long scar on his chin; memento of a killer's knife down across the Mexican border. A killer who had paid in these very mountains, but Alamo Bowie was not thinking of Sonora Lopez.

"Fan out," he said to Buddy. "Keep a little behind me, and not too close. And use yore eyes the way you been taught."

Buddy Bowie dropped back with hand twitching his gun against hang. A change had come over the tall grey gun-fighter who was now leaning over his saddle while the horse walked slowly through the trampled grass of the canyon. Alamo Bowie was reading sign with eyes that missed no tiny detail. Reading it like a man who knows what he will find at the fork of the trail.

"Two hoss-backers rode down here and back again after the herd was long gone," he said softly. "You see that twisted corn-husk yonder, son?"

Buddy Bowie rode up with eyes fixed on the ground. Nodded assent while his eyes slitted to peer through the gathering shadows of twilight. While Alamo Bowie pointed and checked his findings.

"That gent was a Mex, Buddy. You can tell from the way he twisted his quirly. The other was a long-legged gent who chews tobacco. It's them two sure as sin."

"Tucson Bailey and Torio Feliz," Buddy murmured. "Pards of Red Malone, and him killed this morning."

"Tally," Alamo Bowie grunted, and his face was a cold mask of determination. "I didn't say anything at the time, but I saw Bailey watching from up here when old John was making medicine. He waved the tops of the brush, and then he leaned out too far for a better look."

Buddy Bowie felt the comforting glow of confidence Alamo Bowie always stirred within him. Other men would have posed as super-trackers. They would have waited for better light, and the advantage of superior numbers. But Alamo Bowie admitted honestly that he had seen Tucson Bailey, and had chosen to make the odds more even.

"We'll leave the hosses here and cut around through the brush," and Alamo Bowie slid from the saddle and tethered his horse to a sapling with the hair *mecate*.

A moment later he was slipping through the brush with Buddy close to his heels. Not a sound except the lazy buzz of insects, and the sleepy call of birds nesting in the scrub mahogany. With the shadows closing in, and the afterglow on the high canyon walls reflecting a hazy reddish light.

Alamo Bowie stopped abruptly and pointed with his right hand. Buddy could see a rocky trail just ahead. Two horses tied in the brush just beyond a curving bend where a Y branched out to mark the

C

fork. Two men crouching in the shadows, waiting like great silent buzzards.

Alamo nodded and made his way around a screen of growth without making a ripple to mark his passage. Buddy stayed where he was and watched the two out-laws. Steady as a rock now that action was to take the place of uncertain suspense.

He saw a slight movement when Alamo Bowie came up softly. Stopped behind the waiting pair, and his deep voice lost its drawl and crackled like rifle-fire through the gloom.·

"Don't reach, Tucson!"

Tucson Bailey whirled on his high heels with both hands going above his head. Lathy thin and incredibly tall with the crossed belts of the two-gun man cinching his narrow hips. His jaw dropped when he saw Alamo Bowie facing him empty-handed. A stream of amber spouted from his puckered lips before he could speak.

"Alamo Bowie! And you empty-handed back there!"

"Heard you was gunning for me," Bowie said softly. "You and yore Mex pard yonder."

"You must mean two other fellers," Bailey muttered. "We wasn't looking for you, Bowie!"

"Good shooting you did back there in Mimbres Valley," Bowie said slowly. "Did you mean it for a warning when you knocked the sheriff's hat off, or was you aiming to kill him?"

Tucson Bailey clenched his big bony fists. "He never had a chance, Red didn't," and he slowly lowered his long arms. "We found him back there on the river trail, me and Torio. And we sent a shot to tell you that we knew. Me and Torio figgered you'd come chousing back here for to give old John Golden a hand."

"Knew it all the time," Bowie answered softly. "You

left a plain trail from the valley at the mouth of the draw. Any blind man could read it the way you spit tobacco around."

"And you read it," Bailey sneered. "Barged right up here to see how come and what for."

"That's right," Bowie agreed. "Red Malone died the way he done for grabbing the girl."

"Skip the gal," Bailey grunted. "Black Bart had you marked for his own cutter, but I taken up for Red Malone," and the lanky outlaw leaned forward in the gathering gloom. "You never give him a chance!"

"He had first chance, and he made a pass for his guns," Bowie contradicted coldly. "You can have the same if you want to call the turn."

"Up to now I stepped back when Black Bart wanted something," Tucson Bailey said savagely, and hunched his shoulders. "You ready?"

Alamo Bowie moved his head and shifted his feet for balance. Tucson Bailey struck down with both hands; stopped the move as suddenly when Bowie twitched his right arm up and down. The outlaw loosed his clutching fingers and closed his eyes when he saw the leaping muzzle centre on his left breast, and he jerked when a shot roared out from the trail-side brush.

A body hit the ground just behind him, but Tucson Bailey felt no pain. His jaw sagged when he slowly opened his eyes and saw Alamo Bowie watching him over the barrel of his gun. And the gun was not smoking.

His head swivelled around with eyes staring at the man writhing on the ground. Torio Feliz was groaning while a blond young giant crouched across a smoking gun to cover every movement. A long-bladed throwing knife was sticking point-down in the trail, and Tucson Bailey shuddered and raised his hands shoulder high.

"I forgot about yore chip," he muttered hoarsely. "You better shoot, Bowie!"

Alamo Bowie shook his head. "Up to now I ain't ever committed murder," he said quietly. "Take his hardware, Buddy. He just might get foolish and decide to take a chance!"

Buddy Bowie came up swiftly and emptied the tied-down scabbards. Then he jerked a pigging string from his hips while Alamo Bowie smiled coldly and held the drop. Tucson Bailey lowered his arms and shoved his hands behind his back, and Buddy made his wraps and ties like a roper working at the branding fire on the open range.

The lanky outlaw turned slowly and stuck out his jaw.

"You kill my pard, Torio?" he asked hoarsely.

"Naw," Buddy growled. "But that saddle-coloured hombre won't never throw another *cuchillo* unless he's left-handed. Get up on yore hind legs, Feliz!"

Torio Feliz groaned and levered unsteadily to his feet. The shock of the heavy slug had broken his arm, and had knocked him down like a giant hammer. Terror gleamed in his dark eyes when he saw the black gun in the steady hand of Alamo Bowie.

"You will not kill, Senor?" he pleaded. "I have hear that the great Alamo Bowie gives every man a chance!"

"Was you going to give me a chance?" Bowie asked softly. "Hiding back there behind yore pard with a knife in yore hand, and you aiming to split my heart!"

"I bleed, Senor," the Mexican whimpered. "The arm she is nearly broke away from my body. I grow weak and faint!"

"Black Bart," Alamo Bowie said sternly. "You know where a man could find him?"

"Si, Senor," the Mexican almost shouted. "He is in the Goodsight Mountains where a horse he cannot find his way back home!"

"I'm giving you that chance you talked about, hombre," Alamo Bowie warned sternly. "Providing you do what I say."

"Anything, Senor," the Mexican promised. "What is it you would have Torio Feliz to do?"

"Black Bart," Bowie answered. "You are to carry a message back there to him."

"The message, Senor?"

"Tell Black Bart I'm ready to meet him any time he brings it to me. Listen carefully, Feliz. I made a promise, and I never broke my word yet. If Black Bart *brings* it to me——"

"You afraid to take it to him?" Tucson Bailey sneered.

Buddy Bowie stepped forward and raised the barrel of his gun.

"You heard Alamo," he growled hoarsely. "He made a promise ten years ago, and so far he's kept it. Black Bart came over here to kill me and Alamo, and you can tell him I take seconds in case he's lucky!"

"I will tell him, Senor," the Mexican interrupted softly. "He lives only for the day when he meet that great one. I go now, Senor?"

"Mount and ride," Alamo Bowie growled. "Tell his men to get out of the Mimbres Valley or get killed. Black Bart won't leave, and he knows where to find me."

Buddy Bowie led a black gelding out of the brush and jerked his head toward the saddle. "*Vamos, hombre,*" he barked. "And you better ride fast before you bleed to death. The kiyoties would have yore yellow bones picked clean before morning!"

He boosted Torio Feliz to the saddle when the Mexican grabbed the horn with his left hand. The black leaped away when Buddy slapped with his hat; roared away into the gloom and was lost among the shadows. Alamo Bowie holstered his cold gun and came closer to Tucson Bailey.

"Taking you for the sheriff, feller," he announced quietly. "You feel like talking some before we start?"

"I don't talk much," and the outlaw emptied his mouth and sneered insolently at his captor. "You got nothing on me up here in New Mex."

"Except rustling," Bowie reminded. "Bring his hoss up, Buddy. We'll just take a little ride."

Buddy led the outlaw's horse into the clear and muttered thoughtfully.

"Them J Bar G hands, Alamo. You reckon they will string Tucson up when they find out he was one of the rustlers?"

"Wait a minute," Bailey shouted hoarsely. "You can't take me to the J Bar G. I demand my rights, and I'm going to jail down at Deming!"

"The sheriff is at the J Bar G," Alamo Bowie answered quietly. "So that's where we're heading."

Tucson Bailey lost some of his bravado and shivered in the gloom.

"That old Ramrod on the J Bar G," he muttered. "If he sees me, I'll stretch a tight-twist rope shore as hell. What was you wanting to know?"

"That's some better," Bowie grunted. "How many men is Black Bart rodding back there in the brakes?"

"Seven-eight, not counting Red Malone," Bailey muttered sullenly. "He'll get you, Bowie. You won't have a chance when he brings it to you!"

"Boost him aboard and lead him down," Bowie said to Buddy. "I'll go on ahead and get our horses. Joe Grant will want to know."

Tucson Bailey hung his head on his chest until the two men mounted up. "Brazos Day is still rodding the J Bar G, ain't he?" he asked quietly.

"Yeah," Alamo Bowie answered. "And he don't like rustlers none. So you and him know each other?"

"Lead on," the outlaw muttered after a long glance at the gun-fighter's face. "I never heard of any prisoner of Alamo Bowie's stretching rope ahead of time. I'll take another chance."

He was silent during the long ride across the valley to the J Bar G. Opened his eyes when the horses stopped in front of the old house, and Buddy Bowie pulled him from the saddle when Sheriff Joe Grant came down from the porch.

"Name of Tucson Bailey," the big cowboy muttered. "Alamo beat him to the gun and held his shot. Make it rustling for now!"

"We heard a shot back yonder," the sheriff answered. "What about Torio Feliz, his pard?"

"He tried to throw a knife, and I busted his wing," Buddy grunted. "Alamo turned him loose to carry a message back in the Goodsights to Black Bart."

Joe Grant turned and studied the face of the grey gun-fighter. "You should have brought him in, Alamo," he reproved softly. "Mind saying what the message was about?"

"Black Bart came here to bring me show-down," Alamo Bowie answered quietly. "He won't leave until he faces me. I figgered it would save time and trouble to get it over with."

Old John Golden came bristling down from the porch. "You can't do it, Alamo," he growled huskily. "I'd lose every head of beef on the J Bar G before I'd let you go down under outlaw lead now!"

"Don't tell me what to do, Ol' John," and the voice of Alamo Bowie was edged with anger. "A man don't die until his rightful time comes, and Black Bart has waited for ten long years. His owl-hoot pack will make hell here in the valley, and even then Black Bart will bring it to me!"

A short bandy-legged old puncher with barn shoulders stepped out of the shadows with a rope in his hands.

He gripped a finicky loop and held his coils loosely when the noose circled down over the head of Tucson Bailey. The prisoner gasped hoarsely and stumbled against the sheriff.

"I surrender to the law," he shouted. "I'm yore lawful prisoner, sheriff!"

Alamo Bowie spoke softly. "Drop that rope, Brazos Day. I passed my word that there wouldn't be a hanging here on the J Bar G. He gets a fair trial, and they got several good ropes down at the County seat!"

"That tall jigger was with that wide-loopin' outfit," the old foreman growled, and kept his hold on the rope. "We ought to string him high and let him hang and rattle!"

Alamo Bowie caught the wink in the foreman's eye and stepped back. Brazos Day gave a twitch and grinned when the prisoner let out a yell. Sheriff Joe Grant stood by and watched to see what was coming. He too had seen the wink, and he knew Brazos.

"Talk," the old ramrod commanded sternly. "What about that bunch of steers you and yore pards rustled!"

"Black Bart was rodding the drive," Tucson answered shakily. "Me and Torio wasn't there."

"Yo're a liar," deputy Jud Leeds corrected flatly. "Black Bart was back on the Lordsburg road holding up the stage!"

Joe Grant raised his head when a sudden thought struck him. "Yeah," he drawled. "You know why he took my letters from the mail sack?".

"Don't know nothing about it," Bailey growled, and Brazos Day gave a twitch to the rope. "He was afraid you was getting information about his men," Bailey shouted. "You ain't got a thing on any of them over here in New Mex!"

Joe Grant thought for a moment and then faced the

cowering outlaw. "You know anything about Yuma Leslie?" he barked suddenly.

Tucson Bailey stared and shook his head. "Never heard of him," he answered sullenly. "New one on me."

Buddy Bowie turned swiftly. "Tall dark jigger," he explained quickly. "Fast on the draw-and-shoot, and salty for a yearling!"

"That couldn't be Buckskin Frank Leslie," Bailey answered slowly. "On top of that Buckskin is crowding forty."

"You ever hear of the Circle L?" Joe Grant asked softly.

Tucson Bailey nodded. "Heard about it," he admitted. "But the stuff is scattered through the lavas, and the spread carries a salty crew."

"Seven-eight hands," the sheriff prompted. "Riding on the payroll for this here Yuma Leslie."

"Take this damn twine off my neck," the prisoner muttered. "All I know is that one of the boys said young Bowie and this here Yuma Leslie were edging at one another account of a gal. Me, I never set eyes on him."

"You know more than you want to talk about," old Brazos Day growled deep in his crowded throat. "Me and my boys is just itching to pull rope and make cottonwood fruit out of you!"

Tucson Bailey crowded closer to the sheriff. "You can't cut it," he rumbled hoarsely. "I'm a prisoner of the law, and I demand a fair chance right here in front of these witnesses!"

"Fair enough, and you'll get it," Brazos agreed, and looked about for a stout tree.

Joe Grant frowned and flipped the noose loose. "No can do, Brazos," he told the old ramrod. "Neither Alamo nor old John Golden would lie if the word got out we strung this jigger up without the law giving the go-ahead."

Brazos Day muttered under his breath and glared at the prisoner. The sheriff turned to deputy Jud Leeds and barked a curt order when he threw the rope to the ground.

"Saddle up and take Bailey back to Deming, Jud. Me and the posse will ride over to the Circle L come morning, and mebbe so have company for Bailey when we get back to town."

Tucson Bailey sighed with relief when he was again boosted to his saddle. Alamo Bowie was talking quietly with the old foreman. Buddy Bowie stared until Jup Leeds and his prisoner were out of sight, and he started when a hand fell on his arm. Old John Golden whispered from under the drooping cowhorns that framed his stern mouth so that only Buddy could hear.

"Don't go off half-cocked, son. Just forget what you was thinking, and hobble yore bronc till morning."

Buddy Bowie shrugged angrily. "Now looky, Mister Golden," he muttered savagely. "That Circle L outfit borders yore range as well as ours. Then it runs back in the badlands where Black Bart and his gang are holed up!"

"I was giving that some thought, Buddy," the old cattleman answered soothingly. "Alamo and Joe Grant were thinking about it, too. But we got to find out for shore before we go to giving a young dog a bad name. You better shag it back to the cook shack and get you a bait of grub."

Buddy nodded sullenly and walked toward the rear where the yellow lights of the cook shack glowed brightly. Alamo Bowie watched him and took Brazos Day by the arm to follow. The old J Bar G foreman took a seat at the long table and watched the hungry cowboy wolfing his food, and then Alamo Bowie spoke softly.

"Not you, Buddy. I don't want you going up there to the Circle L."

The cowboy dropped his fork and jerked around. "I'm going," he snapped. "I got me a hunch!"

Alamo Bowie smiled and traced a pattern on the oil-cloth with one finger. "Yuma Leslie rides in here several weeks ago and buys up the old Circle L," he said thoughtfully. "Pays cash for the deal, and claims he earned it all. Then Black Bart comes over looking for you and me. He hides back there in the brakes with his killers."

He stopped and sipped at the hot coffee. "That makes two and two," Buddy growled. "He's got something to do with Black Bart!"

"Now we don't know that for sure," Alamo corrected evenly. "That's natural hide-out country, and Black Bart would hole up there no matter who owned the Circle L. That's why the Laskys were anxious to sell out cheap."

"He's a fast gun-hawk," Buddy muttered. "And he brought all his hands over here from Arizona."

"So what?"

Buddy drew a deep breath. "I'll be heading home in the morning," he said sullenly. "On account of the promise I made Nellie."

"Knew you'd see it, son," and Alamo Bowie patted the powerful shoulder. "There's something about this I ain't worked out yet, but we'll give a man a chance until we know for sure."

Buddy Bowie went back to his food and ate in silence. Pushed away from the table while Alamo was still eating, and he stomped into the darkness with lips clamped tight, and pain in the fingers of his right hand.

Brazos Day leaned toward Bowie and spoke seriously. "That young 'un reads sign near as plain as yoreself, Alamo," he began. "What you think about this salty yearlin' up on the Circle L?"

"You ever see him?" Bowie asked.

Brazos nodded. "Seen him and talked some," he answered. "He's a gun-fighter, Alamo. And fast!"

"About a year older than Buddy," Alamo Bowie drawled. "Dark where Buddy is blond. Only difference between them is Yuma Leslie is a killer. He's got it in his blood."

"And Black Bart," Brazos persisted. "Looks funny, Alamo. Damn funny was you to ask me."

Bowie pushed back and rubbed the scar on his chin. "I ain't saying until after I meet Black Bart," but his voice was low and hard. "Right now our job is to track down that herd of steers for old John."

He settled his Stetson down over his eyes and walked out in the yard toward the corrals. Showed no surprise when he saw Buddy saddling his horse up close to the bars.

"Change yore mind, son?" he asked quietly.

Buddy tightened his cinches and nodded his blond head. "I'm lining out for home, Alamo," he answered, and rubbed the fingers of his right hand. "I made a promise to mother, and I'm afraid I can't keep it if I stay down here over night."

"That's man-talk, feller," Bowie praised softly. "And I'll feel better about the girls with you back there on the B Bar G rodding the spread. And Buddy?"

The tall cowboy looked up suspiciously. "Yeah?"

"Asking you to get along with Mary Jane. She's growed up now, and she won't take kindly to bossing. She's gentle, but spirited and proud as a thoroughbred filly, and it might be better to handle her the same way."

"Shore, I savvy, Alamo. Take care of yourself, and I'm wishing you the same as Nellie did."

Alamo Bowie narrowed his grey eyes. "What you mean by that, feller?"

"Back there in the badlands he's on the loose and aching for show-down. If you meet Black Bart," and Buddy jumped his saddle and reined in his roan, "speed to yore gun-hand, pard!"

Alamo Bowie stood in the darkness with hand rubbing the scar on his chin. Watched the tall cowboy roar down through the cedar lane, and after the thudding hooves had died away, he smiled and shrugged lightly.

"Yeah," he whispered softly under his breath. "Same to you, yearlin'!"

Chapter VI

JUDGE AND JURY

TORIO FELIZ stopped his tired horse in the darker
shadows where two high rocky walls shouldered in
to block the canyon. He could see the sugar-loaf peaks
of the Goodsight mountains just beyond the portal.
Weird lights jumped and flickered occasionally from
some hidden pocket deep in the badlands, and Feliz
knew that the outlaw band was gathered around a
roaring wood fire.

He tilted back his head and gave the mournful call
of the hoot owl. *Whoo . . . whoo whoo.* One long call
and two short. While his dark eyes watched the west
wall when the wavering call echoed against the high
canyon pockets of eroded rock. Low and plaintive, a
single cry answered him. The Mexican shuddered and
blessed himself in the darkness before sending his horse
toward the entrance.

" *Quien es ?*" a sharp voice challenged.

"It is me, Torio Feliz," the Mexican called softly.
"I bleed, Pedro. You will not keep me waiting?"

A smothered curse came from the pass, and then a
tall-peaked sombrero bobbed against the skyline. No
face visible under the big hat, but a Winchester covered
Torio Feliz while he rode between the pillars and sagged
wearily in the high saddle.

"You are alone, Torio?" his countryman asked sharply.
"You do not ride with our amigo, Tucson Bailey?"

"Quickly, Pedro," Torio snarled. "Tucson is a
prisoner, and I have make haste with a message for
Black Bart. He is here now?"

"By the fire," Pedro Sanchez grunted. "He will cut off your foolish ears, Torio Feliz. You may pass!"

Feliz grunted softly and gigged his horse forward. Rode down a steep trail that twisted through the lava rocks for a quarter of a mile. Then he was in a sheltered valley where a great fire burned brightly at the far end, and he knew that his mates had heard his call, and awaited his coming.

Three men were lolling on their blankets with rifles close to their hands. A fourth man with black Stetson pulled low, rocked easily on his high heels at the edge of the firelight. Wide shoulders and straight as a pine, with a quality of power about him that easily identified him as the leader. Tall and slender, and dressed entirely in black.

Torio Feliz grunted painfully and slid down from his saddle. His left arm hung limply at his side, and the firelight reflected against the glittering black of his eyes. Face an ashy grey when he dropped bridle reins to the ground and turned slowly toward the grim outlaw chief.

"Where is yore pard, Tucson Bailey?"

The Mexican shuddered slightly when the stern voice leaped suddenly at him. His right hand toyed nervously with the empty holster thonged low on his lean thigh. His voice a thin whisper of sound when he opened his fever-cracked lips.

"He is a prisoner, Senor Bart. Even now the sheriff takes him to Deming."

Black Bart leaned forward. "I know, I know," he repeated softly, and stared unwinkingly into the swarthy face. "And who captured Tucson and winged you in flight, my fine-feathered friend?"

Torio Feliz raised his head and widened his dark eyes. He was proud of the bell-bottomed *pantalones* and tight-fitting *bolero* jacket, and then the look of resentment left his face when he saw the eyes of his chief. His carefully arranged story scattered in his mind like leaves before a mountain wind. Lies would be useless if Black Bart already knew of the capture.

"It was Alamo Bowie," he answered simply. "He came with the sheriff and his men to the place where we rounded up the herd of young steers. Nothing missed his watchful eyes, and the young Bowie was with him."

The tall outlaw stiffened and twitched the fingers of his right hand. "You saw . . . Alamo Bowie?"

Torio Feliz nodded. "His eyes are very sharp, Senor," he explained quickly. "He left the posse and followed us up the canyon like *un perro;* what you call the dog!"

"I savvy *Mejicano*," the tall outlaw said very softly. "You and Tucson Bailey. Why were you down there in the valley?"

Torio Feliz shuddered and lowered his eyes. "Tucson and Red Malone were *amigos*," he whispered hoarsely. "And Red Malone he is dead!"

The tall outlaw made two quick steps and hooked the fingers of his left hand under the Mexican's chin. Raised the drooping head until the dark eyes met his gaze. While the long-barrelled gun thonged low on his right leg gleamed in the red firelight.

"Answer me with a straight tongue, Torio. You and Tucson meant to kill . . . *Alamo Bowie!*"

"*Por Dios, Senor*," the Mexican whispered. "I did not mean to kill. I was riding with Tucson, and I could not leave him as you must know. It is the truth, Senor!"

Black Bart dropped his hand and stepped back. His sharp dark face was like chiselled rock, and his words chipped out like flint when he continued the inquisition. While Torio Feliz squirmed uneasily and waited for the expected lightning to strike.

"So Tucson Bailey wanted revenge for the death of his pard, eh, Torio?" the outlaw purred. "And he thought that he could match guns with an hombre like Alamo Bowie, did he?"

The Mexican nodded, too weak and shaken to speak. Black Bart reached out and stripped the tight bolero jacket away from the wounded arm with no trace of feeling on his face. His strong fingers kneaded the wound mercilessly until Torio fell to his knees with a muffled moan. The outlaw raised him with one hand, and without apparent effort. Called over his shoulder to one of the men by the fire.

"My case, Tonto. Heat the probes and then hold this bravo down while I do something to save his worthless carcass!"

Torio Feliz went to his knees and clenched his white teeth hard. Tonto Fraley gripped him by the arms and locked his muscles. While Black Bart worked like a surgeon there in the ruddy glow of the firelight, with hands that were as steady as the eternal rocks. Probed for the bullet with no emotion on his dark chiselled face.

"Bite down hard, Torio," he advised coldly. "The wound must be cauterized at once to save further trouble."

The Mexican moaned softly when he saw the long-fingered right hand reach toward the fire. Came away with a white-hot probe, and Tonto Fraley held a dead weight in his arms when burning flesh tainted the high mountain air.

His arm was neatly bandaged, and Black Bart was watching him intently when the Mexican slowly opened his eyes. Tonto Fraley passed a flask of whisky and grinned when Torio seized the bottle and swallowed half the contents. Colour came back to the wounded man's cheeks to chase away the ashy pallor, and his voice was strong again when he raised his head and spoke to Black Bart.

"*Muchas gracias, Senor.* I have lost much blood, but now I am the man again."

"Don't thank me," the outlaw answered coldly. "I take care of my horses and my men, and I have a use for you later. Did Tucson Bailey talk before you came away from the canyon?"

Torio Feliz shrugged his shoulders. The tall outlaw cuffed back his black Stetson to show the silver at his temples. Black eyes staring at the face of the Mexican. Probing and reading the hidden thoughts until Feliz broke and nodded his head.

"Alamo Bowie stood there empty-handed," he began. "His gun, Senor. It jumped to his hand before Tucson could clear leather. No one knows why the Senor Bowie did not shoot!"

"I know," the outlaw corrected quickly. "Alamo Bowie never committed a murder in his life. How did you get that bullet through yore wing?"

His piercing black eyes held steady on the Mexican's face while he waited for the answer. "The young Senor Bowie," Feliz muttered. "He was back in the shadows, and we had forgotten him. It was he who shoot me through the shoulder!"

"Yore *right* shoulder," Black Bart said significantly. "Where then is the knife you always carry, Torio?" and his voice was a soft whisper.

"They take my knife and my gun," the Mexican murmured with a shudder. "While that old one hold me under his gun. I thought of a surety he would kill me," and he shook his head eloquently. "But Alamo Bowie spare my life that I might bring a message back here to you, Senor!"

Black Bart stared steadily until the Mexican shifted uneasily. Then: "You tried to get Alamo Bowie with that throwing knife of yours, Torio!"

"It did not leave my hand," Feliz denied emphatically. "I swear it, Senor Bart! Young Bowie was hiding back in the shadows as I have told you!"

Black Bart nodded slowly and kicked a chunk of

greasewood on the fire. His dark vulpine features carried the expression of a man who has found all the answers and had made a decision.

"I'd kill you had you known, Torio Feliz," he said softly. "Because I did not tell you, I will let you live . . . this time. The young Bowie is marked for another gun. The rest of you *buscaderos* keep that in mind!"

Torio Feliz sighed and crossed himself thankfully. He had intended his knife for Alamo Bowie, but the fates were kind. If Black Bart saw fit to believe that his quarrel had been with young Bowie . . .? And then the soft throaty call of the hoot owl drifted mellowly across from the walled-in pass at the upper end of the valley.

Black Bart raised his head and gave the answer. His black eyes were glowing with an inner excitement, and his thin nostrils were flaring wide like a stallion on the fight. The fingers of his right hand began to flex rapidly, and then two horsemen rode down toward the fire.

Torio Feliz stared at the pair and sucked in his breath. One was the lanky Tucson Bailey riding with empty holsters. The other man was a stocky bearded outlaw, Colt McGruder. One of the fastest killers in the gang, and the deadliest shot with a rifle. Now the long gun rode in the saddle-boot under McGruder's left leg, and the breech was powder-grimed. Torio Feliz looked and knew what had happened even before the stocky outlaw spoke.

"That deputy was dead before he fell out of the saddle, chief. I lined my sights on him down there in the valley and shot one time. Brought Tucson back here with me like you said."

Black Bart nodded his head slowly while his black eyes focused on the face of Tucson Bailey. Colt McGruder led the horses away to an ocotillo corral and stripped the riding gear expertly. While Tucson Bailey shifted his big boots and tried to bring a grin to his twitching face.

"What were you doing down in the canyon?" Bart asked quietly.

The lanky outlaw sighed and straightened his drooping shoulders. "Riding around," he answered carelessly. "Figgered you would want to know how many men the sheriff was sending after us."

"And you thought you were faster than Alamo Bowie," Black Bart said suddenly.

"Not me, Chief," Bailey muttered. "He followed us up the canyon. You can ask my old pard Torio yonder."

"I did ask him," the tall outlaw said quietly. "You and him were pointed up Cooks canyon, and you waited there at the forks of the trail instead of hightailing back here. Mind telling me why?"

"We were watching to see that no one followed," Bailey argued desperately. "Eight-ten men in the sheriff's posse, and we thought you would want to know."

"I knew," the tall outlaw answered grimly. "Pedro made the tally, and he heard the shot when Torio was winged. Knowing that you would be in trouble, I sent Colt McGruder to lend you a hand. Looks like you needed one bad."

"Thanks, Chief," and finally Tucson Bailey managed the smile. "You always was a square-shooter that away with yore men."

"I am glad you realize it," Black Bart answered dryly, and glanced at Colt McGruder, who had just returned to the group from the corral.

McGruder nodded and drew a gun from his left holster while the men around the fire watched with narrowed eyes. The stocky outlaw stepped close to Tucson Bailey and pouched the heavy forty-five on the long right leg in the empty tied-down holster.

"Figgered you might need one," he murmured carelessly, and stepped away to take a seat by the fire.

Tucson stared at the gun and raised his eyes to the face of Black Bart. The tall outlaw was watching him intently, chin down on his chest, breathing easily, while the firelight danced high to emphasize the deadly glitter in his beady eyes.

"I am the boss here, Tucson," he began quietly. "When I give an order, I expect it to be obeyed without question!"

Bailey shifted and tried to look away, but the black eyes held him like a magnet. His tongue scraped across dry membrane when he tried to wet his lips, and the sound was like the passage of a snake through coarse sand.

"Shore, Chief. Shore," he agreed hoarsely. "You can count on me till the last horn blows. I ain't never turned you down like you know!"

Black Bart continued to stare for a long moment. "Alamo Bowie," he said at last. "I've waited ten years to match his cutter. Rotted in prison seven of those ten years, and I marked that hombre for my own gun. You ever remember hearing me mention that fact, Tucson?"

"I remember, Chief," Bailey almost shouted. "And I'd say you was the fastest!"

"You ought to know," the outlaw leader murmured dryly. "You've seen us both make our passes!"

"I remembered what you said," Bailey repeated desperately, and the wild gleam in his eyes told that he realized his position. "That's how come me to let Alamo Bowie get the drop when he went for his gun after surprising us down there in the canyon!''

Black Bart relaxed for a moment and allowed a cold sneer to twitch the muscles of his long face. "You let Alamo Bowie get the drop?" he repeated softly, but the contempt in his voice bit like acid.

"Remembered you had him marked for yore own iron," Bailey answered eagerly. "Torio can tell you the same thing."

"Like I mentioned, Torio did tell me," and Black Bart raised his head from his swelling chest. "Yo're a poor liar, Tucson!"

Tucson Bailey jerked erect and craned his head forward. He recognized the menace in that quiet even voice. Knew the nature of the man who had waited ten long years to gain his goal. The privilege of facing the fastest gun-fighter the south-west had ever known. And Tucson Bailey stared intently and felt the chill of death creep into his blood.

He jerked his head down to tear his eyes away from that coldly smiling face while he tried to find some avenue of escape. When the long silence became unbearable, he raised his head again. The fleeting look of hope faded suddenly when he found no change of expression, no sign of mercy.   .

"Not that, Chief," he muttered in a frenzy of fear. "I gave you tops when I signed on to ride with the gang!"

"But you held a doubt in the back of your mind," the tall outlaw said softly. "You knew that the issue between myself and Alamo Bowie would be decided by the split width of a hair. A very fine hair, Tucson. And you meant to rob me of the supreme happiness of my life. You meant to dry-gulch him down in the canyon!"

He ended the words with an accusation that flashed across the fire and filled the night air with breath-taking tenseness. While men stopped all, movement in a paralyzed moment of suspended animation. Hung poised in what they were doing while staring eyes watched Tucson Bailey and saw his sallow face change slowly until it looked like a skull. Eyes swivelled slowly to study Black Bart, and saw in him the grim spectre of Death. That fine split hair of difference in gun-speed which counts the time between the living . . . and the dead.

Tucson Bailey broke the spell when he turned slowly and stared at the wounded Mexican by the fire. Torio Feliz shrugged his shoulders. Danger had been removed from himself and transferred to another. *Bueno Fortuna!* In his language the transition meant Good Luck to one lowly peon who had been christened Torio Feliz. "*Quien sabe?*" Who knows?

Tucson Bailey watched him for a while and slowly shook his head. He had been betrayed, and for a moment his lips tightened while the muscles in his right arm grew tight. Then he saw the empty holster on the Mexican's leg and turned away.

He glanced up when the tall outlaw coughed suggestively. Black Bart was still staring at him. Waiting for him to drag his coat in the dust. And again fear leaped to his sallow face.

"God, Chief! I can't match yuh!"

There it was in all its naked brutality of realism. Jealousy and hatred . . . the vanity of strong fast men. Powder-smoke in the blood of those who had felt the kicking, bucking shock of speeding lead taking the ache and pain from sensitive fingers. Life for the one . . . death for the loser.

Tucson Bailey knew it was coming. Terror rippled across his face and froze there for a moment of silent horror. Faded when the mind had reached its point of saturation. So much and not a drop more. And with all his shortcomings, Tucson Bailey was not a physical coward.

"Red Malone was my saddle-pard," he said slowly, and the terror left his green-grey eyes. "He saved me from a killing one time, and we cut veins and crossed our blood the way the Injuns do. I took up for him, and down in the canyon I met a better man. Well?"

A flicker of admiration flashed briefly across the predatory features of the outlaw chief. "Spoken like a man, Tucson Bailey," he praised quietly, and then his face grew stern. "That's the first truth you have spoken since Colt McGruder brought you in. I reckon you know the answer!"

Tucson Bailey was a changed man when he slowly nodded his head and answered in a low voice: "Reckon I do, Black Bart. You got the killer light in yore hellish eyes, and the taste of yore own blood in yore mouth. Right now I'm dead, but I'll match you with a borrowed gun. Might keep you from thinking about . . . murder!"

Black Bart frowned when a ripple of applause keened across the dying fire. He knew the temper of his men. Men who had come to the forks of the trail and had chosen the owl-hoot branch. Where might is right, and where gun-law proved the survival of the fittest. And because he could understand, Black Bart showed why he was their leader.

"Mebbe you wanted to save me from a killing," he offered suggestively. "That it, Tucson?"

Tucson had committed himself, and he was a man of his convictions. His head shook slowly from side to side when he refused the coward's chance offered to him to save his life.

"Red Malone was my pard," he stated clearly. "We took ourselves a vow to square up for each other. And Alamo Bowie killed my pard up there on the river trail!"

Black Bart cuffed the black Stetson low over his eyes with his left hand to shut out the failing firelight. "Yo're asking for it now, feller," and his deep voice was low. Low like the almost silent voice of approaching death. "You ready?"

Tucson Bailey gathered his failing forces and jerked his head down and up. Right hand shadowing the grip of the borrowed gun on his long right leg. While his mind registered the wish for his own familiar weapon. And then Colt McGruder levered up from his place by the fire and guttered harshly like the wick of a dying lamp.

"Hold it, Bart! I taken the guns from the back of that deputy's belt!"

Black Bart jerked and nodded his head. "Keno," he murmured. "Make the change!"

Colt McGruder high-heeled up to Tucson Bailey and kicked the gun from the lanky outlaw's holster. Bailey stood like a man in a daze without moving a muscle. McGruder's hand slid to the back of his broad belt and came away gleaming with dull metal. Snugged the six-gun deep in holster leather, and shielded the gaunt outlaw while he took a chance with his own life.

"Twitch it, Tucson. It's yore own gun, and she just might hang!"

Tucson Bailey dropped his hand and slapped familiar wood. A smile of appreciation changed his face for a moment. Made it look less like a skull of death. Colt McGruder stepped back then and sank down on his boot heels, and Bailey shifted his big feet for balance.

"I never did like you, Black Bart," he said clearly. "You accused me of wanting to dry-gulch a man marked for yore own gun. But you, Bart. You've brought in a ringer to down young Buddy Bowie. You know you have me faded, but I'll take a chance. Make yore pass, you wide-loopin' son!"

The outlaw chief twisted under the denunciation, and tried to control his anger. Straightened slowly. Like a cold pillar carved from silent ice. Cold . . . with the hot blood of powder-smoke in his veins. Killer blood.

Then: "Right, Bailey. You never put in years behind the grey walls of prison. And you broke the laws of the owl-hoot pack when you tried to cheat me. After you, you gut-ribbed son of hell!"

Tucson Bailey smiled like a man who has proven his mettle. The fingers of his right hand were writhing like snakes. Now his eyes were steady. Steady with the light one sees in the eyes of the newly-dead. And then he made his fruitless bid for a tie. If he could take Black Bart with him. . . .

His right hand dropped swiftly with thumb reaching for the hammer of his own familiar gun. Lifted with a jerk to separate the spasmodic up and down. Black Bart was regarding him with head cocked to one side. His polished left boot stomped out and drew him two feet to the side. Right hand ripping down and up with scarcely a pause to mark the division.

Two guns roared savagely and smoked hazily in the light of the glowing fire. The edge of Black Bart's embroidered vest snapped out like a flag. Tucson Bailey held his stance. Then a red banner began to unfold in the wrinkles of his grey wool shirt. Crimson flaunted boldly and spread out under his heart while he fought for balance.

Fought and lost. His eyes began to droop while the fingers of his right hand opened to spill the smoking gun into powdery ashes. Bart eared back and held the follow-up, and the members of his gang watched in fascinated silence. Here was the essence of living when men duelled for life itself.

Tucson Bailey swayed a mite too far and measured his lanky length on the ground. Torio Feliz crossed himself again. While Black Bart turned slowly and tipped each member of the gang with the smoking muzzle of his killer-gun. Then his deep voice came like the rustling wings of death.

"Did he have a fair shake for his taw?"

Colt McGruder frowned and answered for his mates. "As fair as a jigger could expect under the odds," he stated slowly. "He knew he couldn't match you, chief. You knew it. We all knew it. But he took it to you like a man!"

"So what?" and the voice of Black Bart was like a rasp.

"Thus endeth the reading," Colt McGruder murmured softly, and shoved up to his feet to face the tall gaunt outlaw. "Right back at you, Black Bart. So what?"

Black Bart was a student of men. "So that's that," he answered with stern finality. "Tucson was a brave man, and he died like one. Do I hear any corrections or contradictions?"

"No, not one," Colt McGruder intoned softly, and loosed the curling fingers on his gun handle. "He died like a man. Mebbe all of us will do the same when our time comes."

The outlaw chief holstered his gun and leaned forward. "Anything personal in your remarks, Colt?" he asked softly, and the corners of his mouth began to turn upward.

Colt McGruder stared straight into the glowing black eyes and shrugged. "You call the turn," he suggested softly. "You're fast, Chief. Faster than the greased wheels of slippery hell. But you can't get all of us. You know it, and so do we. Well?"

The tall outlaw studied the stocky outlaw and shifted his eyes to scan each face in the glow of the ruddy firelight. He found no fear or capitulation. Only the stern and ready resolve to die like men if driven too far. They would take just so much from even a gun-master, and Black Bart nodded his head.

"Right," he agreed. "So here's hoping either Alamo Bowie or me takes it just like he took it," and he pointed to the body of his victim.

"Alamo will," McGruder said meaningly. "Like he took that slug from Three-Finger Jack!"

Black Bart stared for a moment and slowly nodded his head. "That's right, McGruder. Now you better turn out and relieve Pedro Sanchez," and he waited to see that his order was obeyed.

Colt McGruder turned slowly and walked away from the fire. Black Bart stayed within the circle of light and showed no fear. Hands dropped away from pistols when he turned his eyes to study each hard face, and Black Bart gave them grudging praise.

"You are men, every mother's son of you. But you will either take my orders without question, or . . . ?" and he pointed to the lifeless body of Tucson Bailey.

"Like you said, boss," Tonto Fraley croaked, and tried to swallow some moisture into his parched throat. "And like Colt said, too," he added softly.

"Tonto," and Black Bart turned like a cat. "Is that meant to be a . . . promise?"

Tonto Fraley was big, strong, and fearless. "We ain't fooling you for a minute, Chief," he said seriously. "And you don't fool us a bit more. What you think?"

Black Bart set his teeth and then his dark face broke into a smile. "I think we understand each other better," he answered, and the smile whisked from his face. "Now you jiggers turn out and dig him a home . . . where the buffaloes roam," and he jerked a thumb toward Tucson Bailey. "That's all I'll ask for myself when the time comes," he finished coldly.

Chapter VII

BLACK BART TAKES A HAND

NELLIE BOWIE sighed softly when she had finished her work in the kitchen. It was easier to wait when one was busy, but little lines of worry were etched deeply on her sweet face when she joined the two girls in the big living-room and seated herself in a low rocker.

Her thoughts fled back down the years of comparative peace she had enjoyed with Alamo Bowie on the big cattle ranch. Years during which she had assured herself that the old gun-fighting days were memories that would never again become realities. She had watched the tall gun-fighter change slightly in his contacts with the children, as though Alamo Bowie realized his responsibilities as a father.

One of these responsibilities had been to teach young Buddy the proper use of a six-gun. The tall woman shuddered slightly and passed a slim hand across her face. Even now he was teaching the tall blond cowboy. Schooling him in those mysteries that went to make up . . . Gun Law.

Mary Jane was standing across the room with an arm around Bonnie Grant, and the sheriff's daughter trembled when she looked through the window and saw the moon coming up over Cook's Peak. Shadows and light, with death lurking in the deeper shadows.

"Daddy," the tiny girl whispered. "I do hope he never finds the rustlers!"

Mary Jane raised her blond head quickly. "Bonnie," she chided gently. "It is the duty of the sheriff to protect property and to keep the peace here in Mimbres Valley."

"Buddy," the trembling girl whispered. "I am afraid for him. The way he looked when you mentioned Yuma Leslie!"

Mary Jane held her answer when a soft knock sounded on the door. Nellie Bowie moved across the room, tall and stately. Opened the door and stepped back when Yuma Leslie swept off his black Stetson and came into the light.

"Evening, Ma'am," he said softly. "I wanted to talk to you while the men folks were away."

Nellie Bowie closed the door and motioned to a chair. "Won't you sit down while we talk?"

"I won't stay long, and I feel better standing," the tall cowboy answered. "It's about Mary Jane going to the dance with me. I'm asking your permission, Mrs. Bowie. I'll take mighty good care of her."

Nellie Bowie studied his dark face and shook her head slowly. "I thought it was decided that you were not to come here until after this trouble was settled," she told him frankly. "And I'm surprised that you would take advantage when you knew that both Alamo and Buddy were away from the B Bar G."

Yuma Leslie showed resentment when the smile faded from his face. In the hard straight lines of his mouth, and the angry glitter in his black eyes.

"Just trying to avoid trouble," he muttered. "Not that I am afraid of trouble," he added quickly, and raised his head defiantly. "But I was thinking of Mary Jane," he added, and once more his voice was gentle.

Mary Jane came over from the window and tried to take his hat. "Please sit down, Yuma," she requested softly. "And don't frown that way when you speak of trouble."

Yuma Leslie held tightly to his hat and raised his eyes to her face. His dark good looks contrasted with her blond beauty under the yellow glare of the lamps, and then he shook his head and tried to smile.

"I've always had to fight for what I wanted," he stated clearly. "Looks like it won't be any different up here. Will you go to the dance with me Saturday night?"

Mary Jane glanced at Nellie's face and slowly shook her head. The light caught the golden yellow and played among the curls until the movement stopped. While the tall cowboy watched her and read her answer even before she spoke.

"Not until after this trouble is settled," the girl answered with a little sigh. "I promised Daddy, and we Bowies never break our promises."

Nellie Bowie smiled happily until she caught the swift expression of anger that swept across the cowboy's face. Yuma Leslie made no effort to conceal his emotions when he reached out and caught Mary Jane by the hand and turned her to face him.

"How about that promise you made me?" he demanded sharply. "Seeing that you Bowies never break your spoken word?"

Mary Jane caught her breath and tried to release her hand. Thudding hooves roared into the yard and slid to a stop in front of the big porch. Then Yuma Leslie dropped the girl's hand and slapped down for the six-gun on his black chaps when he faced the door in a crouch.

Buddy Bowie jumped to the porch and threw the door open with a rush. His blue eyes blinked rapidly to shed the light, and he stiffened slowly when the voice of Yuma Leslie spoke sharply from behind the heavy gun in his right hand.

"Don't draw, feller. Yo're covered!"

Buddy Bowie turned slowly and stared at the six-gun. Moved his head to glance at the face of Nellie Bowie. While Mary Jane covered her lips with a trembling hand and stared with fear mirrored in her eyes.

"You came here just to make trouble," she whispered accusingly. "I wouldn't have believed it!"

"I didn't expect him to get back," Yuma Leslie almost snarled, but his eyes were watching the crouching Buddy. "And I'll let him have it if he does what he is thinking and makes a pass for his gun!"

Buddy Bowie relaxed his muscles and leaned back against the wall. Again he turned his head to glance at the face of Nellie Bowie, and then his eyes hardened when he spoke quietly to Leslie and watched the dark face behind the gun.

"I found Jud Leeds a while back!"

Yuma Leslie returned the stare without winking. "Meaning that deputy sheriff?" he grunted.

Buddy Bowie nodded slowly. "Found him down on the river trail with a bullet in his back!"

Yuma Leslie crouched lower while the angry blood rushed to his face and narrowed his blazing eyes. "Damn you, Bowie," he grated. "You trying to say that I shot that lawman in the back?"

Buddy Bowie curled his lip. "Saying it out loud," he answered scornfully. "You dry-gulched him without giving him a show!"

"Take it back!" and the dark cowboy jabbed out with his gun. "Unsay them words before I slip hammer!"

"Don't shoot!" Mary Jane screamed. "Please don't shoot!"

"Take back them words!"

Nellie Bowie stepped forward, but Yuma Leslie slipped to the side like a cat. Buddy Bowie stopped the sudden urge of his straining muscles, and the Circle L owner smiled grimly and waved Nellie Bowie to a chair.

"Sit down!" he barked. "Unless you want him to die!"

"Like Jud Leeds died," Buddy interrupted softly. "Shot in the back on a sneak before he could even start for his gun!"

"Please, Buddy," Nellie Bowie pleaded desperately. "Let's talk this thing over. When was deputy Leeds killed?"

"Me and Alamo caught two of Black Bart's outlaws," Buddy growled deep in his throat. "We took Tucson Bailey back to the J Bar G and turned him over to the sheriff. Joe Grant sent Bailey to Deming with Jud Leeds, and this hombre killed the law!"

Yuma Leslie flicked his eyes from face to face. Tightened his lips when he saw contempt and horror written plainly. The three women believed him guilty, and he shrugged his shoulders.

"How long was this feller dead?" he asked quietly.

"He was still warm," Buddy Bowie muttered. "And I didn't see yore hoss when I rode up to the house."

"I'm asking you to read the sign the way it is, Bowie," Yuma Leslie answered softly. "I rode down the mesa trail and tied my horse out back. I didn't even see Jud Leeds, and I never shot a man in the back in all my life!"

"You can tell it to the sheriff," Buddy Bowie sneered. "Right now I want to know what you are doing here on the B Bar G."

"He came over to ask me again to go to the dance with him Saturday night," Mary Jane interrupted quickly. "I refused, so please don't make any trouble, Buddy."

Yuma Leslie turned his head slightly to glance at the girl. "Do you believe I killed that deputy?" he asked softly.

Mary Jane raised her head proudly. "I was watching your face, Yuma," she answered steadily. "I am sure that you are innocent!"

Buddy Bowie growled in his throat and glared at his sister. "That jigger knew me and Alamo were away from the spread," he barked hoarsely. "He came sneaking over here because he was afraid to take a chance. And he killed the law!"

D

Yuma Leslie shifted his feet and came out of his crouch. "I didn't kill the law, Bowie," he said quietly, but his voice was edged like a file. "If the women were not here, I'd holster my iron and give a chance to draw me evens!"

Buddy Bowie changed at once and smiled eagerly. Anticipation in his blue eyes while the fingers of his right hand began to flex rapidly. With a song humming in his deep voice when he made a suggestion.

"Ride out, Leslie. Hit yore saddle and head for the Circle L. I'll bring it to you come sunrise!"

Nellie Bowie interrupted with a soft cry of protest. "Buddy! You made me a promise. Have you forgotten so soon?"

Yuma Leslie parted his lips and waited. Smiled when the eager look left the tanned face of Buddy Bowie. Curled his lips into a sneer when the blond cowboy dropped his eyes.

"Dogging it, eh?" he taunted.

Buddy Bowie raised his head and stared for a long moment. "Did I dog it this afternoon when you stepped out of the brush?" he asked quietly. "Did I hop on you when you went to sleep?"

"Buddy," Nellie Bowie whispered. "What do you mean?"

"Him," Buddy sneered. "He was hiding when we rode out to see the body of Red Malone. Called me for a skull-and-knuckle ruckus, and I lowered the boom is all!"

Yuma Leslie nodded slowly. "He fought fair, Mrs. Bowie. Bested me out there on the trail like he said. And he didn't kick me to death when I went down like most cowboys would do."

Buddy Bowie stared uncertainly and slowly shook his head. "You still think I'm dogging it now?" he asked.

"Buddy made a promise," Mary Jane tried to explain. "He said he wouldn't use a gun unless . . ."

"Yeah; unless . . .?"

"Unless it was brought to him," Nellie Bowie finished soberly. "And Buddy always keeps his word."

Yuma Leslie shifted uneasily. "Makes a difference," he conceded. "Saying you didn't dog it, Bowie."

"I'm glad," Nellie Bowie murmured. "You better go now, Yuma Leslie."

Yuma Leslie shifted his boots and narrowed his eyes. "You made that kind of a promise?" he whispered.

A soft laugh came from the open door. Buddy Bowie jerked around and stared at a tall man dressed entirely in sombre black. The stranger was balanced easily on hand-made boots of soft calf-skin, but the forty-five in his right hand was steady and eared back ready to go.

"Don't turn, Yuma Leslie," he warned softly. "You brought it to him, and now is as good a time as any!"

Yuma Leslie stood perfectly still. "Who are you?" he asked in a strained voice.

The stranger chuckled again. A low sardonic laugh without mirth.

> *"Before you jiggers make a start,*
> *I'll introduce myself . . . Black Bart!"*

His deep voice murmured softly across the room tinged with a deadly undertone. Buddy Bowie turned slowly and stared with an intensity that took in every little detail. Long-tailed black coat, with broadcloth pants tucked down in polished boots. Black Stetson, and a string tie flowing over the embroidered vest. Piercing black eyes, thin bloodless lips; high cheekbones. The outlaw who recited or wrote poetry. Black Bart!

"You can't do this thing," Nellie Bowie whispered and her strong voice trembled with fear. "It isn't human!"

"Can't?" and the outlaw threw back his head and laughed. "Black Bart does what he wants to do. I'm saying that young Leslie is faster with his tools than this chip Alamo Bowie trained. Holster your gun and give him a chance, Yuma!"

"Just a minute," Yuma Leslie answered evenly. "He thinks I killed a deputy by the name of Jud Leeds. The women thought I killed him. Well?"

The dark cowboy stared at the outlaw and waited for him to speak. Black Bart grunted and shrugged his square shoulders.

"They thought that, eh?" he murmured. "They found out about Jud Leeds so soon?"

"I found his body down on the river trail," Buddy Bowie growled. "He was taking Tucson Bailey to jail down in Deming."

"Tucson Bailey was one of my men," Black Bart answered gruffly. "I settle my own troubles without any help from the law. One of my men killed that deputy, and I'm not saying which one!"

Buddy Bowie stared at the hard face and turned to Yuma Leslie. "Taking back them words of mine, cowboy," he muttered grudgingly. "But that don't make me feel any different about you!"

Yuma Leslie nodded. "Same here," he answered. "That lets you and me start from scratch again."

"So you might as well start now," the tall outlaw interrupted coldly. "Holster yore hardware and wait for the word!"

"About Tucson Bailey," Buddy said quietly. "You said he *was* one of yore men."

"He's dead," Black Bart answered without emotion. "When I give an order to my crew, I expect to be obeyed. If I'm not . . ."

"The law would call it murder," Buddy barked.

"Do I care what the law would call it?" the outlaw asked softly. "I gave Bailey a chance, and he took it."

"You pick 'em easy," Buddy Bowie taunted. "You knew you had Tucson Bailey beat before the start. Alamo never thumbed hammer when he took him prisoner!"

"That's the difference between me and Alamo Bowie," the outlaw answered lightly, and turned to Yuma Leslie. "Better seat that six-gun in holster leather," he suggested quietly.

Yuma Leslie swivelled his wrist and pouched the gun on his right leg. Buddy Bowie squared around with a smile curling his full lips. Jerked erect when a throaty voice spat from the shadows near the window like a wildcat protecting her young.

"Don't you move, Black Bart. You're covered!"

The tall outlaw held the drop on Buddy Bowie and turned his head slightly. Frowned when he saw Bonnie Grant covering him with a Bisley forty-one. Dark eyes glittering to match the fire in his own, and then his head nodded one time.

"Shoot," he answered softly. "It might save Alamo Bowie, but I'll get his chip!"

Yuma Leslie cleared his throat to attract attention. "I'm walking out," he stated clearly. "I'm riding back to the Circle L where I belong!"

"Stand hitched," the outlaw barked. "You and him have been edging at each other long enough. You brought it to him, and he made a promise. The best man can cut a notch when the smoke clears off!"

His eyes held steady on the gun in the hand of Bonnie Grant while his deep voice filled the room. Bonnie Grant set her little chin defiantly and contradicted his order.

"He rides, and you won't take a chance, Black Bart. Not after waiting ten years to meet a better man."

Black Bart stiffened. "You mean . . . Alamo Bowie?"

"You know I do!"

"Ten years," the outlaw echoed, and he made no

move to interfere when Yuma Leslie squared his shoulders and started for the door.

The silent duel remained at a stalemate until hooves roared away in the darkness, and there was no evidence of anger in the outlaw's voice when he spoke to Buddy Bowie. Like a judge pronouncing sentence.

"You'll face him some day, yearling. I can see it in your eyes, and in the way you hold your hand. Like your fingers were itching with a pain. A pain that nothing but a kicking gun can heal!"

"No!" Mary Jane contradicted hoarsely. "Tell him he is wrong, Buddy!"

Buddy Bowie twitched his right shoulder. "He's right," he answered heavily. "Yuma Leslie is a brave man, and some day he will bring it to me."

"Promises," Black Bart sneered. "Don't forget that I made one myself."

"You didn't come down to bring it to Alamo," Buddy taunted. "You came down here because you knew he was away!"

"And a posse is hunting for you right now," Bonnie Grant added. "For rustling J Bar G stock."

"I rustled that stock," the outlaw admitted calmly. "Rustled it just to bring Alamo Bowie out into the open. Up to now he's been hiding behind petticoats!"

Buddy Bowie forgot the menacing gun and started across the room. "Yo're a liar!" he shouted angrily.

Black Bart thumbed back the hammer and waited. Buddy Bowie slid to a stop with muttered curses twisting his lips, and the outlaw smiled.

"I heard about you," he said softly. "Heard that you had taken seconds in case I was lucky," and then he shook his head. "It isn't luck with me when I face a man for show-down," and his voice began to vibrate. "I had Tucson Bailey beat . . . and Alamo Bowie won't be any different!"

"No different than he always is," Buddy retorted. "And up to now he has never shot second!"

"You forget about Yuma Leslie," the outlaw said, and smiled when the cowboy leaned forward. "So you won't be here," and Black Bart slowly raised his gun.

Buddy Bowie braced himself for the shot he expected while his wide blue eyes studied the deeply lined face a few paces away. Almost at once he realized that Black Bart had no intention of killing him. He might shoot to cripple, but every line of his strong body suggested maturity and experience. He considered Buddy a boy, and men did not kill boys.

The tall cowboy was humiliated by the knowledge. Anger flooded across his brain, and with it the desire to prove himself. Black Bart regarded him coldly, impersonally. No emotion in his probing black eyes. Only a searching penetrating quality that seemed to look through and through, and read the minds of men.

"You won't," he stated quietly. "Like you did for Torio Feliz, I will put a slug where it will do the most good, and pull your stringer. You ain't man-growed yet, yearling."

He talked quietly and without excitement, while the gun in his long-fingered hand covered the tall cowboy carelessly. Buddy Bowie had the sensation of shrinking in stature, and he stepped back with hands hanging loosely at his sides. Not until then did the outlaw raise his head and smile at Bonnie Grant, and the gun that covered his heart.

"You won't shoot," he told her softly. "You might do it if I slipped hammer to down the button," and he shook his head slowly to make the silver gleam at his temples. "But I won't shoot him, and you won't shoot me!"

The tiny girl felt her eyes wavering. Something about this dreaded killer dominated all who came under his spell. Even Nellie Bowie felt the influence, and she seated herself in the low rocker and closed her eyes to shut out sight of his face. Mary Jane stood by the window where the moonlight streamed in to emphasize her blonde beauty, and Black Bart turned his eyes toward her.

"You don't like Yuma Leslie?" he asked softly.

Mary Jane jerked up her head. "I—I hardly know him," she faltered. "He seemed to be two different persons," and she avoided the outlaw's eyes and stared at the black gun in his hand.

Black Bart smiled. "He is two persons," and then the smile vanished. "Do you recognize something familiar about him?"

The girl shook her head. "I can't place it," she whispered more to herself than to the outlaw. "But there is something vaguely familiar. I think it is because of the way he wears his gun!"

"Yeah, the way he wears his gun," the outlaw repeated, and shrugged irritably. "But you were too young to remember," he growled under his breath.

Both Mary Jane and Buddy Bowie leaned forward as though some forgotten memory had filtered through their minds. The girl was the first to express herself, and her voice sounded faint and far away.

"Something about Three-Finger Jack," she whispered.

"By God," Buddy growled hoarsely. "He tilts his gun-handle out the same way Three-Finger did it!"

"That's reading sign," the tall outlaw praised quietly. "I doubt whether Yuma Leslie knows it himself, but handling a gun that away seems to run in the blood."

Mary Jane caught her throat with one hand to stifle a little scream. Buddy Bowie stood straight as a pine and stared with his mouth open. Bonnie Grant was trembling like a whipped horse, and the gun rested in her lap, quite forgotten. A silence gripped the occupants of the room until Nellie Bowie opened her eyes with a soft sigh.

"I felt it the first time I saw the boy," she said with a catch in her voice. "You are trying to tell us that he has the same blood as Three-Finger Jack!"

Buddy Bowie leaned forward and waited for Black Bart to answer. The outlaw was enjoying himself, and he seemed to be entirely without nerves. The gun that covered the tall cowboy was steady with the muzzle depressed toward the floor, but ready for instant use. The outlaw's voice was deep and vibrant; ringing with overtones.

"The very same blood," he stated positively. "Yuma Leslie is a half-brother to Three-Finger Jack!"

"You are cruel," Nellie Bowie answered in a hushed voice that expressed her horror. "You knew this, and you tried to goad him into killing Buddy!"

"I did," Black Bart answered bluntly. "The yearling done served notice on me. Him and Yuma Leslie will meet sooner or later for a draw-and-shoot!"

"They won't," Mary Jane contradicted fiercely. "It isn't fair to do this thing to Yuma, and now I can't possibly see him any more."

"You'll see him," the outlaw answered carelessly. "When I tell him what I know. . . ."

Nellie Bowie rose to her feet and set her firm lips. "I could almost wish that Alamo was here to seal your lips forever," and her throaty voice rang like a bell.

She shrank back involuntarily at the sudden change that swept over the tall outlaw. A reddish light blazed in his black eyes, and the thin lips grimaced like a soul in torment when Black Bart fought for control. His shoulders stooped forward while the gun swivelled up to centre on Buddy's heart, and his deep voice was harsh and metallic.

"If Alamo Bowie were here now he would die! Slow; that's what he was. So slow that Three-Finger found him with a bullet to spoil my chances. You spoiled my chances, too," he accused hotly, and glared at Nellie Bowie with eyes narrowed to glittering slits.

The tall woman nodded with a smile. "Yes," she agreed. "I made him promise because I knew he wanted to accept your challenge. And then they sent you to prison!"

Black Bart sucked in a deep breath and controlled himself. "Ten years," and his deep voice was a wind-roughened whisper. "I've waited ten years . . . to bring it to him!"

"You won't have to wait much longer," Buddy interrupted hoarsely. "When Alamo hears about you coming right here to his own house, all hell won't hold him back!"

"That's why I came," the outlaw answered. "Tell him I was here, and tell him that I will come again. I heard all about that promise he made. That he wouldn't pull killer's trigger unless it was brought to him. I'll bring it!"

Nellie Bowie started to speak, and then closed her lips. One look at the face of the outlaw was enough. Here was a man who had lived the hard way. One who had endured the torments of prison without complaint. Had waited and schemed until a chance had come for escape. With only one thought in his cruel distorted mind.

Buddy had made a promise to Alamo, but he was young and might forget in the heat of anger. She could see the tall youth tensing his muscles with some inner excitement. Black Bart would shoot to cripple if Buddy leaped, and Nellie Bowie spoke sharply.

"Yuma Leslie. You brought him up here?"

She saw Buddy relax and raise his head. A strange light came to the eyes of the outlaw when he turned his head to study her face. Then he shook his head slowly.

"I didn't bring him like you know," he answered. "But I did know Three-Finger Jack, and now the time is here to tell Yuma Leslie. They both had the same mother, him and the Kid. They were half-brothers."

"You can't do that," Nellie Bowie whispered. "You must not. Can't you see?"

Black Bart stared. "See what?"

"It would send Yuma Leslie up here to revenge his brother!"

The outlaw poised and muttered to himself. Then he backed swiftly toward the door with a savage bewildered expression on his craggy seamed face. For once he had overlooked an important detail.

"I'd kill Yuma Leslie if he beat me to it," he whispered. "Alamo Bowie will answer to me!"

"You are a free man," Nellie Bowie suggested quietly. "You can ride out of the country and save your life. Alamo will never follow you."

"You tell Bowie I was here," the outlaw barked. "And tell him I will come back!"

He was gone like a shadow into the outer darkness before she could answer him. They heard the roar of hooves echoing back from the mesa trail that led to the Goodsight Mountains. Buddy was the first to recover from the spell that held them all, and he went to Nellie Bowie and put his arms around her.

"Don't you worry none, Nellie," he whispered with his lips close to her ear. "Alamo is the fastest!"

Chapter VIII

THE ARREST

BLACK BART rode his sweating horse through the guarded pass deep in the Goodsights. Colt McGruder was waiting with Winchester in his two big hands. One glance at the face of his chief was enough to seal the sentry's lips, and the tall outlaw passed him and rode to the fire.

One man was rolled in his blankets close to the dying embers, and he roused out when he heard the thud of hooves. Stomped into his rusty boots and took the bridle rein when Black Bart swung down, and the short gunman led the horse away and stripped the riding gear before turning the black into the ocotillo corral.

"Come over here, Tonto!"

Tonto Fraley stared and approached the fire slowly. "You have any trouble, Chief?" he asked slowly.

Black Bart raised his head and nodded. "I made one mistake," he almost whispered. "After waiting ten years."

Tonto Fraley stared at the fire and waited. He knew the uncertainty of the tall man's temper; the cruelty that lurked in that savage mind when Black Bart was thwarted.

"Yuma Leslie," Bart said suddenly. "To-morrow you will bring him here for a talk with me. Don't give him a chance to go for his gun, or one of you will die. Get the drop on him, and tell him I want to see him pronto."

"He's dangerous, Chief," Tonto muttered. "Might

be just as well to let him have what that deputy got, and in the same way."

Black Bart reached out and gripped Fraley by the shoulder until the cringing outlaw gasped with pain. "I said bring him in alive!"

"Yeah, alive," Fraley hastened to agree. "You don't have to take it out on me," he added sullenly, and rubbed his arm.

"I'll take it out on any man that tries to beat me to Alamo Bowie," Black Bart muttered.

Tonto Fraley leaned back and nodded. "So that's it," he grunted. "The Kid figures to make a pass at Bowie."

Black Bart nodded. "He takes young Buddy Bowie," he answered grimly. "But if he cuts down on Alamo Bowie——"

"I get it, Chief," Fraley answered quickly. "And we'll bring him in if we have to slap him to sleep with a gun-barrel."

Black Bart raised his head and stared moodily at a new grave under a tall pine. "Tucson Bailey was a fool," he said harshly. "I gave him a chance for an out, but he wouldn't take it. First Red Malone and then him!"

Tonto Fraley shrugged. "That's what comes of fooling with women," he answered carelessly. "Red tried to kiss the sheriff's daughter, or he would be alive to-day."

Black Bart leaned forward and stared at the glowing coals. "That gives me an idea," he muttered. "Go up and tell Colt McGruder I want to see him. It's just about time for you to relieve him."

Tonto Fraley straightened up and settled his gun-belts. Started for the narrow pass without further comment until he called to the hidden guard in the shadows.

"Hi yuh, Colt. The chief wants to see yuh."

Colt McGruder came out of the darkness. "Lacks

all of a half hour before you come on watch," he grunted. "What's he got on his mind?"

"Something about women," Fraley answered. "I'm glad it's you and not me."

"Yeah? You know something?"

Tonto Fraley shrugged. "I mentioned that Red Malone would be alive if he had left the sheriff's ga' alone, and Bart said it gave him an idea. Then he sent for you."

Colt McGruder stared and shook his head slowly. "He's got an idea that the sheriff will lay off if he can get the girl," he explained slowly. "It sounds like a good idea to me, and I don't make love to 'em like you know."

"Well, better get down there and see him," Fraley suggested. "And don't forget what happened to Red."

"Now look, Tonto," McGruder said grimly. "You know what we talked over with the boys when he rode out after killing Tucson. The next man Black Bart jumps here in camp will be his last!"

"I ain't forgetting," Fraley muttered. "If I was you, I'd try to talk him out of this idea he's hatching. Women of any kind don't mix with this business we are in."

"Yeah," McGruder murmured. "But you likewise know what happens to a jigger who argues with Black Bart when he gives an order."

He hitched up his gunbelt and walked slowly to the fire where the tall outlaw was waiting. Black Bart glanced up and jerked his thumb toward a log.

"Sit down," he grunted. "I got a job for you."

"Like the one I did to-night?" McGruder grinned.

Black Bart frowned. "No killing," he barked. "I rode down to the B Bar G. Yuma Leslie was there arguing with young Bowie. Refused to meet him when I called for show-down, and the sheriff's daughter got the drop on me with an old .41."

"So you killed young Bowie," McGruder said softly.

"I didn't! That's for Yuma Leslie to do, but the young squirt fell in love with Bowie's adopted daughter, Mary Jane."

Colt McGruder scratched his grey head. "Spell it out, Chief," he muttered. "It don't make sense to me."

"The girl's name is Bonnie Grant," the tall outlaw explained. "I want you to get down there and watch for a chance to grab her. Joe Grant will have business some place else if we hold his daughter."

"Was just thinking," McGruder said slowly. "We lost two good men account of that same gal. Red Malone . . . and Tucson!"

Black Bart straightened slowly and stared at the short outlaw. "What about it?"

Colt McGruder shrugged. "Nothing, but they were both pards of mine," he answered thoughtfully. "First Red was killed by Alamo Bowie, and then——"

"Then I killed Tucson Bailey for not obeying orders," Black Bart finished softly. "That's the law in this owl-hoot camp, Colt. Are you taking orders?"

Colt McGruder flushed and shrugged his wide shoulders. "I'm doing what I was told to do," he growled. "Not because I'm afraid of you, Bart. I know you can fade me with a six-gun, but like I pointed out once before, you can't down the whole outfit."

"You or the whole outfit," the tall outlaw answered grimly. "But you buscaderos will obey me without question. That straight?"

"Straight as a die," McGruder answered, and dropped his eyes before that piercing gaze. "Guess I'll be turning in now."

Black Bart stared when McGruder walked to the deep shadows of a pine bosky where a log-house sheltered the sleeping crew. Then he seated himself on the

log and smoked brown-paper cigarettes until the grey
light in the east warned of approaching dawn. He
arose quietly and walked over to the corral, and a
moment later he was saddling the black gelding.

"Might as well make sure," he muttered under his
breath, and rode across the valley.

Tonto Fraley shook his head when the tall outlaw
rode through the pass without offering any explanation,
and Black Bart scratched with the spurs when he was
out of sight and headed towards the Circle L. He had
given orders, and mutiny threatened in his own ranks.
They would either do what he told them to do, or
they would join Tucson Bailey.

He stopped abruptly when the clank of steel against
rocks warned of approaching riders. A grim-visaged
army was winding through the lavas of the badlands.
The tall outlaw cupped a pair of old glasses to his eyes
and swore softly. Then he started through a twisting
trail of underbrush until he could see better.

Alamo Bowie was riding in the lead with Sheriff
Joe Grant, while Brazos Day and old John Golden of
the J Bar G made the second pair. Young Jim Golden
was bringing up the drag with the posse, and the men
whispered among themselves while their leaders talked
in low tones.

"He might go on the fight, Alamo," Joe Grant suggested. "After what happened yesterday back in town."

Alamo Bowie shrugged carelessly. "You handle it,"
he grunted. "I only came along to read the sign.
The herd was moved up this way, and the Circle L
always has been hide-out range."

"You think Yuma Leslie was in on this rustling?"
the sheriff asked curiously.

"Do you?"

Sheriff Grant studied the question he had asked,
"I don't know much about that yearling," he admitted.
"But I do know that he ain't afraid of any man alive."

"Neither is Buddy," Alamo Bowie said bluntly. "We got to keep those two apart if we can."

Joe Grant nodded. "That's why Buddy high-tailed away from the J Bar G last night," he guessed shrewdly. "I could see it in the fingers of his gun-hand."

"Yes," and the deep voice of Alamo Bowie was filled with regret. "He's gun-fighting stock, Joe."

The sheriff raised his head and studied the trail ahead. Now they were through the pass and entering a deep grassy valley surrounded by low hills. Cattle grazed on the valley floor, and far ahead a cluster of buildings marked the headquarters of the Circle L. A man came out of the house and shaded his eyes, and Joe Grant spoke softly.

"It's Yuma. Pass the word back for the boys not to make a play."

Alamo Bowie dropped back and spoke to the posse. All nodded except young Jim Golden, and he stared ahead with sullen hatred in his clear grey eyes. Bowie watched him for a moment.

"Jim," he said quietly. "Don't go to fighting yore head, cowboy."

Jim Golden jerked his head around and nodded when he caught the look in the older man's eyes. "Count on me, Alamo," he said earnestly. "I ain't forgetting that I'm riding for the law."

Alamo Bowie smiled and gigged his horse to take his place with the sheriff. Yuma Leslie was waiting at the broad front porch; the only man visible on the place. Joe Grant reined in and swung down while he called a greeting.

"Howdy, Yuma. Just rode over to ask if you saw anything of a bunch of two-year-old J Bar G steers. They were headed over this way."

Yuma Leslie shook his head while his dark eyes watched the face of Alamo Bowie. "Didn't see any," he answered quietly. "You gents must have started early from the J Bar G."

Alamo Bowie narrowed his eyes. "You knew we were at the J Bar G?" he asked quickly.

Yuma Leslie waited a moment before answering. "One of the boys saw you about sundown," he explained. "Said he heard shooting down the canyon aways."

The sheriff glanced at Alamo Bowie. The grey gunfighter was sitting his saddle easily with right hand hooked in his worn gunbelt. His left arm hung limply at his side, and he was studying the face of the Circle L owner intently.

"Buddy done that shooting," Alamo volunteered. "Winged a Mex by the name of Torio Feliz. Yore man tell you that?"

Yuma Leslie shifted his boots and shook his head slowly. "He didn't. How come you to keep yore gun clean?"

"Tucson Bailey was slow," Bowie answered evenly. "And I never kill a man just to be killing."

"Interesting if true," Yuma Leslie drawled. "I always thought Tucson was fairly rapid with his hardware."

"Then you know him?" Bowie countered swiftly.

Yuma Leslie smiled and refused to be trapped. "Most every one around Yuma knew of him," he answered carelessly. "I told you the same thing yesterday down in Deming. Them two was pards of Red Malone. And one of them took a shot at you down on the river trail when the Coroner was there with the body."

"Yeah; forget about it," Bowie agreed. "Right now Tucson is in jail."

Yuma Leslie smiled and shrugged his shoulders. "Mebbe," he said slowly, and his face hardened. "Anything else bring you and yore army up this away on my range?"

Sheriff Joe Grant took a step forward. "That's

right, it did," he answered sternly. "We aim to run this gang of outlaws out, or kill every one of them. So we rode over here to make a start."

Yuma Leslie crouched forward with hand shadowing his gun. "Meaning just what?" he whispered.

"Meaning that the Circle L always has been outlaw range," the sheriff barked. "You got any objections if we ride around for a look-see?"

Yuma Leslie relaxed and waved his left hand. "Fly at it," he invited. "And don't get yoreselves lost in the tangles."

The sheriff mounted and spoke to his men. While back in a black-jack thicket a hundred yards from the house a tall man lowered the hammer of his Winchester and sheathed it in the scabbard under his saddle fender. Then he mounted a tall black gelding and walked the animal into the timber.

A pair of blue eyes watched him for a moment, and then a calloused thumb lowered the hammer of another rifle with a sigh. The second man was Buddy Bowie, and he sent his horse around to circle the thicket, keeping out of sight of the Circle L house. A few minutes later he rode through a narrow draw and waved his hat at a pair of riders coming in from the other end.

"It's Buddy," Alamo Bowie told the sheriff. "Something must have happened to bring him up here on the Circle L!"

"Let him talk first," Joe Grant advised. "He's learning to keep his head like an old-timer, Alamo."

Buddy Bowie rode up fast and came straight to Alamo. "I wanted to kill him back there," he began, and his voice was strained and husky with repressed emotion.

Alamo Bowie gazed levelly. "Yuma Leslie?" he asked quietly.

The tall cowboy shook his head. "Black Bart. He

was hiding in the black-jack thicket with a rifle trained on either you or Leslie. I couldn't make out just who, and I had him under my sights the whole time, with my finger aching to press trigger."

Alamo Bowie nodded his grey head slowly. "I had a feeling back yonder," he answered. "And you had Black Bart under yore sights?"

"And the sights drawed fine," Buddy muttered. "But I was all tangled up in my own loop. I made a promise to you, and one to Mother Nellie. I had no call to be on the Circle L any way you look at it. When that damn outlaw ramrod lowered hammer and rode away, I done the same thing and followed you and Joe Grant down here."

"Something funny about all this," the sheriff muttered. "Mebbe Tucson Bailey will talk some more if we put on the pressure."

"He won't," Buddy growled savagely. "That's one of the reasons I rode up here so early. Tucson was killed last night!"

Joe Grant straightened suddenly. "Can't be," he barked. "I sent him to Deming with Jud Leeds like you know!"

"Yeah," Buddy agreed. "But Jud Leeds was killed first. I found his body on the river trail on my way home from the J Bar G."

"Who killed Jud?" and the sheriff waited tensely for the answer.

"One of Black Bart's gang," Buddy answered. "I'd say it was that killer by the name of Colt McGruder, him being the best rifle-shot in the outfit. At first I thought Yuma Leslie had done it, and I told him so!"

Alamo Bowie rode closer and gripped Buddy by the arm. "Mebbe you better start at the beginning, and tell us the whole story," and his voice was edgy with restraint. "How come you to meet Yuma Leslie again?"

Buddy Bowie rolled a brownie and filled his lungs

with smoke. Then he began his recital. Talked himself out while the two pardners listened intently, and without interruptions. When he had finished, Alamo sighed deeply.

"It had to come," he stated quietly. "I'll be there to meet Black Bart next time."

"Gun Law," Buddy jerked out. "Black Bart could have killed me last night, and he could have killed you this morning. Then I had him under my sights and let him go!"

"That's Gun Law," Alamo Bowie answered softly. "It's the mark of a brave man no matter which side of the law he rides on. A gunman will shoot another feller in the back without giving him a chance, but a *gun-fighter* don't tally that away. He calls for show-down according to the code."

Buddy Bowie did not seem to hear. He was gazing across the valley toward the distant buildings of the Circle L. Right hand twitching with fingers writhing like snakes. Joe Grant saw it and nudged Alamo. The grey gun-fighter spoke softly.

"Not yet, son. He didn't bring it to you up here!"

Buddy jerked around with a snarl ripping from his lips. "He brought it to me last night, and Black Bart held me under his gun. Me and him would have settled it then if Bonnie had kept out of the play!"

."You can't force these things, son," Alamo Bowie remarked thoughtfully. "They work out when the time is right, and not before. But something about Yuma Leslie strikes me as being familiar," he added slowly. "Something I've seen before and can't call back."

Buddy Bowie leaned across the horn of his saddle. "Think hard," he whispered. "You ever know a gent who carried his gun with the handle pitched out that away like Leslie packs his?"

"That's what sticks me," Alamo Bowie admitted. "I've seen it before, but it gets away from me."

"You was shot up bad one time," Buddy persisted. "And you laid there in the hotel for a spell of time like a dead man. That tell you anything you ought to remember?"

Alamo Bowie slapped down with his right hand. "Three-Finger Jack!" and his voice rang triumphantly. "He wore his gun thataway!"

Then his deep voice died away while he stared intently at Buddy. Memories of the dimly remembered past crowded through his mind with startling clearness. The day in the desert when he had faced the dreaded outlaw; the fastest gun-fighter in Arizona. They had both struck at the same time, and Three-Finger Jack had died.

Alamo Bowie's right hand reached slowly across and gripped the useless muscles of his broken left arm. Three-Finger Jack had died, but he had left something for Alamo Bowie to remember him by. His bullet had crippled that arm, and the duel had almost ended in a draw.

"Three-Finger Jack wasn't married," he said slowly. "But Yuma Leslie carries the mark of him."

"Black Bart could tell you," Buddy growled hoarsely. "Like he told us last night there at the B Bar G!"

Alamo Bowie leaned forward and gripped with all the strength of his fingers. "Spell it out," he commanded sternly. "Read the sign, yearling. I ought to know!"

Buddy Bowie winced under the incredible strength of those biting fingers. "Turn me loose," he snarled. "Unclutch yore fingers, feller!"

Alamo Bowie jerked back and loosed his fingers. "Sorry, son," he murmured contritely. "Get it told now."

"Yuma Leslie and Three-Finger Jack both had the

same mother," Buddy stated bluntly. "That makes them half-brothers!"

Alamo Bowie stared and began to mutter to himself; as though he were seeing ghosts of the past, and found them unpleasant. While sheriff Joe Grant watched and waited and held his tongue. Finally the grey gunfighter shook his head positively.

"Yuma wouldn't have been but ten or eleven years old," he said slowly. "Three-Finger Jack never taught him what he knows!"

"He might have remembered," Buddy contradicted. "I can remember how you wore the twins when you were packing two guns."

"And he came up here to avenge his brother," Alamo whispered. "I can't throw down on a yearling like him!"

"I can," Buddy cut in promptly. "But he didn't come up here to whittle for you, Alamo. He don't know that he is the brother of Three-Finger Jack."

Alamo Bowie shrugged irritably. "You mean Black Bart never told him?"

"That's what Black Bart said," Buddy answered. "You see, they had different fathers. Three-Finger drifted to Tombstone and his mother married again and raised Leslie in Yuma." He leaned forward suddenly and pointed a finger at Joe Grant. "Sheriff."

"Yeah, Buddy. You think of something?"

"It just come to me," the tall cowboy answered quickly. "Black Bart was covering Yuma Leslie in case he talked with his mouth!"

Joe Grant stared and scratched his head. "Meaning that them two is in cahoots?" he asked slowly.

"You take last night," Buddy continued. "Yuma Leslie was holding me under his gun when Black Bart came up on the porch. He seemed to know Leslie, and he told us later about him being kin to Three-

Finger Jack. Then I catched him holding Yuma under his rifle back there not more than an hour ago!"

Alamo Bowie was rubbing the scar on his chin. "Guess work," he grunted. "Best thing we can do is to ride back there and make medicine with Leslie."

His face grew craggy and hard when he saw the look of happiness leap to the blue eyes of Buddy. "I'd tell uh man," the cowboy whispered. "I've waited long enough to make the kind of medicine that will do him the most good!"

"There's Nellie," Alamo reminded sternly, and felt a tug at his heart when the light faded from Buddy's bright eyes. "You made her a promise, son."

"I can't keep it now," the tall cowboy muttered, and bit his lip between strong white teeth. "You got to give me quits on it!"

Alamo Bowie shook his head slowly. "You and me are riding with the law now," he pointed out. "It's up to the sheriff to call the turn the way he sees it."

"I'll handle it," Joe Grant growled, and kept his eyes from the face of Buddy. "Asking you two just to stand by and listen. C'mon."

Back across the rolling mesa to the ranch-house where Yuma Leslie was saddling a fresh horse. He turned slowly with flame in his dark eyes when the sheriff swung down and hitched up his gunbelt. Alamo Bowie was staring at the long-barrelled gun on Leslie's leg, and the Circle L owner dropped his hand automatically.

"Leave it in leather," Joe Grant barked. "You didn't tell us all you knew, Leslie!"

Yuma Leslie turned slowly, and locked glances with Buddy Bowie. "You told," he accused hotly. "And this is as good a time as any!"

Buddy Bowie looked away and shook his head. Alamo Bowie sighed and dropped his gun back in the holster when Yuma Leslie unloosed his clutching fingers. But it was the sheriff who finally broke the deadlock.

"I'm the law, Leslie. Why didn't you say something about Jud Leeds getting rubbed out?"

"And have Alamo Bowie gunning me down?" the dark cowboy grated harshly. "Use yore head, lawman!"

"And about Black Bart cutting in on the play last night," Joe Grant continued. "You want to talk some?"

"I ain't talking," Leslie growled. "I'm out here on my own spread, minding my own business. You and yore law business don't interest me none!"

Joe Grant half turned and then jerked back. Now his forty-five was cradled in his hard fist with the muzzle covering Yuma Leslie. The dark cowboy snarled like a trapped wolf, but the sheriff eyed him coldly.

"Yo're under arrest, Yuma Leslie," he said quietly. "You are mixed up with a crooked crowd, and I aim to hold you while I look around some more. I got to find the answer."

"You got nothing on me," Leslie sneered, but his two hands came up at a level with his heart when he recognized the glint in the sheriff's eyes. "What's the charge you aim to put again me?"

"Accessory after the fact," Joe Grant recited clearly. "You knew about Jud Leeds, and you withheld knowledge from the proper authorities."

"That," and Leslie shrugged carelessly. "Black Bart admitted that one of his own men did it. Young Bowie heard him."

"Then there is a little matter of rustling," the sheriff continued. "You know more about it than you care to tell."

"I don't know anything about it," Leslie contradicted. "Keep on talking."

"Black Bart," Joe Grant said softly. "How long have you knowed him?"

"He's been up here about two weeks," and the Circle

L owner stared belligerently. "Law or no law, you wouldn't have got the drop on me if you hadn't pulled a sneak!"

"The law don't have to pull sneaks, yearling," the sheriff told him coldly. "And a lawman don't draw his pay for fighting duels. Now you better talk straight!"

Yuma Leslie swung his head around and stared out across the yards. Buddy Bowie caught the look and curled his lips. His voice held a boyish sneer when he spoke.

"He's gone now, Leslie. I saw him ride away."

Yuma Leslie whirled like a wild cat. "Who you talking about?"

"Black Bart. He was hiding back there in the thicket covering you with a long gun!"

Yuma Leslie studied his young rival's face for a long moment, and then drooped his shoulders. "Yo're telling the truth, cowboy," he rapped. "I figgered mebbe he would."

"He was fixing to press trigger if you talked," the sheriff added. "Looks like he don't trust you any too much after Tucson talked last night."

"And Bart killed Tucson," Buddy added. "Just like he aimed to kill you!"

Chapter IX

THE SHERIFF RIDES ALONE

THE heat devils were beginning to dance across the high desert while the four men kept close to the shadow of the porch. Joe Grant held the drop on Yuma Leslie and waited for the cowboy to speak. Even he was unprepared for the sudden reaction that motivated the young Circle L owner.

"Damn Black Bart!" and Yuma Leslie started to drop his hands fast. "I'll settle with him for that!"

"Keep them gun-hooks up," the sheriff warned sternly. "I might make a trade with you if you want to shoot square with the law."

Yuma Leslie hung poised and then relaxed with a sigh of defeat.

"I ain't talking," he muttered. "And I don't need any help."

Joe Grant studied the defiant cowboy for a long moment. He admired the courage with which Leslie met the web of circumstances that was drawing in about him. Against odds that an older man would have conceded too great for his experience and strength. The law on one side; with the ranchers of the Mimbres Valley openly suspicious. Then the sheriff shook his head when a new thought struck him.

A man in such a position would need help to hold his own. And he might find such help in the owl-hoot pack of Black Bart now hiding out in the lava badlands bordering the Circle L. Yuma Leslie had declared positively that he was not afraid of rustlers, and Joe

Grant nodded gravely when he thought of the J Bar G steers that had been driven away.

"The way you wear yore gun, Leslie," he said suddenly, and his deep voice was reminiscent. "I knew a feller who wore his cutter just like you do. Mebbe you knew him?"

The dark cowboy glanced up suspiciously.

"Mebbe I did," he answered softly. "You never can tell."

"He's dead now," the sheriff continued meaningly. "He finally met a faster man with his tools."

"They come and go," the cowboy remarked carelessly, but his dark eyes stared intently at the sheriff's face. "Every gent has to die sometime or other," he finished lamely.

"This feller died over Tombstone way," Joe Grant murmured. "Up to then he was tophand in that high desert country."

Yuma Leslie jerked around and skinned back his full lips.

"What you getting at?" he burst out. "I know damn well yo're talking about Three-Finger Jack!"

"Yeah," the sheriff agreed quietly. "But you wasn't old enough to remember much about him. You couldn't have been over ten-eleven years old at the time he passed on."

"He had his gun-handle tilted out for a fast draw," the Circle L owner growled. "I saw him many's the time. Practised wearing my gun the same way if you can make something out of it!"

Joe Grant smiled slowly. At last he had shaken the confident cowboy out of his defiant calmness. He studied the scowling dark face and flashing eyes with quiet satisfaction, and when he turned to Alamo Bowie, the grey gun-fighter was listening intently and checking his findings over in his mind.

"I got nothing personal against you Leslie," Bowie interrupted quietly. "But I did want to know how come you to wear yore hardware that away."

"And I don't give a damn what you thought," Leslie barked angrily. "I never did think you was so all-fired fast!"

"You wouldn't know," the tall gun-fighter answered lightly. "My life is mostly behind me; yores is mostly all ahead of you."'

"And so far I've worked it out without any help," the cowboy retorted. "Mebbe you wanted to know about that, too."

Alamo Bowie shrugged and turned to the sheriff. "Tell him, Joe," he suggested softly. "Seems to me he ought to know."

Yuma Leslie lost some of his anger while he watched the face of Joe Grant. The sheriff shook his head slightly, and the dark cowboy lowered his voice when he spoke. Pleaded softly as an admission of his curiosity.

"He said I ought to know. Well?"

"I figgered mebbe you knew all the answers," Grant murmured. "And I likewise figgered you had some answers Bowie and me are looking for."

"Yo're clouding the sign," Leslie barked. "Riding around in circles."

"Did you come up here to match guns with Alamo Bowie?" Joe Grant demanded sharply.

Yuma Leslie stared for a moment and shook his head slowly. The expression on his face left no doubt as to his honesty when he answered clearly and without hesitation.

"No, sheriff. Like he told me, most of his gun-fighting is all behind him. He ain't so fast as he used to be!"

Alamo Bowie started and then checked himself. At one time *both* his hands had been trained in gun-magic. Now he depended solely upon his right hand, and for a moment he felt a wave of doubt assail him. Was he getting as old as Leslie intimated?

"Gun-fighter," the sheriff muttered, and shook his head while he studied the Circle L owner. "With gunpowder salt in yore blood. Means you've killed yore man, and you not yet of age."

"Pass that," Leslie muttered. "You agoing to tell me?"

The sheriff drew a deep breath and sighed. "Three-Finger Jack," he murmured. "You and him were half-brothers!"

Yuma Leslie straightened slowly and threw back his shoulders.

"Is that all you had on yore mind?" he asked quietly.

"Ain't that enough for now?" the sheriff countered.

Leslie shook his head. "Not near enough," and his eyes widened with some secret relief. "I knew about that all the time."

The sheriff scowled and stepped forward. Jammed his gun deep in the lean belly and emptied Leslie's holster with a little vicious jerk. The tall cowboy started to twitch his hands down and changed his mind. Then the sheriff stepped away and pointed to the saddled horse.

"Mount up," he ordered gruffly. "And I'll put the cuffs on you the first crooked move you make. You and me are going to Deming!"

"Just a minute, sheriff," Leslie said slowly. "What you expect to gain by a play like that?"

Joe Grant smiled coldly. "If I can't count on any help from you, at least I can put you where you won't hinder the law," he answered bluntly. "There are several points I'm not clear about in my mind, and I want to know where you are while I'm trying to run down what sign there is."

"Yo're the boss," Leslie grunted, and closed his lips tight when he stepped across his saddle. "Only I was thinking about what happened to Jud Leeds when he was taking Tucson to Deming."

Joe Grant turned swiftly and stared with narrowed eyes.

"One of Black Bart's men shot him in the back," he snapped. "And Bart had us both under his sights not long ago!"

"Thought you'd remember," Leslie murmured.

The sheriff set his lean jaw. "Putting it that away, it might not be such a bad idea after all," he said quietly. "Taking you in just might bring him out in the open."

Yuma Leslie's face changed instantly. "Using me for bait, eh?" he growled.

"Something for you to think over," the sheriff answered. "Up to now you've been pretty well satisfied with yoreself."

Yuma Leslie turned in the saddle to glance at Alamo Bowie.

"I get it," he growled. "That gives Bowie a chance to bring up the drag and shoot Black Bart in the back."

Alamo Bowie leaped forward and closed down on the cowboy's wrist with a grip of steel. While his cold grey eyes narrowed and held the cowboy in a motionless trance.

"Think it over and unsay them words!"

Bowie's voice was deep and vibrant when he spoke softly, yet with a terrible strength that would not be denied. As though the weight of all his years of living were behind the power of his eyes, and in the strength of his fingers.

"I was wrong," Yuma Leslie admitted with a new humility. "Just got back at you like a kid button, Bowie. Right now you'd give yore other arm for the chance to meet Black Bart for a draw-and-shoot. Saying I'm sorry I talked out of turn with my mouth!"

A peculiar light changed the colour of the stern eyes holding the cowboy's gaze. Admiration and respect for a man of courage who admitted he was wrong. Not because he was afraid, but because he was honest.

"Thanks, Yuma," and Alamo Bowie twitched his fingers a time or two gently against the cowboy's muscles. Then he stepped away and climbed his saddle awkwardly with his good right arm.

"Let's get going," Leslie barked at the sheriff. "I won't make you any trouble."

Sheriff Grant nodded and touched his horse with the spur. Rubbed stirrups with his prisoner on the long ride through the valley, and two members of the posse fell in behind when they reached the outskirts of Deming and rode slowly into town.

The sheriff knew the temper of cowboys, and both the O Bar and the Diamond A had lost stock recently. If word got around that Yuma Leslie was mixed up in some way with the outlaws, someone was sure to suggest a rope.

When they reached the jail, Leslie swung down to the ground in front of the tie-rail and turned to his captor.

"I'm telling you one more time yo're wrong, sheriff," he stated earnestly. "Better change yore mind and turn me loose. I'll be right there at the Circle L any time you want me!"

Joe Grant shook his head firmly. "Got it to do for now," he answered. "It's one way to keep you and Buddy Bowie alive. In a day or two . . .?"

"A day or two might be a day too late," the cowboy murmured. "But yo're rodding the drive."

Hooves pounded down the street when the sheriff pushed the cowboy into his office. One of the deputies turned his gun on Yuma Leslie when the sheriff stepped back to the open door. The horse slid to a stop outside, and then Mary Jane Bowie was up on the steps facing Joe Grant while she panted for breath.

"Easy, Mary Jane," he told her gently. "Get back yore wind and tell me what brings you here in such a burning hurry."

"It's Bonnie," the girl gasped. "She's gone!"

The sheriff lost some of his composure while the colour drained from his deeply-tanned face. Then his eyes swung around to stare at the prisoner.

"Gone!" he whispered hoarsely. "Spell it out, Mary Jane!"

The girl looked at Yuma Leslie and frowned at the gun in the hands of the deputy. Joe Grant touched her impatiently on the shoulder, and Mary Jane swung around and caught her breath.

"Bonnie was worried about Buddy," she recited rapidly. "She saddled up and took a ride early this morning. When she did not return for breakfast, I went out to look for her!"

Yuma Leslie watched the sheriff's face and interrupted harshly.

"Black Bart did that," he stated grimly. "Turn me loose and I'll ride out there and get the girl!"

The sheriff whipped around like a flash. "You mentioned something might happen," he barked. "Said a day or two might be a day too late," and his hand went to his gun when he jumped in front of the cowboy. "Did you know about this?" he demanded icily.

"You was with me since sun-up," Leslie answered evenly. "You ought to know the answer to that one."

E

"But I wasn't with you last night," the sheriff shot back. "And you was with Black Bart!"

"Now you use yore head," Leslie suggested. "I was talking to Mary Jane . . . and her . . . brother. They can tell you I left before Black Bart did!"

"And the chances are he knew right where to find you," Joe Grant accused.

Yuma Leslie shrugged and turned his head. "I offered to go after the girl," he murmured.

"I'll ride out and get her myself," the sheriff shouted, and then a startled expression leaped to his eyes. "Meaning you could get her where I couldn't?" he asked slowly.

Yuma Leslie returned the stare without winking. "Meaning I'm younger than you are," he corrected, and rubbed his empty holster suggestively. "You and Alamo Bowie are about the same age."

Joe Grant turned abruptly to one of his deputies. "Take him back and lock him up. I'll talk to him again when I get back, but right now I'm riding out there to see what happened!"

"And you won't ride back," Yuma Leslie cut in grimly. "You can't match Black Bart, and you can't beat Colt McGruder to the gun!"

· "Colt McGruder, eh?" the sheriff repeated softly, and nodded his head when Yuma Leslie flushed. "That's the jigger who shot Jud Leeds in the back, and you knew all about it. And you didn't tell me," he continued harshly. "That's why I brought you down here to jail!"

"While Bart and McGruder are still on the loose," Leslie pointed out softly.

"You ain't on the loose," the sheriff shouted. "Take him back there and see that he stays put!"

He glared angrily when the deputy marched the prisoner back through the cell block and opened one of the doors. He turned quickly to Mary Jane and studied her face for a long moment. Then the girl spoke jerkily.

"They got her, sheriff. I saw where she struggled, and I found her Bisley .41 in the brush where she dropped it. I looked around for sign, and found the tracks of two horses heading toward Cooks Canyon!"

"Cooks Canyon! That's where Black Bart is hiding," the sheriff growled. "I'm going out there if I have to face the whole owl-hoot pack," and then he leaned toward the girl. "You, Mary Jane. I need yore help now. I want you to ride out toward the Circle L and let Alamo know."

"We were afraid of that," the girl whispered. "Afraid it was a play to make Daddy break his promise."

"Buddy made one, too," the sheriff reminded. "Which is one of the reasons I brought Yuma Leslie down here to jail."

"Buddy," the girl whispered faintly. "He rode over that way early this morning."

"We saw him," the sheriff admitted. "Alamo and I were talking to Leslie at his house. Black Bart was back in the brush covering Yuma with a rifle. Buddy had Black Bart under his long gun——"

"Don't you see?" the girl pleaded desperately. "Black Bart wants to throw suspicion on Yuma. He took Bonnie to make you give up the hunt for him so he can meet Daddy Alamo!"

"I aim to find out," and the sheriff quieted down and filled his pockets with fresh shells. "You ride out and get word to Alamo."

He ran from the office before she could answer and hit his saddle with a flying leap. Mary Jane called sharply, but the sheriff was spurring out of town at a dead run. She turned when the two deputies came back to the office from the cell block.

"Where's the sheriff?" one of the officers asked.

"Gone," the girl answered brokenly, and faced

them with hands clenched. "He is going back there to Cooks Canyon by himself. You men better follow him!"

"He must be out of his mind," the deputy growled. "He told us to stay here in the office, but I figger he's going to need plenty of help. C'mon, Jim!"

Mary Jane held her breath and watched them mount their horses. Her face twisted when they hesitated; cleared when the two men reined sharply and roared up the street after Joe Grant.

"Gun Law," she moaned softly, and caught her breath when the sound of her own voice brought her back to her surroundings.

She seated herself on the edge of the sheriff's desk and ran over the events of the last two days in her mind. The deaths of Red Malone and Tucson Bailey. The visit of Black Bart to the B Bar G while the men were away following rustler sign. The quarrel between Buddy and the young Circle L owner, and Mary Jane slid to her high heels quickly and stared down through the corridor of cells.

"He might tell me," she whispered, and started for the far end.

"Yuma," she called softly. "Where are you?"

"I'm in jail," a sarcastic voice answered gruffly. "You come back here to hooraw me?"

The girl bit her lip and walked back to the cell. "You should be ashamed of yourself," she said pridefully. "I told you that I believed in you, and then you act like a spoiled boy."

"I'm just a boy like Buddy," he mimicked, and the girl turned away. He had repeated the same words she had used just the night before.

"I made a mistake," she whispered, and started for the office.

"Mary Jane," he called swiftly. "Saying I'm sorry

for talking that away. I was just blowing off my mad."

The girl stopped and turned to face him.

"I came back here to ask your help," she told him slowly. "It all seems so mixed up, and everyone tries to hide what they know. Even you and Buddy," she continued.

"Leave Buddy out of it," the cowboy answered harshly. "About Alamo; I had a talk with him not long ago. I figgered some sort of a play like this was coming up, but neither him nor the sheriff would listen."

"You told Alamo and Joe Grant?"

Yuma Leslie nodded. "And the sheriff threw me in jail because I wouldn't say any more," he muttered.

"But don't you see, Yuma?" the girl pleaded. "You said either too little or too much!"

"It can't be done," he grunted. "The best thing a feller can do is take a hitch in his jaw and hold tight to his tongue."

"Buddy," the girl said softly. "He was out at the Circle L this morning."

"Let's leave him out of it," Leslie barked.

"But can't you see?" the girl argued. "He promised not to take trouble to you, and he was covering that outlaw when Black Bart had you under his rifle."

"Yeah? What about it?" Leslie growled.

"He kept his promise," the girl continued. "A Bowie always does that."

"The Bowies haven't got a corner on that," Leslie grunted. "But you said you wanted to talk."

"Bonnie," the girl said thoughtfully. "She thinks a lot of Buddy. That's why I brought up his name, and he will be killing-mad when he hears about this."

"A gent can't do his best work when he's mad," Leslie muttered. "He wouldn't have a chance again either of those two if he cut their sign while he was fighting his head."

"But he would try," Mary Jane moaned. "Nothing could keep him from hunting them down if he had to go right into Cooks Canyon to find Bonnie."

"Something would stop him before he got that far," Leslie said grimly. "A forty-five slug placed between a gent's shoulders would do the trick, and that owl-hoot gang don't take many chances!"

"You can take it that coolly?" the girl demanded almost hysterically. "When the only brother I have is in danger?"

"How come he is?" Yuma Leslie asked slowly. "He don't even know the sheriff's daughter is missing."

Mary Jane stared at his face for a moment and started back toward the office. Yuma Leslie called softly, but the girl entered the office with her shoulders shaking. She could not let him see her crying, and she paid no attention when he called her name repeatedly.

Yuma Leslie drew back in his cell and lowered his head while he thought swiftly. Then he was at the barred door shaking the lock until it rattled. When he received no reply, he retreated sullenly to his bunk and threw himself on the rough blanket.

"Yuma," a faint voice called some minutes later. "You wanted me?"

"Wanted you?" and the cowboy laughed bitterly. "You better go away now."

"But you called me," the girl almost sobbed. "I thought perhaps you had thought up a plan to help me."

"I'd do anything for you, Mary Jane," he growled deep in his throat, but he stayed back in the dark shadows where she could not see his flushed face.

"You mean that, Yuma?" the girl asked breathlessly. "You really mean you would help?"

"Help?" he repeated ironically. "And me locked up in here with nothing but my two hands?"

"You could use your mind to think with," the girl suggested. "If both of us think real hard, we might find a way to help."

"The only help that would do any good is fast gun work," the cowboy grunted softly. "And Black Bart is the fastest killer I ever saw. Colt McGruder ain't but a shade behind his boss."

"They will kill the sheriff," the girl whispered. "What can we do?"

Yuma Leslie laughed grimly. "We?" he mocked. "We're here in jail, and you sent what help you had to help Joe Grant. If they ever come in sight of him," he added softly.

"He brought you down here and put you in jail," the girl said thoughtfully, and bit her lip. "Why did they arrest you, Yuma?"

"For obstructing justice and not telling the law about deputy sheriff Jud Leeds getting killed," the cowboy answered bitterly. "I was supposed to blab my head off as soon as the sheriff rode up to the Circle L."

"You didn't tell him?" the girl asked. "After what you heard last night at the B Bar G?"

"That's why I couldn't tell him," Leslie growled. "Alamo Bowie was with the sheriff, and they both looked at me like I had rustled that J Bar G herd of steers. So I just sat tight and kept my mouth shut!"

"You came up here a stranger," the girl said thoughtfully. "You didn't tell anyone very much about yourself, Yuma. And when you don't tell about yourself, they are bound to talk about you."

"Let 'em talk," he grunted. "I've taken care of myself up to now, and I'm not asking for any help."

The girl studied his face for a long moment. "I believe in you, cowboy," she told him frankly. "Or I would not be here talking to you now."

The caged man came to the bars and peered down into her pretty flushed face.

"You believe in me, Mary Jane?" and his voice held a new note of gladness. "After what they said about me?"

Mary Jane nodded slowly. "I don't know much about you yet, but it seems that we have lived years in the last three days," she answered, and he thrilled to the tremble in her throaty voice.

"You are the only one here in the Mimbres Valley who does," he muttered. "I wonder why you believe?"

"You have a temper like Buddy's," the girl went on, and set her lips when the cowboy's face darkened. "You are a fighter . . . a gun-fighter," she said sadly. "But you tell the truth when you talk!"

"Thanks, little pard," he growled huskily. "What do you want me to do?"

"I want you to put yourself in the place of Joe Grant for a time," the girl answered, and lifted her blonde head sharply. "What would you do if you were out there following the sign?"

The tall cowboy half-turned and cupped his chin in his left hand.

"That would be easy," he said finally, and his dark eyes gleamed in the shadows of his cell. "I'd come up on that McGruder killer and give him a chance."

"You'd take a risk like that?" the girl whispered.

Yuma Leslie nodded his curly head. "Every man is entitled to a chance," he said earnestly. "Him being wrong that away, and me having the right on my side, I'd outspeed him when it come to show-down!"

"But he might kill you," the girl whispered under her breath.

Yuma Leslie swelled his chest and squared his broad shoulders. "He wouldn't," he stated quietly. "You kinda know when you see a gent work a gun one time, and Colt McGruder don't have what it takes."

"The sheriff," Mary Jane whispered. "Can he . . .?"

"McGruder would beat Joe Grant," Leslie muttered positively. "If I could only take his place!"

Chapter X

THE PAROLE

MARY JANE left the cell without speaking and walked to the sheriff's office. She opened a drawer and took a bunch of keys from a hidden corner. Held her head high when she returned to the cell of Yuma Leslie and called him to the door.

"You are a prisoner now, Yuma," she began earnestly. "Will you make me a promise?"

Yuma Leslie studied her serious face and shuffled his feet. "You mind giving it a name?" he asked suspiciously.

"I want you to give me your promise to surrender again if I release you on parole," the girl said slowly. "Will you promise?"

The prisoner studied the question for a long moment. "You mean you will turn me loose?" he asked doubtfully.

Mary Jane nodded. "I will turn you loose so you can ride out there and help Joe Grant . . . and Bonnie. She loves Buddy, and she is such a child. Just past seventeen."

"Me help the sheriff?" Leslie almost sneered. "After what he did to me, and what he thinks about me?"

"Yes, and I am sure you will, Yuma."

Yuma Leslie reached a hand through the bars and caught her fingers. "I'd go to hell for you in my bare feet, Mary Jane," he whispered huskily. "And you know it!"

The girl nodded. "I'm asking you to help little Bonnie," she repeated firmly. "You know the secret

trails back there in the badlands. You can get in where
the law would fail."

A startled look leaped to his dark eyes. Was carefully
hidden when Yuma Leslie bowed his head. Then his
fingers touched the keys and jingled them softly.

"I could take the keys and get out without making
any promise," he growled, and closed his fingers over
them.

Mary Jane waited until he raised his head and stared
deep into her wide blue eyes. "But you won't," she
stated positively. "Because I trusted you. Will you
promise, cowboy?"

"Open the door," he answered gruffly. "I promise
on my word of honour, and I ain't never broke it yet.
I'll get Bonnie Grant out of that canyon if it can be
done!"

Mary Jane fitted a key in the lock and swung back
the cell door. Walked into the sheriff's office and opened
the top drawer of the desk. Lifted a heavy forty-five
six-gun and handed it to Yuma Leslie by the long
handle.

"It's your own gun," she told him. "I saw the
sheriff put it there for safe keeping. Please hurry now,
Yuma!"

Yuma Leslie holstered the weapon and moved like a
cat. His arms went around the girl and tightened.
Mary Jane closed her eyes and made no attempt to
escape, and the tall cowboy bent his head and kissed
her warm red lips. Closed his eyes when he felt her
answer, and then he stepped back with a little cry of
dismay.

"Saying I'm sorry to take advantage of you that
away, dream girl," and he leaped across the floor and
jumped his saddle with a flush of shame colouring his
dark face.

Mary Jane stood perfectly still and watched him
thunder up the narrow street. Something had happened

to her. Something that brought a glow of happiness to her heart. Then she uttered a little cry when she thought of her brother Buddy. He would be riding with Alamo Bowie, and the sheriff had her word to ride for help.

Now she moved fast and raced from the office to mount her sweating horse. The Circle L was miles away, and if Buddy and Yuma Leslie should meet on the trail . . .? What would he say when he learned that she had turned Yuma Leslie loose?

Men stared at her when she raced through town and headed for the broad open valley. Twenty miles to Cooks Canyon; several more to the hide-out of the outlaws back in the Goodsight Mountains. If the sheriff had only waited for help. But Joe Grant was a man of action, and now his only child was in danger.

She knew what he would do. Knew what Buddy would do when he heard the news. Buddy didn't say much, but she remembered the way he had looked at the tiny girl when he was sure no one had been watching him. Her heart missed a beat when she thought of Yuma Leslie riding out to help Joe Grant. And the sheriff thought the dark cowboy was a prisoner in Deming jail.

A moving speck far out in the valley caught her eye, and the girl reached to her saddle-bags for the glasses she always carried. She cupped them to her eyes and turned the pin to regulate the focus; tried to still the tremble in her hands. Joe Grant leaped into her vision for a brief moment before he rounded a bend in the trail. Then another bobbing dot far in the rear of the sheriff, and the girl sighed thankfully when she recognized Yuma Leslie. The two deputies had evidently taken the long way and were nowhere in sight, and the girl cased the glasses and turned her horse toward the distant Circle L.

Out on the rough mountain trail leading away from the valley, Joe Grant was muttering hoarsely to himself while he reined his horse to a walk. He came to a fork in the trail and stopped briefly to study the sign. Hoof tracks led both ways and the sheriff pointed toward the left.

"Closest to the B Bar G," he muttered. "If I find him . . .!"

His hand twitched the heavy gun against crimp when he started through the timber leading to Cooks Canyon. Rode along in silence for an hour until the sun told him that it was noontime. Then he swung down and loosed his cinches to allow the horse to drink when they came to a cold spring.

"If he hurts Bonnie," and his deep whisper was like the growl of a bear. He whirled with eyes narrowed when a twig cracked off in the trail-side brush to the right.

"Hold it," a deep voice warned softly, and entirely without excitement.

Joe Grant stiffened with his right hand close to his gun. A tall man stood near a black gelding not more than ten yards away. Dressed entirely in black from polished boots to high Stetson, and the sheriff felt the hot blood of anger surge madly through his veins.

"Black Bart," he ripped out hoarsely. "Where's my girl?"

The tall outlaw smiled with his black eyes. "Safe enough," he answered carelessly. "And she will stay thataway if you come down off your high horse and listen to reason."

Joe Grant crouched forward. Black Bart faced him fearlessly with long arms hanging loosely at his sides. Empty handed. While his glittering black eyes watched the sheriff and dared him to take a chance.

"I came up here to get Bowie," the outlaw said very softly. "Now that we have met, I suggest to you that you have important business somewhere else for a while. I figgered to make my argument more convincing if I took the girl."

Joe Grant experienced the purgatory of indecision while he stared at the long cruel face across the trail. His only child was in danger, but he had taken an oath to do his duty and to uphold the law. His heart was torn with physical pain when he thought of the tiny girl, and then his right hand wrenched down to grip the handle of his gun.

Black Bart saw the grey eyes narrow just before the clutching fingers touched wood. His own right hand moved swiftly. So fast that flame and smoke belched out from his fist before the sheriff's gun had cleared leather. Joe Grant felt a tearing, searing pain just below the heart when he swung around and shocked to the ground, and then a curtain of velvety blackness enveloped him.

Black Bart stared for a long moment and jacked the spent shell from his smoking weapon. Plucked a bullet from his belt and thumbed it automatically through the loading gate while his head nodded slowly. After which he mounted the black gelding and rode slowly up the trail with an indifferent shrug of his powerful shoulders.

Down the back trail, Yuma Leslie came to the branching fork and stopped his horse to study the trampled ground. He jerked his head up when a soft echoing explosion rattled through the trees from far off in the timbered distance.

"Six-gun," he whispered softly, and turned to stare at the two paths. Both were lined with brush and led through a thicket of scrubby post oak. The left-hand trail pointed toward the B Bar G; the right was a little used short-cut to the Goodsight Mountains.

Yuma Leslie hung in the saddle and tried to solve

the puzzle. Sheriff Joe Grant was somewhere ahead
of him; had probably met with one of Black Bart's
gang. Sound was hard to trace through timber and
echoing rocks, and one guess was as good as another.
Then the dark-eyed cowboy leaned far over and
stared at two sets of fresh tracks leading off to the right.

His spur raked back and sent his horse in that direction,
and Yuma Leslie rode hard until he came to a trickle of
water seeping down across the trail. A whorl of mud
eddied up in the clear water like drifting smoke, and
the cowboy nodded his head and loosed the gun in his
moulded scabbard.

"Five minutes ahead of me at the most," he whispered,
and narrowed his eyes to study every moving leaf and
trail-side sign.

The minutes dragged away while he sent the horse
at a fast walk through the timber. Ears tuned to catch
every sound, and he reined to a stop when the creak
of saddle leather came to him from around a sharp
bend just ahead. He pulled a saddle string loose and
made a loop around the nose of his horse to prevent a
whinny, after which he started to creep slowly up the
trail. Placing his thin-soled riding boots carefully to
make not the slightest sound.

"Right now yore old man is a corp," a heavy voice
boomed brutally. "Bart was riding up that other trail
yonder, and he never misses when he drops hammer!"

Yuma Leslie stopped suddenly and waited. He knew
that voice; knew the man just around the bend. Colt
McGruder; second in speed only to Black Bart himself. The deadliest shot in the gang with a rifle, and
the killer of deputy sheriff Jud Leeds. The tall cowboy
poised, and then came the answering voice he had
expected.

"Please take me back," a girl pleaded earnestly.
"Do anything with me, but let me go to my father now.
He needs me!"

Bonnie Grant! Yuma Leslie knew that the tiny girl was sobbing. Could picture the terror and grief in her brown eyes, and his right hand began to twitch when Colt McGruder laughed coarsely.

"Joe Grant don't need you now, gal. He got what Alamo Bowie will get. What Yuma Leslie will get if he tries to run a blazer on the boss!"

"It wasn't Daddy," the girl sobbed hysterically. "He was riding with Alamo Bowie. I know it wasn't him!"

"It was that lawman," McGruder answered positively, "Right now he's all through doing what he tried to do, and Bowie won't be no different when he meets Black Bart!"

The tall cowboy straightened slowly and began to move forward. Stretched his neck around a shoulder of rock until one eye could see, and then he jumped sideways like a cat and landed lightly on the balls of his feet.

Now his dark eyes were glowing with a feral light that changed to a soft luminous red while he stared at the broad back of Colt McGruder. Bonnie was sitting her saddle with feet tied under the belly of her horse. Both hands tied behind her back; staring at the man on the ground tightening the cinches.

Two heavy guns thonged low on the short powerful legs, with handles tilted out rustler-style for a quick draw. Coarse black hair hanging down on the wide, heavily-muscled shoulders. Grinning through the black stubble that covered the lower part of his face, and the girl shuddered when his thick fingers touched her.

"Yuma Leslie is not your kind," she said positively. "I know it now after what you said about Black Bart!"

"Keep on guessing," the outlaw chuckled. "But the boss will know what to do when he meets that good-lookin' cow nurse."

Yuma Leslie spoke softly through tight-clenched teeth. "Turn slow, Colt McGruder. I ought to shoot you in the back for a killing lobo!"

The stocky outlaw jerked suddenly. His hands darted down toward his twin guns and stopped as quickly. Then he turned slowly like a man in a trance. A grin split his heavy face when he saw Yuma Leslie regarding him coldly with right hand hooked in his belt.

"I was just now talking about you, Yuma," and Colt McGruder tried to make his voice sound careless. "What you doing way back here in the brakes?"

"Trailing a skunk," Leslie snapped. "Since when has Black Bart started to make war on women folks?"

"Since last night," the outlaw answered promptly. "You ought to know, seeing that you was there!"

"You wasn't," Leslie barked. "And I was accused of something you done!"

Colt McGruder shrugged. "I done lots of things in my time," he murmured. "Like yoreself."

"You killed that deputy," Leslie accused harshly, and fought for control. "For a while I was blamed for it. You shot him in the back without giving him a chance!"

"Just another good guess," McGruder sneered. "Finding the answer is something else again!"

Yuma Leslie shook his head one time. "We got the answer," he told the sneering outlaw. "Black Bart came to the B Bar G like you might have heard. Admitted it was one of his men got Jud Leeds with a long gun, and you claim to be tops with a rifle."

"Yeah?" and Colt McGruder leaned forward with a scowl on his bearded face. "So I shot Jud Leeds with a rifle. What about it, feller?"

"Every man deserves a chance," the cowboy answered more quietly. "Alamo Bowie gave Tucson one, and his chip threw off his shot when Torio Feliz tried a sneak with a throwing knife. Those two are gun-fighters, but you wouldn't know the difference!"

"Mebbe you do?" McGruder sneered. "I don't fight to lose, and like you might have heard, Tucson Bailey is dead!"

"Black Bart killed him, but he gave him as much chance as Bart ever gives a man," Leslie said quietly. "Which is more than you gave Leeds."

"And Black Bart told that, eh?" McGruder muttered softly. "The boys will be glad to know."

"You won't tell them," the cowboy answered pointedly.

Colt McGruder set his boots wide and spat from the side of his mouth. "What you gettin' at, feller?" he asked thickly.

Yuma Leslie leaned forward. "Did you meet Joe Grant?" he asked in a whisper.

Colt McGruder grinned and shook his head. "Black Bart met that nosey lawman like as not," he chuckled. "That's why for I snatched the girl. Bart figgered Joe Grant would pull in his horns and find some pressing business over around Silver City if we got the girl. Looks like the sheriff was stubborn."

"Mebbe," and the cowboy spoke softly. "I'm taking the girl back with me," he added suddenly, and watched the face of the outlaw.

Colt McGruder growled savagely under his breath and shifted his big boots for balance. "Over my dead body, and you ain't going back," he muttered. "You won't live to shoot it out with young Buddy Bowie!"

Bonnie Grant swayed in the saddle and tried desperately to catch the eye of Yuma Leslie. The cowboy was watching McGruder, and the fingers on his gunbelt were tapping a rapid tattoo against the worn leather. The girl had been too terrified to speak, but now her voice broke the grim silence.

"Please, go away, Yuma. He means to kill you!"

Yuma Leslie smiled with his lips. A hard smile that ridged his jaws with muscle, and entirely without mirth. Watching Colt McGruder while the outlaw inched his big hands up slowly toward the guns on his thick legs. While Leslie read the intention of the killer in the little greenish-grey eyes.

He felt the throb of tingling blood in the ends of his fingers when he saw the little V wrinkles leap to the corners of McGruder's eyes. The outlaw was sure of himself. Was going to take a chance. Both had said what had to be said, and both were all talked out.

It came like a bolt of lightning from a clear sky when Colt McGruder twitched his shoulder muscles and wrapped fingers around the handles of his tilted guns. Yuma Leslie dropped his right hand and made his draw with thumb earing back the hammer on the up-pull. Gunlight winked out from the naked muzzle like a flash of sunlight, and Colt McGruder stumbled with both arms trying to lift his holstered guns.

The heavy weapons hung in leather while the stocky outlaw leaned against the shock that battered his swelling torso. A startled expression leaped briefly to his eyes before he swayed back and crashed to his wide shoulders. The fall jerked his twin guns free, and both roared futilely when the reflexes jerked spasmodically to mark the passing of life.

Yuma Leslie leaned forward then and lowered the hammer of his smoking gun. Bonnie Grant stared at him wide-eyed in the grip of a terror that had paralyzed all her muscles. She had heard Alamo Bowie and her father tell about men dying, but the recitals had always seemed unreal and far away. Now she knew why their eyes held that peculiar look that only comes with actual experience.

She was unable to speak when the tall cowboy came to her to cut the thongs that bound her tiny hands. After which he slashed the ropes that held her boots and lifted her lightly to the ground. Bonnie Grant leaned against him and began to tremble violently with sudden reaction.

"You killed him!" she sobbed. "It was terrible!"

"It had to be done," he answered slowly, and there was no regret in his voice. "He meant to kill me, and take you back there to the owl-hoot hide-out in the Goodsights."

"Oh," the girl sobbed jerkily. "I just couldn't tear my eyes away, and I didn't want to look!"

"You better stretch yore muscles so's we can ride," Leslie answered practically. "We want to make tracks out of here pronto," and his eyes glanced briefly at the dead man.

"He caught me down by the river," the girl whispered between sobs. "Said he was taking me to the camp you mentioned, and I lost my gun in the brush."

"I know," Leslie muttered, and patted her shoulder gently. "Mary Jane went to look for you, and she found your gun. Then she rode in to tell the sheriff, and he sent her to get word to Alamo Bowie and Buddy."

Bonnie Grant stopped crying and straightened up to grip him by the arms. "You must go," she panted, "If Buddy should find you now——"

"Yeah? And if he should?"

The girl stared at his dark face and smouldering black eyes. She had seen him kill . . . knew that he would kill again. And yet he had risked his life to save her. He had ridden into danger to help her father.

"You mustn't," she whispered, and her eyes widened when she glanced at Colt McGruder and thought of her father. Yuma Leslie read her thoughts and patted her shoulder.

"Brace up, Bonnie," he muttered. "We must hurry and see if we can do anything to help the sheriff."

"No, no," the tiny girl cried. "I will go alone. There has been enough killing, and I am in your debt more than I can ever repay!"

He shrugged with a gentle smile softening his dark face. "Wrong," he contradicted. "No woman is ever in my debt. You feel alright to ride now?"

Bonnie Grant stared at his face and knew that she could not change him. He helped her to the saddle when she nodded, and the girl took the bridle reins and shuddered when she pointed to the body in the trail.

"Him," she whispered. "It seems cruel to leave him so."

Yuma Leslie shrugged. "Some of his pards will be down to find out about the shooting," he answered carelessly, and touched his horse with the spurs. "Right now I'm thinking about the living, and there might be something we can do for the sheriff."

"Daddy," the girl whispered. "If he met Black Bart . . . ?"

"Now you buck up," the cowboy growled irritably. "We don't know that he met Bart. We won't know till we get back there and check on that one shot."

Bonnie Grant bit her lips to keep back the tears, and followed him down through the timbered trail. Neither spoke until they came to the fork where Yuma Leslie had taken the branch leading to the right. There he swung down again to study the ground.

"No one has come down this way since I passed," he muttered. "The sheriff must have been up ahead of me," and he turned with a frown. "You keep behind me now, girl!"

Bonnie Grant stared at his straight back and the strong column of his bronzed neck. A stranger in a strange and unfriendly land, fighting his battles against outlaws as well as the law. She felt a warm wave of sympathy for him when she remembered how he had looked in the lamp-light the night before on the B Bar G. When Mary Jane had told him that she could not keep her promise.

She knew that he had wanted to fight it out with Buddy Bowie; had holstered his gun to ride away because of the women. Even under the naked gun of Black Bart, leader of the outlaws. And yet the tall outlaw had talked as though he knew him intimately.

Yuma Leslie was riding slowly with eyes watching the trail ahead. She saw him jerk suddenly, and turned his horse swiftly to bar her view. She neck-reined aside; gasped when she saw a body huddled on the ground with a saddled horse grazing nearby. Then she slid to the ground with a little cry welling up from her aching throat.

"Daddy," she called. "Speak to me, Daddy!"

Yuma Leslie threw his reins down and hit the ground in front of her. She tried to push him away, but he held her firmly and turned her around.

"Better stay back, Bonnie," he urged gently. "Better let me look after him first!"

The girl struggled frantically and finally slipped from his hands. She ran up the trail and fell to her knees beside the sheriff. Searched the deeply-tanned face without touching him. Yuma Leslie ran to her when she cried out with a note of new-born hope in her sobbing voice.

"He's alive, Yuma! He is still alive!"

"Shore he is," Leslie growled, and hunkered down on his high heels. "You couldn't kill a feller like him unless you cut off his head and hid it from him!"

"Do something," the girl pleaded. "Hurry, Yuma!"

The cowboy stared at the soggy stained shirt with a frown of doubt. Then he reached down inside and explored gingerly with his fingers. Shook his head slowly and stopped the gesture abruptly.

"Bad," he whispered, and then his face lighted up. "Bonnie," he almost shouted. "The bullet just creased him. Hit him high above the heart to knock him out, but I'm sure he will rouse around!"

Bonnie Grant stared at him, and her teeth chattered when she tried to keep back the tears of relief. "Are you sure?" she whispered in a faint voice.

"Certain sure," he answered quickly. "It made a bad wound in his side, but not enough to keep him down for keeps. These o'-timers are a tough breed, Bonnie. You just can't kill 'em!"

Bonnie Grant closed her eyes and moved her lips slowly. "Thank God," she whispered. "I felt all the time that he was . . . still alive and waiting for us. Please do something to help him, Yuma."

"Yo're brave for a gal-chip," he praised gruffly "And I'm telling you Joe Grant will be alright!"

Chapter XI

YUMA LESLIE'S TEACHER

YUMA LESLIE unbuttoned the sheriff's heavy wool shirt and reached for his knife. Then he cut the undershirt into pieces and handed them to the girl. She leaned forward to stare at the ragged wound just over the heart on the left side, and he noticed the tremble of her lower lip.

"Little canteen on my saddle," he growled. "Bring it so's we can wash out that bullet burn!"

Thankful for some action that would help control the fear in her mind, Bonnie Grant ran back to the horses and fumbled with the strings that held the cloth-covered canteen. Yuma Leslie was cutting strips from the torn undershirt when she returned, and the girl studied his dark face as though she were seeing a miracle performed.

The tall cowboy was applying a pad to stop the flow of blood, and his black eyes were soft as he watched the pallid lips of the wounded sheriff. No woman could have been more gentle, and now the stern fighting lines were gone from his mouth. Bonnie Grant caught her breath and went to her knees beside him with the stopper removed from the canteen, and a new feeling of security in her heart.

"He will live?" she whispered.

"Shore he will. And he ought to be rousing around most any time now."

He applied a cold-water press and washed the wound clean, and the girl marvelled at the ease with which he lifted the sheriff to pass strips of cloth under the broad shoulders. Made his ties as neatly as a surgeon . . . or a cowboy who knew how to fashion knots. Then he fashioned a bandolier bandage from the left side up over the right shoulder.

"You have almost stopped the bleeding," the girl whispered.

"We want it to bleed some to keep the wound clean," he muttered. "But we know the bandage won't slip."

So engrossed was he in his work that he did not hear the muffled hoof-beats coming up the trail. His head jerked back and he came snapping to his feet when a deep hoarse voice growled savagely behind him.

"Reach, you killin' son! Reach high before I slip hammer!"

Buddy Bowie was straddling the narrow trail with his forty-five spiking out from his big right hand. Blue eyes slitted and blazing with menace while his face twisted in a scowl of hatred.

Yuma Leslie glanced at the gun and curled his full lips in a sneer. "You ain't no hero, Bowie," he said coldly. "Holster yore gun and lend a man a hand."

Buddy Bowie turned his head and parted his lips with surprise. He had come roaring up the trail ready to kill, and the man he hunted was refusing his challenge. Then his eyes rested briefly on the sheriff.

"You got him on a sneak," he accused hotly. "Account of him taking you down to jail!"

Bonnie Grant recovered from her surprise and ran to him with a little cry. Breasted right up to the gun and threw her arms around his waist. Buddy Bowie jerked sharply and lowered the filed hammer when the gun was muffled against her firm breast, and a bewildered expression widened his blue eyes when Yuma

Leslie shrugged and refused to take the advantage offered him.

"Black Bart shot Dad," Bonnie Grant whispered swiftly. "Yuma and I have just finished bandaging the wound!"

Buddy spoke jerkily. "That was a fool play, Bonnie. My thumb might have slipped the hammer when you barged in that away!"

"I knew it wouldn't," the girl answered confidently. "Who told you, Buddy?"

Buddy Bowie pushed her away and turned to Yuma Leslie with the gun in his hand. "Yo're still under arrest, Leslie," he barked gruffly. "Don't forget it!"

The Circle L cowboy shrugged again. "But I'm not your prisoner," he answered bluntly. "I made Mary Jane a promise, and I aim to keep it. She turned me loose on my honour, and when she comes I will surrender my gun to her."

"I'll take that gun now," and Buddy stepped forward.

Yuma Leslie went into a crouch with his right hand shadowing the smoke-grimed weapon on his leg. "I'm warning you, Bowie," and his voice was husky. "You try to take my iron, and I'll take a chance. I'll match my draw against yore drop as shore as sin!"

They glared at each other until Bonnie Grant spoke softly. "Don't, Buddy. I don't know what might have happened if Yuma hadn't come when he did. Colt McGruder was taking me back to the hide-out in the Goodsights!"

The blond cowboy lowered his gun slightly and stared at Leslie. "You kill Colt McGruder?"

Yuma Leslie nodded grimly. "I killed him!"

Bonnie Grant shuddered. "Colt McGruder had me tied to my saddle," she interrupted quickly. "With my hands bound behind my back. Black Bart was going to hold me, figuring to force Dad to leave him and his gang alone."

Buddy Bowie changed expression and shook his shoulders as though the task he had to do was distasteful. "Thanking you for what you did, Leslie," he growled ungraciously.

"You ain't thanking me for anything," Leslie retorted sharply. "I'd do the same for any woman, and you needn't act so high and mighty about it!"

His hand moved down slowly and rested on the tilted grip of his gun. Buddy Bowie watched him and holstered his own weapon smoothly. Then he turned his back on Leslie and hunkered down beside the sheriff. Yuma Leslie stared when a faint far-away voice spoke softly.

"I heard you, feller, but yo're still under arrest!"

Leslie smiled then and raised the sheriff up to rest against his knee. "Yeah, Grant," he agreed quietly. "How you feeling along about now?"

"A long ways off," the sheriff answered, and tried to look around. "Black Bart," he muttered hoarsely. "You get him?"

Yuma Leslie shook his dark head. "Never even saw him," he answered quietly. "You might feel some better if you are strong enough to have visitors."

Joe Grant stared coldly until a pair of soft plump arms circled his neck. Then he tried to sit up when Bonnie Grant laid her cheek against his own.

"Bonnie baby," he breathed hoarsely. "You alright, gal?"

"Daddy," the girl whispered, and held him close. "We thought Black Bart had killed you. We came as soon as we could."

"Colt McGruder is dead, Joe," Buddy Bowie told the sheriff. "Leslie beat him in a draw-and-shoot up on the other fork of the trail."

Joe Grant raised his grey eyes and studied the

two hard young faces above him. Buddy Bowie was watching Bonnie, while Yuma Leslie made no attempt to conceal his dislike for the blond cowboy. The rattle of hooves jerked all eyes toward the lower trail, and the sheriff sighed with relief when he saw Alamo Bowie coming up fast with Mary Jane just behind.

Yuma Leslie stepped back and folded his arms. Alamo Bowie reined his horse to a stop and slid from the saddle. His keen eyes took in the situation instantly and stopped a moment to stare at Yuma Leslie. Then he spoke quietly to the sheriff.

"You meet up with Black Bart?"

Joe Grant nodded. "Met him and lost the deal," he answered heavily. "He's fast, Alamo."

"Get you bad, pard?"

The sheriff grunted. "Just a scratch over the heart. Bonnie and Leslie found me laying here in the trail. Looks like we made some of a mistake, Alamo."

Yuma Leslie curled his lip and turned to Mary Jane when she dismounted and came toward him. His right hand made a slow draw, and then he reversed the heavy gun in his hand and extended it to the girl.

"I'm surrendering my iron to you," he said simply. "I'm ready to go back to jail now."

Mary Jane took the weapon and held out her right hand. "I knew you would keep your promise, Yuma," she answered softly. "And I'm thanking you for helping our little Bonnie."

Yuma Leslie smiled happily and held her hand for a long moment. Joe Grant looked at Alamo Bowie and shook his head slowly one time. Buddy Bowie scowled and turned his face away, and then the wounded man spoke.

"I'm releasing you on yore own word, Leslie," and now his deep voice was stronger. "You mind stepping back there aways with Mary Jane while I make medicine with Alamo?"

Yuma Leslie dropped the girl's hand and turned slowly to study the wounded officer's face. "Like you said, sheriff," he answered finally. "But I don't want you to say anything about Mary Jane. I'll take the blame for what I did."

Joe Grant took a deep breath and gathered his strength. "Turning a prisoner loose is serious business, and I'll handle it my own way. Just remember that you are on parole, Leslie!"

Yuma Leslie did not answer. He turned to Mary Jane and started down the trail with her while Buddy glared after them with smouldering eyes. Joe Grant waited until they were out of hearing distance, and his face was grave when he turned back again to face Alamo Bowie.

"Fine looking pair of young 'uns," he muttered. "But there can be no compromise with the law in a time like this."

Alamo Bowie studied the remark with a frown. "Looks to me like Leslie did what had to be done like a man," he said slowly. "He did what both you and me came back here to do."

"And I'm not forgetting," the sheriff growled, and knotted his brows while he stared intently at Bowie. "Did you ever see Black Bart make his draw?" he asked suddenly.

The grey gun-fighter shook his head. "Never did," he answered. "But you said he was fast."

"Faster than that," the sheriff answered soberly. "I saw him, and I can't figger it out clear in my mind."

"Black Bart has always been a gun-fighter," Bowie answered with a shrug. "He's practised all his sinful life, and he's killed eight men that we know of."

"That," and the sheriff dismissed the remark with

a shrug. "I'm talking about what I saw just before his slug knocked me down and put out the lights!"

Alamo Bowie leaned forward and waited. His grey eyes were lighted with repressed eagerness as though he knew what was coming. And his voice was low and vibrant when he prompted Joe Grant.

"You saw . . . ?"

Joe Grant turned his head slightly and glanced at the pair down the trail. "It could have been Yuma Leslie," he whispered. "His hand moved down and up in just the same way!"

Buddy Bowie leaned forward breathing hard. "Any one who saw both me and Alamo work could tell Alamo had taught me all I know about guns," he began excitedly. "You mean——?"

Joe Grant nodded slowly with hard lines curling the corners of his mouth. "I mean that Black Bart taught Yuma Leslie to come out of holster leather," he answered positively. "How do you read that one, Alamo?"

Alamo Bowie was staring at the couple down the trail. Trying to piece out the puzzle while his right hand rubbed the worn grip of his gun, and his useless left arm swayed limply at his side. When he spoke, his deep drawling voice was low and thoughtful.

"Leslie came up here and paid cash for the old Lasky place," he murmured. "A couple of weeks later Black Bart drifted in with his gang. Yuma Leslie is half-brother to Three-Finger Jack, and Black Bart lives for nothing except to match guns with me."

"That's the way she lays," the sheriff agreed. "And Black Bart was Yuma Leslie's teacher!"

"He can't chouse around with my sister," Buddy growled angrily. "I got the answer right now, even if you old-timers do let somebody ride in to cloud up the sign!"

"Meaning what, yearling?" the sheriff asked quietly.

"Meaning that Yuma Leslie was trained and brought up here to rub me out," the tall cowboy declared hotly. "Black Bart figgers he is faster than Alamo, and he means to make a clean sweep to wipe out old scores. I'll take care of my end!"

"Now don't you go to fighting yore head," the sheriff warned soberly. "All you are doing is to make a guess."

"A mighty good guess," Alamo Bowie interrupted quietly. "If you remember what Black Bart told the folks back there on the B Bar G when you and me was out cutting for rustlers' sign with old John Golden."

Bonnie Grant came slowly to her feet and laid a little hand on Buddy's arm. "Please be reasonable, Buddy," she pleaded. "Yuma Leslie made Mary Jane a promise to surrender after he had done his work, and he rescued me from that terrible outlaw. And if you could have seen his face when he was dressing Daddy's wound. Soft and gentle as a girl's, and he could have killed you when I stepped up to your gun."

Buddy Bowie wrinkled his face in a scowl while the two older men listened. "Something in what she says, Joe," Alamo Bowie murmured. "Yuma Leslie ain't afraid of man nor beast, and he kept his word like a man."

"He's a damn rustler," Buddy growled. "And all I ask is a chance to prove it!"

"Hard words, son," Alamo reproved. "Fighting words. Mebbe you better leave them unsaid until you have some proof."

"I aim to get the proof," Buddy barked. "You mind if I cut away from here now, and ride out on my own?"

"Might be better that away," Alamo Bowie agreed slowly. "But don't you go to make a play at Yuma Leslie when you pass him on the trail."

The two older men looked away when Bonnie Grant threw her arms around the tall cowboy. "He isn't bad, Buddy," she whispered earnestly. "He is an awful lot like you because he is cow folks."

Buddy tried to release himself, and then his big hands patted her curly brown hair. "There's good in every man, Bonnie," he said huskily. "And plenty of bad," he added under his breath.

"You won't make trouble here, Buddy?"

"Not now," he growled. "You stay and take care of the sheriff while I ride on over the hill to see what I can see."

He glanced at the older men and hugged the girl tightly while a flush of colour stained his face. Then he tore himself away and vaulted to his saddle without touching the oxbows. Roared down the trail without a glance at his sister or Yuma Leslie, and Mary Jane caught the hand nearest to her.

"I do wish you and Buddy could be friends," she whispered. "He is an awful lot like you, Yuma."

Yuma Leslie growled in his throat and turned away. "If he wasn't yore brother it would be easy. He bristles up his hackles every time I cut his sign."

Mary Jane held his hand and stroked the long brown fingers. "I know," she agreed. "And you ruffle up every time you look at him. Why is it, Yuma?"

"Because I don't like him and his high and mighty ways," Leslie muttered. "He even tried to thank me for coming up here after Bonnie. I didn't do it for him, and I told him so."

The girl faced him squarely and stared into the angry black eyes. "Buddy thinks a heap of little Bonnie," she said softly. "You can't take advantage of him, Yuma. He thinks he is under obligations to you, and it hurts his pride a lot right now. He will get over it in a few days."

"He don't have to get over it on my account," Leslie

growled. "Let's be getting back there to that jail in Deming."

"But you forget what the sheriff told you," the girl reminded. "You are free under parole, Yuma."

He faced her with his jaw jutting out like a shoulder of granite. "Asking you for my gun, Mary Jane," he muttered, and refused to meet her blue eyes.

The girl slipped the heavy gun from her belt and snugged it deep in the scabbard on his right leg. Then she put a hand under his chin and tilted his head until the scowling eyes looked at her. Glittering and angry, and full of fight.

"There's your gun, Yuma," she began softly. "You will need it after what you did to Colt McGruder. You must take care of yourself, and I know you won't draw it against Buddy."

"I didn't say that," the cowboy muttered. "But like you mentioned just now, I aim to take care of myself!"

Bonnie Grant came down the trail and called softly.

"Dad wants to talk to you now, Yuma," and her brown eyes stared at the gun in his holster. "He just wants to talk," she added meaningly.

"Did I ask, and him down on his back?"

Yuma Leslie squared his shoulders after that; stalked up the trail stiff-legged. The two girls followed at a distance, and Bonnie Grant caught Mary Jane's hand in a tight grip.

"Isn't he wonderful?" she whispered.

Mary Jane gripped the tiny hand in her own. "I think he is," she answered sincerely. "And I know Daddy thinks so, too."

"But Buddy don't," Bonnie whispered with a frown. "I'm glad he rode away just now. The way those two edge at each other!"

Yuma Leslie stopped a few paces away from the

F

two men and balanced on his high heels. "You wanted
to say something, sheriff?" he asked quietly.

Joe Grant nodded and glanced up at the recovered
gun. "I see you got yoreself dressed again," he began
slowly. "You mind letting me take a look at yore
gun?"

Yuma Leslie leaned forward and searched the face
of the wounded .man. Then his right hand rapped
down swiftly and drew the weapon. Reversed it in his
hand and tendered it to the sheriff handle first. Joe
Grant nodded and made no attempt to take the proffered
forty-five.

"Keep it," he said quietly. "I just wanted to make
sure." .

Yuma Leslie stepped back and studied the sheriff's
face with a puzzled gleam in his dark eyes. Alamo
Bowie watched silently, and nodded his head slowly
one time. As though he had settled a point in his
mind.

"You mind telling a man?" Leslie asked brusquely,
and his hand pouched the gun smoothly in the oil-
moulded holster.

Joe Grant studied the suspicious features and nodded.
"I'll tell you," he began slowly. "I just met a faster
man. His hand moved so fast that I couldn't see for
looking. I am speaking of Black Bart like you might
have guessed."

The cowboy caught his breath sharply and looked
away. "I get it," and his voice was strained.
"Well?"

"Mebbe you want to explain," the sheriff suggested.

Yuma Leslie shrugged carelessly. "Nothing for me
to explain," he muttered. "Figgered it out for yoreself.
You and Alamo Bowie rode up here to read sign for
yoreselves."

"I figgered it out," the sheriff said very softly. "An
experienced hand can watch any yearling go for his

gun and tell who his teacher was. Looks bad for you figgering it that away, Leslie."

Alamo Bowie was watching the cowboy closely with eyes that missed no little detail. Yuma Leslie tightened his lips and stared at the sheriff with no sign of weakening in his stubborn jaw.

"Meaning that I am under arrest?" he asked stiffly.

Joe Grant shook his head. "We can find you if we want you," he answered with a grim smile. "But what I wanted to say was that you couldn't fight both sides, Leslie."

The Circle L owner turned slowly and glanced at Alamo Bowie. "I can shore as hell try," he answered sullenly. "I ain't afraid of Black Bart and all his killers, and I don't back down the trail for no other gun-hawk in Mimbres Valley!"

Alamo Bowie walked over and looked the younger man fully in the eye. "Meaning just what?" he demanded sternly.

Yuma Leslie returned the stare without winking. "Meaning just what I said," he growled. "I taken all I'm going to take for one day, and you can figger that out for yoreself!"

Alamo Bowie tightened his jaw, and then his right hand shot out and fastened on the cowboy's right shoulder. "You've taken plenty, cowboy," he agreed softly. "More than either me or Buddy would take in yore place. I'll give you that much, but it looks to me like you aim to take the wrong fork of the trail."

"If I do, I'll ride it alone," Leslie grunted. "I ain't asking for any help."

"Every feller needs some at one time or another," Bowie answered thoughtfully, and shook the cowboy lightly to gain attention. "Mebbe you'd rather have good friends in place of bad enemies," he suggested.

Yuma Leslie started to answer and dropped his eyes.

Alamo Bowie released his grip and stepped away
The cowboy raised his hand and dropped it when
Bowie turned his back, and his voice was husky when he
tried to find words.

"I don't want to——"

Bowie turned slowly. "Then don't do it," he
answered quietly. "Take time to think over what I
now said, Yuma."

Yuma Leslie became suddenly awkward. He studied
each face in the little group and could find no enmity.
The two girls were smiling at him like they would smile
at an old friend, and his anger faded away and disappeared for lack of fuel on which to feed.

"I won't pay no mind," he ground out suddenly.
"Damn his soul, I'll take it to him!"

Alamo Bowie changed instantly. He had the un-
canny ability to read the faces and the minds of men,
and he caught Yuma Leslie by the arm and viced down
with all the incredible strength of his right hand.

"You won't," he contradicted sternly. "Black
Bart will answer to me. That clear in yore mind,
feller?"

Yuma Leslie tried to wrench free and failed. His
black eyes glittered and changed colour, and then
the harsh grating voice of Alamo Bowie battered against
the sensitive tuning of his ears.

"He's waited ten years to match my speed. Ten
years; do yuh hear? With the hate of hell in his black
heart while he whipped up the speed in his gun-hand!"

"Unclutch me, Alamo Bowie. I'm my own man!"

Alamo Bowie glared for a moment and then loosened
his fingers. "Sorry, Leslie," he murmured contritely.
"But you came riding up here to bring me grief. You
didn't find what you expected, and right now you don't
know what to do about it."

The cowboy muttered under his breath. "I can
do it!"

"You can't," and Alamo Bowie glanced at the face of Mary Jane.

Yuma Leslie caught the glance and shifted uneasily. "If he brings it to me," he muttered sullenly.

"He won't," Bowie answered. "Buddy made a promise to the sweetest woman any of us ever met. And a Bowie never breaks a promise even if it means his life!"

Yuma Leslie swallowed hard and growled under his breath. "Black Bart will be looking for me now. If he finds me——?"

"He won't," Alamo Bowie barked. "Right now that black-hearted son is looking for me. We know what he did, Yuma. Know it just the same as though we had seen him training you to slip yore cutter!"

Yuma Leslie jerked back as though a lash had stung him. He looked like a small boy who had been caught stealing apples. His dark eyes darted from face to face and came back to lock glances with Alamo Bowie.

"Yo're guessing, and I ain't talking," he muttered defiantly.

"Yo're a pore liar, Yuma," Bowie whispered.

Yuma Leslie slapped down and then held his hand when the grey gun-fighter moved his shoulder and got the drop. The cowboy stared at the long gun-barrel. Lifted his head high.

"You called me out of my name, Bowie. I won't forget!"

Alamo Bowie moved his hand and the gun disappeared "I said you was a pore liar, Yuma. Well?"

The cowboy stared into the cold grey eyes and then nodded slowly. "Like you said," he capitulated. "But I'm still not talking!"

"Knew you wouldn't," Bowie praised quietly. "Now I'm asking you to give me a hand with the sheriff. We got to get him in the saddle and back to the B Bar G. And Yuma?"

"Yeah," Leslie answered gruffly.

"Sometimes a feller can make mighty good friends with his enemies. There's good in every man, but sometimes it takes a good woman to bring it out. Think it over, son."

Chapter XII

THE SHOT FROM AMBUSH

BUDDY BOWIE was a changed man when he rode the river trail toward the southern boundary of the J Bar G. It had been three days since his last meeting with Yuma Leslie. Three days in which he had searched for some evidence that would link the Circle L owner up with Black Bart and his outlaw gang. He had found no trace of the missing J Bar G steers, and he felt sure that the rustled herd would provide the key he sought.

His usually smiling face was sombre and serious while he turned over all the evidence that pointed to Yuma's Leslie guilt. There had been reasonable doubt up to the time when Sheriff Joe Grant had met Black Bart. The outlaw had taught Yuma Leslie his famous draw, and Black Bart never did anything without some definite purpose.

Buddy reined into the trail-side brush from force of habit when a horse rounded a bend leading down from the high mesa. He waited when he looked through the branches and recognized young Jim Golden, old John's nephew. The J Bar G cowboy was evidently reading sign, and his hand slipped down to his gun when Buddy called softly from his hiding-place.

"Howdy, Jim. Hold your shot until I come out. You find anything yet?"

Jim Golden loosed his gun handle and answered without smiling. It seemed that he, too, had forgotten how to smile, and Buddy knew the reason. Jim was·in

love with Mary Jane; was anxious to prove that Yuma
Leslie was an outlaw and an impostor.

"You drive any stock up through the canyon?" he
asked sharply.

Buddy shook his head. "Not recent, Jim," he
answered. "We've been shoving out shippers down
this away since Black Bart started rustling. Brought a
new bunch down yesterday."

"I knowed it," young Golden muttered. "I saw
fifty-sixty big three-year-old steers high-tailing up the
canyon back aways, but one of those new Circle L
riders stopped me with a Winchester when I cut over
for a look-see. Thought I better ride over and let you
and Alamo know."

Buddy Bowie stared for a moment during which
his blue eyes narrowed bleakly. "I mis-trusted that
Circle L jigger right along," he said grimly. "What
say you and me take a ride over to his spread? I know
a cut-off where we can catch his house without being
seen. I was up there just the other day."

Jim Golden nodded assent. "The one you took that
day when you had Black Bart under yore gun," he
muttered, and his next words expressed the thoughts
that had changed him during the last week. "If we
get the proof on Yuma Leslie, mebbe so Mary Jane
won't be so keen about him!"

He was taller and broader of shoulder than Buddy
Bowie. Would some day be the owner of the J Bar
G. Serious in his work, and a tophand with horses
and cattle. Like most range-bred men, he didn't
talk much, and hardly at all in the presence of
women.

"I dunno," Buddy answered thoughtfully. "Things
are changed around some since he saved Bonnie from
that owl-hoot pack."

"They ain't changed any with me," Golden muttered.
"I don't just trust him none, and I aim to prove that he

is in with those rustlers. It can't be no other way!"

"There's an old forgotten trail leading down from Fort Cummings," and Buddy changed the subject. "We can take it and come out in that strip of timber right in back of Leslie's house. It looks right down into the holding corrals, and we might find something as long as they don't know we are close."

He wheeled his horse and took the lead when Jim Golden nodded agreement. Both straddled mountain horses. The kind that raced up and down the steep slopes without slackening speed. A deadfall blocked the old brush-grown trail, and both horses cleared it without hesitation. Buddy reined down to a walk after the jump and signalled for caution.

"We leave the horses here, Jim," he whispered. "It means a bullet if we get ourselves caught back here."

Jim Golden smiled then. A hard fighting smile that made his face look old. He slid from the saddle and pulled his Winchester from the saddle-boot, and the two fastened the horses in a little clearing. Hung spurs on saddle-horns before stepping out to follow a dimly-marked path down through the cactus-studded *malpais*.

Buddy Bowie again took the lead and headed for the spot where he had discovered Black Bart on the morning after Jud Leeds had been killed. The sun was high when he stopped in a little pocket of rocks and parted the brush with both hands. Sucked in his breath and raised a hand to warn Jim Golden when he saw a group of riders standing their horses near the bread porch of the old Circle L ranch-house.

Jim Golden hunkered down and swore softly when he took in the scene. Yuma Leslie was facing three men, and each of the three had a six-gun centred on the tall black-eyed cowboy. One of the three was Torio Feliz, and Buddy Bowie lined his sights on the Mexican while his mouth tightened at the corners.

Jim Golden stared and lowered the barrel of his rifle. Shook his head doubtfully and turned to look at Buddy. He had been so sure of Yuma Leslie's guilt. Buddy motioned for silence when the Mexican began to speak.

"You will come with us for a little ride, no?" he purred silkily. "Señor Bart he would like the talk with you. He send us over to show you the way."

Yuma Leslie had both hands hooked in his broad gunbelt. Boots spread wide for balance with black Stetson pushed well back on his curly head. His eyes moved slowly to study each face, and then he shook his head emphatically.

"Not me," he contradicted the Mexican. "If Black Bart wants to *habla* with me, he knows where to find me. Now you gents might as well ride on back, and you can tell him what I said."

"Now looky, Kid," a stocky rider cut in harshly. "The boss made you like all of us knows. Took you under his wing when you was a raw button without no savvy. Taught you all you know about six-guns, and right now the sheriff knows it."

Yuma Leslie stared levelly at the speaker. "Like you said, Bisbee Trent," he admitted quietly. "But I didn't know then what I know now. And the lot of you know that I never worked with the gang even when Black Bart was teaching me!"

"Mebbe it wasn't yore fault," Bisbee Trent sneered. "He was saving you for something else, and all of us knows what it was. You fell in pretty soft, but the boss drives a hard bargain!"

Yuma Leslie continued to stare at the outlaw. "I'll pay what I owe," he said softly. "Tell him what I said!"

"It was Bart's money paid for this Circle L outfit,"

Bisbee Trent continued. "Money that the chief hid away before they sent him to the Pen. What you reckon the sheriff would say if he finds out about that?"

"Tell him," Leslie answered shortly. "I'd tell him myself, but like you know, I'm not a squealer!"

Buddy Bowie almost stopped breathing. He had wondered how Yuma Leslie could have earned so much money in so short a time. Ever since the night Black Bart had visited the B Bar G ranch-house, he had been sure that Leslie and the outlaw were connected closely in some secret way. Now he had the answers.

He glanced at the face of Jim Golden and motioned for silence when he saw the J Bar G cowboy getting ready for action. Golden scowled and fingered the trigger of his rifle nervously. They could hear the voice of Bisbee Trent plainly when he answered Leslie.

"You ain't hoorawing us?" the outlaw asked slowly.

Yuma Leslie shook his head soberly. "I ain't," he stated. "Black Bart might own the Circle L the way you put it, but as long as I'm rodding the spread it won't hide any rustled stock. Tell him I said so!"

The stocky outlaw turned his head just far enough to glance at Torio Feliz. Yuma Leslie knew what was coming, and set himself to match the three-to-one odds. And in that moment of deadlock when tensed muscles were waiting for the call to deadly action, Buddy Bowie shouted harshly from his hiding-place.

"Don't draw that knife, Torio! Reach high, gents!"

The four men in front of the rambling porch jerked erect like puppets drawn by the same string. Yuma Leslie was the first to recover, and he leaped backward to the porch floor and slid through the door like a shadow. The three outlaws turned to face the hidden voice, and Buddy Bowie stepped into the clear with his Winchester at the ready.

"Just take a chance, Bisbee," he growled with a tinge of hope in his husky voice. "Save the law a heap of trouble and time!"

He came slowly across the clearing and down into the big yard with Jim Golden behind him and a little to one side. The three outlaws were crouching forward and watching for some sign of carelessness. Torio Feliz dropped the knife back into its sheath. A Bandanna sling held his wounded right arm close to his chest, and a sickly pallor changed the colour of his swarthy face when he recognized young Bowie. Bisbee Trent curled his thick lips in a sneer.

"So that's how it is?" he said thickly. "You and Yuma done decided to call off yore ruckus and be pards!"

"I don't pard up with an outlaw," Buddy barked. "Now you gents turn slow and keep yore grub-hooks up high. Take their hardware, Jim. Any of them make a pass——"

Jim Golden circled carefully so as not to come between the outlaws and Buddy's rifle. Bisbee Trent moved his lips and hunched his powerful shoulders, and a barking voice rapped out from the house to stop the J Bar G cowboy.

"Hold it, feller! I'll square up with them three, but I'll do it my own way and without no help. You and Bowie ain't the law up here in these parts!"

Buddy Bowie held the drop of the three outlaws and turned his head to find Yuma Leslie. The Circle L man stood just inside the door with his six-gun held high and thumbed back for a chopping shot. His dark eyes were glowing with a strange fire that told of conflicting emotions, but the lines around his stubborn lips also told of a grim determination.

"Knew it all the time," Buddy growled. "I should have let yore pards get on with their getting!"

"It might have been better that away," Leslie agreed quickly. "And I didn't ask for any help!"

"But you needed plenty," Jim Golden almost shouted. "A gent can't play around with skunks without smelling like one!"

He twitched his wide shoulders and set his boots for a spin. Yuma Leslie read the signs and spoke softly.

"Don't do it, Golden. It's bound to cost you!"

"Stand hitched, Jim," Buddy advised in a low voice. "You just look on and listen, and let this chuck-walla tangle himself all up in his own coils. It won't take long."

Yuma Leslie smiled with his lips and nodded his head. "Thanks, Bowie," he murmured. "I'll do the same for you sometime."

He turned to Bisbee Trent and his two companions, and now his dark face was like craggy granite. "Hit leather, you three," he growled icily. "You can't hide that rustled stock on my place while I'm rodding this outfit. Now you ride off Circle L range and tell Black Bart what I said!"

"Just a minute," Buddy Bowie interrupted. "Yo're forgetting that them three are still under my gun, and it ready to go!"

"And yo're forgetting that you and yore pard are under mine," Leslie countered dryly. "What you make of that?"

Jim Golden had recovered from his anger, and he spoke the word that Buddy needed. "Better let 'em go, pard," and he turned slowly to Yuma Leslie. "I'd hate to be in yore boots now," he added very softly.

"I'll wear 'em as is," the Circle L owner clipped. "Get going, Bisbee. And tell Black Bart that if he wants to see me, he knows where I live!"

Bisbee Trent shrugged his heavy shoulders and

walked over to his horse. Gave Torio Feliz a boost up to his saddle and mounted his own horse without haste. The third man followed suit in stoical silence and Trent reined his horse around and spoke to Leslie.

"You can't play both sides again the middle, yearling," and his voice was harsh. "I'll tell Black Bart just what you said!"

He hit his horse with the spurs and led his two companions across the valley without looking back again. Buddy Bowie watched them go and slowly lowered the hammer of his Winchester. Then he turned to face Yuma Leslie. Widened his blue eyes when he saw that the Circle L man was empty-handed.

"Sorry I had to do it that away, Bowie," Leslie murmured. "Now I'm passing the deal back to you!"

The scowl faded from Buddy's face and was replaced by a smile of happiness. He shifted the rifle to his left hand and shadowed his six-gun with the right. Holding himself in check like a hound on leash, and once more Jim Golden spoke the warning word softly.

"Hold it, pard. You can't bring it to him up here account of yore promise!"

The tall blond cowboy stared for a moment and drooped his shoulders. Yuma Leslie saw the hopeless gesture and interrupted to make a compromise.

"I'm saying it wasn't a fair shake, Bowie. You get on yore horse and hit a line for the B Bar G. You got it coming, and I'll bring it down there to you."

Buddy Bowie stood perfectly still and stared at the dark face for a long moment. Then he shook his head slowly and drew a deep breath. While the Circle L owner watched every move and balanced easily while he waited for his answer.

"That can wait, Leslie," Buddy muttered. "But

you were talking about rustled stock just before Jim and me bought chips in yore little game."

Yuma Leslie set his jaw grimly. "Keep on talking," he clipped. "You was saying?"

"Saying that me and Jim cut sign on that last bunch of B Bar G steers we lost," Buddy answered quietly. "Right now they are held somewhere on Circle L range, and we aim to do something about it."

"Damn you, Bowie," Leslie blazed savagely. "You know I wasn't in on that play. You and him hid back there and heard the whole thing!"

"I know it now," Buddy answered promptly. "The sign leads over there toward the lavas just at the edge of the Goodsights. I don't see any of yore hands around," he added quietly.

"The boys are all out riding," Leslie growled. "That's what I pay them to do!"

"Yeah!" Jim Golden interrupted harshly. "Riding over there in the badlands toward the Goodsight Mountains."

Yuma Leslie ignored the J Bar G rider and turned to Buddy. "I don't like you, Bowie," he admitted frankly. "But I'm riding out there with you and him just to make sure. If we find any of my men with that rustled stuff, I'm asking you to stay out and let me handle them on my own."

"You can ride along," Buddy answered bluntly, and his young face was hard. "But I'm all through making promises. Rustlers are rustlers, no matter what outfit pays them, and you don't fool neither me nor Jim!"

Yuma Leslie studied the last remark deeply. "They get a chance," he answered quietly. "Every man deserves that much, no matter how bad things look against him."

"Not rustlers," John Golden growled. "Them hands you brought over from Arizona, Leslie. They're the same bunch that rides with Black Bart and his gang. Desert cowboys who ain't used to this high mesa country!"

Yuma Leslie turned his head and smiled mockingly. "Yo're guessing because you got yore mad up, Golden," he answered quietly. "I'm not talking, and we better let it pass for now."

"Actions speak louder than words," Golden retorted angrily. "I'm watching you mighty close if you ride with us!"

Yuma Leslie stared at the big cowboy and repressed a sneer. "Do all the watching you want, Golden," he answered carelessly. "But if you see something you don't like, better keep yore hand away from yore gun. You don't measure up to fast company."

Jim Golden set his teeth and leaned forward. "If I see you pull something I don't like, I'll take a chance," he grated. "I might not be so fast as some, but I'd get you before I quit kicking!"

Buddy Bowie walked between the pair and spoke jerkily. "Get yore hoss, Leslie. I'll be watching you, too!"

Yuma Leslie smiled then and walked to the corral for his horse. Mounted and waited until Bowie and Golden rode down from the brush, after which he took the lead, then loped across the valley. At the mouth of a dry wash he pulled up and pointed.

"Short cut this away, Bowie. I got a hunch, and I'm playing it."

Buddy Bowie tried to read the expression on the dark face and gave up with a shrug. "Line out," he grunted. "I got a hunch of my own,"

Yuma Leslie made no reply. He gigged his horse into a narrow trail where the three had to proceed single file. Twisting and winding through molten lava rock where the sun beat down to make a furnace. Not a word spoken for an hour, and Yuma Leslie broke the long silence when he came out in a little grassy park and reined in on a bench.

For a long moment his eyes squinted to stare into another valley dotted with grazing cattle. Buddy Bowie pulled up beside him and cupped his old field glasses to his eyes. Even with this help, Leslie was the first to make a discovery.

"The rustling sons!" he growled deep in his throat. "You fellers stay out of this, and leave it to me. Three of my hands down yonder!"

He hit his horse with the hooks and raced across the valley on a dead run. Buddy Bowie cased the glasses and eased the gun in his holster. Spoke softly to Jim Golden.

"If they're his hands, that makes them rustlers. Let's go, Jim!"

Jim Golden pulled his Winchester from the saddle-boot and pounded down the gentle slope with the gun across his knees. Yuma Leslie was up ahead and going fast. The three riders at the far end wheeled their horses when they heard the drum of hooves, and Buddy Bowie was close enough to hear when the Circle L owner slid his horse to a stop and barked a question.

"Those B Bar G steers. You have a hand in that?"

A lathy thin man with a wispy moustache answered for his mates. "We was rounding up strays back here, boss. We just now come across this bunch of shippers."

"You see who drove them in here?" Leslie asked. "I want the truth, Gila!"

Gila Towers scratched his head. "I saw that barn-shouldered jigger riding away," he answered slowly. "The one you pointed out as Bisbee Trent."

Buddy Bowie was standing his horse off side. A rifle barked sharply just as Jim Golden cut around in front of Yuma Leslie. The J Bar G cowboy threw up his arms and pitched from the saddle, and a blur of shots rattled out before Bowie could swing his horse around.

Yuma Leslie was facing a fringe of brush where a smoke ring was circling above the tops. His long-barrelled six-gun was also smoking in his hand. Buddy smothered a curse and raked savagely with both spurs. Rocketed across the short grass and through the brush with gun leaping to his hand.

Yuma Leslie was right behind him when he swung down and crouched above a writhing figure on the ground. The man twisted suddenly and tried to raise his gun, and Buddy Bowie kicked the weapon into the brush with the toe of his scarred boot.

"Like I thought," the blond cowboy muttered. "It's Bisbee Trent!"

"Water," the outlaw gasped. "I'm shot through the middle and burning up inside!"

Yuma Leslie sat his saddle and stared without emotion. "No water," he answered sharply. "You meant that shot for me, Trent!"

The wounded man drew himself to a sitting position with both hands clutching his middle. "I'd have got you, too, if that big jigger hadn't run right under my sights just as I pressed trigger!"

Buddy Bowie reached for his whangs and vaulted to the saddle. "I'm going back to Jim," he growled at Leslie. "He was a better man than you!"

"Hold yore hoss, yearlin'," the outlaw shouted hoarsely. "I'm due to cash, and I know it. But before I pass there's something about this damn traitor you ought to know. He was brought up here to match guns with you. And Black Bart trained him to do it!"

Buddy Bowie stared down at the wounded man and nodded his head. "I knew it," he said softly, and spurred his horse when Yuma Leslie jerked around with hand above his gun.

The three Circle L cowboys were grouped around

Jim Golden when Bowie slid to the ground and hunkered down beside his pard. Jim Golden opened his eyes and tried to smile, but his tanned face was twisted with pain.

"He get that dry-gulcher?" he asked weakly.

Buddy nodded. "It was Bisbee Trent," he answered bitterly. "I had a hunch, but he beat me to it. Bisbee won't last long," he added grimly.

"Reckon I owe Leslie one for getting him," Golden murmured. "Glad he ain't a rustler, Buddy."

Buddy Bowie turned his face away. "That shot was meant for Leslie," he growled. "You rode right under Trent's gun, and it saved that Circle L waddy!"

Jim Golden jerked his head for Buddy to lean closer. "Mary Jane," he whispered. "She loves him, Buddy. I never had a chance, but I want you to tell Mary Jane it's all right with me."

Buddy felt the hot blood rush to his face. Jim Golden had loved Mary Jane for years, and had been afraid to speak. His blue eyes widened when the wounded cowboy lowered his dropping lids, and then the three Circle L men took off their hats.

"He's gone," Gila Towers whispered hoarsely. "Out there on the long trail where they don't come back."

Buddy stared at the tanned face and bit his lip. "Naw," he growled. "Why, him and me was talking just now!"

The three cowboys turned their faces away when Buddy knuckled a hot tear from his eyes. "Yonder comes the boss," Towers said, just to be saying something.

Buddy Bowie stretched to his feet and turned to meet Yuma Leslie. His eyes were blazing hotly, and Leslie swung sown and took a long look at Jim Golden. His head jerked suddenly, and his deep voice was shaky when he spoke to Buddy Bowie.

"He's dead, Bowie!"

"Yeah, he's dead," Buddy repeated bitterly. "And yo're still living!"

Yuma Leslie fell to his knees and gripped the dead man by the hand. Muttered softly under his breath, and then he straightened up to face Buddy. Shrugged his shoulders back, but his face looked years older than when he had ridden down into the valley.

"Like I said before, Bowie," and his voice was pitched low. "Ride on back to the B Bar G. I'll follow with this bunch of steers, and I'll . . . bring it to you!"

Buddy nodded his head slowly. "I'll be waiting," he answered softly, and glanced at Gila Towers. "Give me a hand with my pard, cowboy. I'll be taking him back to the B Bar G. Old John Golden will want to know first."

Yuma Leslie watched while they raised the dead cowboy to the saddle and fastened hands and wrists for the long ride. Then Buddy Bowie mounted up and took the lead reins from Towers. No expression on his tanned face when he turned to Yuma Leslie.

"I'll be waiting," he promised quietly, and walked his horse slowly across the little valley.

Chapter XIII

BAIT FOR SHOW-DOWN TRAP

MARY JANE BOWIE moved restlessly and blinked at the brilliant sunlight. Sheriff Joe Grant was out of danger and resting easily in a shaded back room on the B Bar G. Nellie Bowie and Bonnie Grant were with the wounded man, and Mary Jane breathed a little sigh of thankfulness. She had taken her turn at nursing, and the long hours of confinement were beginning to tell.

Alamo Bowie was working in the tack room. She could see his tall figure sitting at a saddle bench working over a bridle. For three days he had worked feverishly, and she knew that he was trying to burn up some of the nervous energy brought on by waiting. He had always been a man of action; always would be.

She could see the black-handled gun cradled in leather on his long right leg. Lying close to his hand. She knew the dynamic force of this grey gun-fighter who had fathered her during the past ten years. Added lines were etched deeply in his craggy face while he worked . . . and waited.

Mary Jane watched him for a while and then moved quietly to the other side of the big house. Her full lips pouted when she turned to the horse corral and watched the big red sorrel Alamo had given her for her last birthday. Three days since she had saddled the gelding, and she moved swiftly across the yard when the animal saw her and whickered a welcome.

Mid-afternoon, and Buddy would be returning from the J Bar G by the river trail. The girl glanced around to make sure that she was unobserved, after which she led the sorrel from the corral and slipped the bridle over his sleek head. Saddled up like a cowboy and circled the barn until she came to the river trail leading through the lower valley.

Buddy would scold when he saw her riding alone, but the blue-eyed girl shrugged and sent her horse through the under-brush bordering the river. She could take care of herself, and her hand strayed down and felt the light six-gun tied low on the right leg of her high-cuffed Levis. Buddy and Alamo laughed at her for carrying a .38 calibre Colt, but Mary Jane shrugged when her fingers wrapped around the familiar grip.

The laugh froze on her pretty face when a bush rustled off to the right. The gun leaped to her hand and centred steadily on the spot, and her throaty voice backed up the threat of the cocked weapon when she called a sharp command.

"Come out reaching high!"

Her eyes widened when a Mexican in a high-peaked sombrero stepped into the trail. His right arm was carried in a bright-coloured sling close to his chest. The left hand was held shoulder-high, and his purring voice spoke softly when he introduced himself.

"I am Torio Feliz, Señorita, I have the message for you."

Mary Jane stared for a moment. "I don't trust you, hombre," she said coldly. "But keep on talking."

"Me, I owe my life to your brother," the Mexican murmured. "This morning he ride to the Circle L with the young Señor from the J Bar G. They talk to Yuma Leslie for the long time, and then all three ride away to search for cattle."

Mary Jane lowered the gun while her mind raced swiftly. Could it be possible that Buddy and Yuma had made up their differences? And Jim Golden. Why would he be riding on the Circle L?

"I don't believe you, Torio," she stated bluntly. "What is this message you were talking about?"

"They find the cattle, Señorita," the Mexican answered readily. "But the young Golden he was very much hurt. Your brother have taken him to the J Bar G, and he asks that you come at once. The young Señor Golden he is very sick."

Mary Jane stared at his saddle-coloured face and tried to read what was going on behind the glittering black eyes. "Yuma Leslie?" she asked sharply. "If they were on the Circle L, what became of him?"

Torio Feliz shrugged. "Yuma Leslie he cannot go to the J Bar G," he answered softly. "I go now, Señorita. Your brother spare me my life, and I have given you his message. He waits for you at the J Bar G."

Mary Jane half raised her gun when he turned his back and walked slowly toward the horse she could see tethered back in the brush. She did not hear the whirring loop that circled over her head and dropped down to pin her arms with a jerk. The gun flew from her loosened fingers and fell in the short grass, and she was jerked from her saddle when her horse snorted with fright and made a sudden jump.

She twisted her supple body when she was pulled over the cantle and she took the sting from her fall when she rolled on her shoulders in the grass trail. A pair of strong arms caught her arms and twisted savagely, and Mary Jane struggled like a wildcat until a rawhide thong fastened both hands behind her back.

She jerked around when the hands released her, and the colour drained from her face when she saw a tall man dressed entirely in black regarding her with a mocking smile in his dark eyes. The same man who had ordered Yuma Leslie to shoot it out with Buddy that night in the living-room of the B Bar G.

"Black Bart!"

Her voice was a low frightened gasp that only deep-
ened the smile in the outlaw's black eyes. "At yore
service, Señorita" he answered quietly. "And Alamo
Bowie, yore father? I hope he is well!"

Mary Jane bit her lips and tried to look away. She
had been warned against riding alone, and she had
not heeded. She saw the whole devilish plan when
Torio Feliz came riding out from the brush with a
mocking smile on his dark face.

"You meant to shoot me, Señorita," he taunted.
"But you *Americanos*. I knew you would not when
I turned my back."

"Enough of that, Torio," Black Bart told the Mexican
sharply. "You ride back to the B Bar G like I told
you. Being wounded that away you will be safe enough.
Carry out the plan as I have told you, and you will
have nothing to fear."

Mary Jane tensed her muscles and came to her feet.
"You can't do this thing," she almost screamed.

Black Bart continued to smile. "And why not?"
he asked softly. "I have waited ten years to meet
the great Alamo Bowie, but he has made the promise.
To a woman. But when he hears that I am holding you
a prisoner——?"

The girl shuddered and faced him proudly. "You
can't win," she told him positively. "You forget
Buddy, and there is one other!"

"Yuma Leslie?" and the smile faded from the
outlaw's dark face.

The girl nodded. "I mean Yuma Leslie."

Black Bart came forward in a crouch, and his voice
rasped like a file. "Yuma Leslie is the brother of
Three-Fingered Jack," he grated savagely. "I found him
nearly three years ago, and I trained him to use a six-
gun for only one purpose. He was a Kid button on the
loose, and even he didn't know why I wasted my time
on him!"

"You did that to a boy?" the girl whispered. "Gained his confidence only to betray it and ruin his life?"

"His life," the outlaw snapped. "What do I care about his life? Alamo Bowie killed his brother, and Alamo Bowie has an adopted son!"

"Buddy!" the girl whispered. "You mean my brother!"

"Smart girl," the outlaw sneered. "My money paid for the Circle L, and mebbe you can guess the rest!"

Mary Jane stepped back with eyes staring at his scowling face. Black Bart had released the venom of years, and his dark eyes glittered with the feral light of a savage beast. The girl caught her breath and strained against the thong that held her hands.

Now she knew why Yuma Leslie could pay cash for the Circle L before he was of age. She understood why the outlaw had ordered him to shoot Buddy back there in the big living-room. Why the tall dark cowboy held such an enmity against her brother, and she bit her lower lip to hold back the sudden tears.

"He didn't know," she murmured. "I am sure Yuma didn't understand what you were doing to him."

"He understands now," the outlaw answered shortly. "Alamo Bowie dies, and after Yuma has settled with yore brother Buddy——"

The girl stared at his distorted face. "If Yuma should win?" she whispered faintly.

"Then he answers to me!" the outlaw growled. "For talking too much, and for what he did to Colt McGruder and Bisbee Trent!"

"I knew it," the girl sighed thankfully. "I knew he wasn't bad."

"He's a trained gun-fighter," Black Bart corrected. "I've seen to that. Prideful as all get-out, and he won't be able to rest until he meets that brother of yores. Alamo Bowie's chip!"

The girl shook her head slowly. "Buddy made a promise," she whispered. "And he won't break it no matter what happens!"

The outlaw smiled and turned back to Torio Feliz. "Ride on back to the B Bar G," he ordered shortly. "I will be waiting down where the river makes the big bend. That place is on B Bar G range, and Alamo Bowie can keep his precious promise!"

The Mexican wheeled his horse and started down the back trail at a fast lope. His dark eyes burned with the desire for revenge against the man who had made him a cripple. And when he came to the cottonwood lane leading up to the big ranch yard, he rode into the B Bar G without hesitation.

Alamo Bowie glanced up from his work and came swiftly to his feet. His right hand darted down and came up to cover the Mexican, but Torio Feliz smiled gently and raised his left hand slowly, pointed to his wounded arm and waited until the grey-gunfighter had lowered his weapon.

"I come with a message for you, Señor Bowie," he began softly.

Bonnie Grant came running from the house before Alamo Bowie could answer. "Have you seen Mary Jane?" she called anxiously, and then drew closer to Bowie when she recognized the man on horseback.

Alamo Bowie turned his head and stared at the tiny girl. "You mean she is not in the house, Bonnie?"

"She left nearly two hours ago," Bonnie Grant answered. "She said she was restless, and she wanted to take a ride."

"She take the ride," the Mexican interrupted with a smile. "I meet her not more than an hour ago!"

Alamo Bowie stepped close and jabbed with his

gun. "Talk up, Mex," he barked savagely. "Before I blow you out of yore saddle!"

"But no, Señor," the Mexican answered with a shrug. "You cannot shoot the wounded man, and I have come to bring you a message."

Alamo Bowie stared and stepped back. His hard face tightened until the skin pulled against the high cheekbones and narrowed his cold grey eyes. When he spoke his voice was low and far away like wind in distant trees.

"This message, hombre?"

"You have make the promise long ago," the Mexican began. "Not to draw the gun on Black Bart unless he brings it to you," and he shrugged suggestively.

Alamo Bowie leaned forward with an eager expression sweeping across his craggy face. "He going to bring it to me?"

Torio Feliz nodded. "He have bring it, Señor. He holds the Señorita to make sure that you will come!"

"You mean . . . Mary Jane?"

The Mexican nodded. "Sí, Señor. He waits down where the river she make the big bend. What you call B Bar G range, and there Black Bart he brings it to you!"

Alamo Bowie smiled coldly and holstered his gun. The front door slammed loudly in the big house. Nellie Bowie came swiftly across the yard, and Alamo Bowie knew from the expression on her face that she had heard. He did not speak until she touched him on the arm.

"I heard, Alamo. Must you go now?"

He turned then and looked deeply into her brown eyes. "Ten years, Nellie," he said softly. "He has waited ten years, and I have kept my promise to you. You heard about Mary Jane?"

Nellie Bowie repressed a shudder and her voice was firm when she answered. "I heard, Alamo. But will he keep his word?"

Alamo Bowie stared. "What do you mean?" he grunted.

"I mean about Buddy and Yuma Leslie. You know what Black Bart will do to Yuma after what has happened."

Alamo Bowie thought deeply and turned to the Mexican. "You heard," he said sharply. "What about Yuma Leslie?"

Torio Feliz shrugged. "That I do not know, Señor," he murmured. "One cannot be sure about Black Bart."

Alamo Bowie reached out and gripped the Mexican by the arm. Viced down with all the cruel strength of his fingers until Feliz whimpered and nearly came unseated.

"Talk," Bowie barked. "What about Yuma Leslie?"

"This morning he kill another man," the Mexican whispered. "You break my one arm, Señor. I beg you to release me."

Alamo Bowie opened his fingers and stared into the dark eyes above him. "Keep on talking, hombre," he prompted quietly. "And talk with a straight tongue if you want to live."

"It was Bisbee Trent," the Mexican muttered sullenly, "He go for to kill Yuma, but the young Golden ride his horse between. I think that one is dead, and then Yuma Leslie draw very swiftly and kill Bisbee!"

"Buddy," Alamo Bowie said sternly. "Where was he all this time?"

"He think Leslie rustle cattle," the Mexican muttered. "He was talking to Yuma, and they make much angry talk. Then he take the dead man back to the J Bar G. After that——"

Again Alamo Bowie reached for a grip. Torio Feliz jerked away just out of reach and began to talk rapidly.

"He too have make the foolish promise," he almost

screamed in his haste. "So Yuma Leslie will bring it to him. One of them will die Señor. Black Bart will finish the other!"

Nellie Bowie placed a hand on her lips while the colour drained swiftly from her face. "Alamo," she whispered. "So much depends on you now. He does not mean to release Mary Jane, and he knows that nothing will stop Yuma Leslie when he hears. If Buddy and Yuma should meet first——"

"There is one chance," Alamo Bowie muttered, and turned to study the face of Bonnie Grant. "Will you do it?" he asked gruffly.

The tiny girl looked up at the tall gun-fighter. "I don't know what you mean," she faltered. "Please?"

"Saddle a hoss and take the short-cut to the J Bar G," Bowie rasped hoarsely. "Try to catch Buddy before he hits our range. Keep him from reaching here as long as you can!"

He turned back to Torio Feliz when the girl raced toward the horse barn. "I'm holding you here, hombre," he growled. "Light down out of that kak!"

The Mexican stared at him for a moment with hate smouldering deep in his dark eyes. Then he gripped the horn with his left hand and swung down with the horse between himself and Bowie. The tall gun-fighter stepped around the animal just as the Mexican slapped his left hand to the back of his belt. Bowie leaped forward and caught the sinewy wrist when it flashed up holding a keen-bladed throwing-knife.

Something snapped loudly when Alamo Bowie wrenched the arm back and to one side. Torio Feliz screamed like a wounded horse, and grovelled to his knees. Alamo Bowie threw him aside and drew his gun, and his voice was low and savage when he crouched over the wounded man on the ground.

"I ought to kill you for that. Now you get up on

yore feet and shag over to the barn. Come along, Nellie. I might need yore help."

The Mexican moaned with pain when he came to his feet and started for the big barn. Nellie Bowie followed with sympathy· showing plainly in her' brown eyes, but she took the rope Alamo handed her. Came close to Torio Feliz and ran her fingers over his free arm.

"We can't tie him up, Alamo," she told her husband. "His left arm is broken."

Alamo Bowie stared with· emotion. "Get into the granary," he barked at the Mexican. "I'm locking you up in there until I get back!"

Nellie Bowie faced Alamo and looked deep into his angry grey eyes. "Do you mind if I set his arm?" ,she asked softly.

"I don't trust him," and Bowie shrugged his shoulders, "But suit yourself," he muttered, when she continued to watch his face. "With both arms done for, he ought to be harmless enough."

Nellie Bowie smiled then and kissed him on the cheek. "You have your work to do, Alamo," she reminded gently. "I know you won't fail because you are right. Black Bart cannot win because he is wrong."

Alamo Bowie was flexing the long fingers of his right hand. Once more the old eager light of battle was shining in his narrowed grey eyes. His hand blurred down and made the swift pass Nellie Bowie had seen so many times, and there was no fear in her eyes when he leaned over to kiss her.

"Yuma Leslie," he said quietly. "What do you think of that young 'un, Nellie?"

"I like him," she answered without hesitation. "He was filled with hatred when he came up here to Mimbres Valley, and then he met Mary Jane. He is a different boy, Alamo."

"If he gets here ahead of Buddy, you talk to him,"

Bowie answered slowly. "I kinda like that yearling myself."

He turned away and started for the door. "Joe Grant," she called softly. "Are you going to tell him?"

Alamo Bowie jerked his head. "Got it to do," he answered gruffly. "He ought to know, being the law."

No haste when he walked across the yard and entered the big house. Black Bart had waited for ten years; he could wait a few minutes longer. Joe Grant sat up when Bowie entered the sick room. The sheriff was pale and restless after enforced inactivity, and he sensed that something was wrong from the look on his partner's face.

"Bad news, Alamo?" he asked quietly.

"It's come, Joe," Bowie answered slowly. "Mary Jane went for a ride this afternoon, and Black Bart got her. Right now he's holding her down by the river bend until I come to keep my word!"

The sheriff twitched at the old hardness in that low raspy voice. This was the old Alamo Bowie he had known eleven years ago. They had met on old John Golden's J Bar G spread when Bowie was special Agent for Wells Fargo. Both had pooled their savings to buy the B Bar G, but in his heart Alamo Bowie had never changed.

Joe Grant remembered the leaping fires in those grey eyes when fast gunmen were mentioned. Alamo Bowie had been the fastest in his day; was still the fastest in spite of the passing years, and the injury to his left arm. Joe Grant remembered the famous twins; the long-barrelled forty-fives Alamo Bowie had worn on his legs for so many years. Then the sheriff spoke softly.

"Yo're taking it to him, Alamo. We knew it had to come."

"Yeah," and Bowie moved restlessly. "In case I don't come back, Joe. What do you think about Yuma Leslie now?"

"Guilty," the sheriff answered promptly. "Black Bart trained him and sent him up here. Black Bart bought the Circle L with stolen money. He used the spread as headquarters for his rustling operations. Reckon you know the answer!"

"Not sure that I do," Bowie murmured. "Stop and think a spell, Joe. Yuma is only a yearling. Black Bart poisoned his mind and set him up against Buddy. And then we got to think about Mary Jane."

"You mean to tell me——?" the sheriff began.

Alamo Bowie eyed him steadily. "There was Nellie and me," he answered quietly. "She made me the man I am to-day, Joe."

"But you rode on the right side of the law," the sheriff argued. "Yuma Leslie chose the wrong fork of the trail!"

"That's right," Bowie agreed. "But he's done a right smart bit of yore work since you've been laid up, Joe. And don't forget that it was him saved Bonnie."

Joe Grant stirred restlessly. "I'll do my duty as I see it," he muttered stubbornly. "He's part of that outlaw gang!"

"And to-day he killed another one of them," Bowie continued slowly. "You've heard of Bisbee Trent. Trent killed young Jim Golden, and Yuma downed Trent before the smoke had cleared away. Buddy taken Jim back to old John on the J Bar G. Only kin old John had."

"Look, Alamo," the sheriff said slowly. "Them two yearlings ain't no different than you was. Each thinks he is the fastest, and nothing can keep them from finding out which one is best!"

"Something might," Bowie murmured thoughtfully. "Something made me lay aside my guns for ten years."

Joe Grant leaned forward with a frown. "You mean love," he almost sneered. "You sit there and tell me it's all right with you if Mary Jane loves that young outlaw?"

"Love is something you can't change," the grey gun-fighter answered softly. "You know that as well as I do, Joe. Take Buddy and yore gal chip for example. They think a heap of each other."

Sheriff Joe Grant stared down at his hands. "I get what you mean," he muttered. "I kinda like that Leslie boy in spite of his failings. He's fought both sides without giving back a step." Then he jerked upright again. "You said he was coming here to the B Bar G?"

Alamo Bowie nodded. "Buddy made a promise to Nellie, and Jim Golden died to save Leslie. Yuma is coming down so's Buddy won't have to break his word."

"There ain't the flicker of an eye between them two," the sheriff muttered slowly, and groaned because of his helplessness. "I wish I was up on my feet," he barked fretfully.

Alamo Bowie smiled. "I sent Bonnie up the short-cut to talk to Buddy," he told the sheriff quietly. "You couldn't do any more than Bonnie will do, and mebbe not as much."

The sheriff paled. "You sent Bonnie out there with this owl-hoot pack on the loose?" he whispered hoarsely.

Alamo Bowie nodded again. "Most of them are pretty busy right now," he answered dryly. "Torio Feliz is locked up in the barn. He brought me the message from Black Bart. There's only one thing, Joe."

"Yuma Leslie," the sheriff growled.

"That's right. We ought to give the boy a chance."

G

Joe Grant continued to frown and drew a deep breath. "Let's hold our heads a spell and see what comes of it," he suggested finally. "The Circle L is bought with stolen money, and Leslie knows it by this time."

"Dirty money gets clean when it changes hands one time," Bowie murmured. "And you couldn't find the rightful owners of that money nohow. Being sheriff, you could sell the Circle L for what ever you could get when the smoke clears away."

Joe Grant mumbled under his breath. Alamo Bowie hitched up his gunbelt and held out his hand. The sheriff gripped hard and forced a smile on his seamed face.

"Good luck, pard," he said simply. "And don't throw off yore shots!"

Alamo Bowie did not answer. Now his grey eyes were narrowed and cold. He had said what had to be said; had thought of others instead of himself. Black Bart was waiting out there on the river trail. A few minutes more or less would not matter to a man who had waited ten long years.

"Be seeing you, Joe," and the grey gun-fighter walked stiff-legged from the room with the old familiar pain in the fingers of his gunhand. A pain that nothing but a bucking gun could heal.

Chapter XIV

WAITING WILL END

MARY JANE BOWIE was tall for a girl, but her stature was dwarfed by the tall frame of Black Bart. When Torio Feliz had disappeared around a bend in the river trail, he turned to the girl with a grim smile changing his predatory features.

"There's a little clearing back aways where we can be comfortable, and also undisturbed," he began quietly. "Perhaps we can talk some and become better acquainted."

Mary Jane studied his dark face and repressed a shudder. Aside from Alamo Bowie, she had never met so commanding a personality. The outlaw radiated a strange power that influenced every one he contacted. Dominating and sure of himself. Ruthlessly cruel and self-contained.

She offered no resistance when he took her arm and led her up a shelving bank, and guided her to a grassy park screened on three sides by heavy brush growth. Black Bart led her horse; tethered the animal to a sapling close to his own black gelding. Then he returned to the clearing and gestured with his left hand.

"Be seated," and his request was more like a command. "It will be at least two hours before my appointment."

Mary Jane sank down on the grass and rested her back against a log. "Will nothing change this mad plan of yours?" she asked earnestly. "Must you bring trouble to all of us?"

Black Bart smiled and shook his head. "Nothing will change me," he answered softly. "Ten years is a long time to wait, but it will be worth every hour of it."

He leaned forward and stared intently when the girl spoke vigorously. "Did you bring Yuma Leslie up here to the Mimbres Valley?"

"I sent him up here," the outlaw answered coldly. "When I heard that Alamo Bowie was training that brother of yores to carry on for him!"

The girl sighed. "The four of you," she whispered. "Believing in nothing except what you all call . . . Gun Law!"

Black Bart nodded. "Alamo Bowie has lived by it all his life, and so have I," he answered slowly. "It is the only final law we know."

"But Buddy and Yuma are so young," the girl argued desperately. "I remember the night you tried to make them kill each other. But there was something stronger than you that kept them apart."

The outlaw shrugged. "The issue was only postponed," he said carelessly. "Nothing on earth can keep those two yearlings from matching speed."

"Yuma had done well for a boy so young," the girl answered softly, but her carefully-veiled blue eyes were watching the outlaw. "And up here he could settle down and be happy."

"With you?" the outlaw asked softly.

Mary Jane flushed and then raised her blonde head proudly. "Yes, with me," she answered without attempt at evasion. "He is honest down in his heart, and nothing will ever change that part of him."

Black Bart smiled with his eyes and studied her face. "Yuma Leslie had too much money," he said slowly. "And I needed him. I saw to it that his plans would be arranged for him. I don't mind telling you, because now it can make no difference. He killed a man near Yuma, and had to leave there in a hurry."

The girl stared at his cruel face and caught her breath sharply. "You did that to a boy?" she half whispered.

The outlaw nodded. "His father left him a lot of money, but Yuma couldn't touch it until he was of age. Two-three years seems a lifetime to a button, and most of them won't wait for the time to pass. Right-now money in the hand always looks bigger than a fortune he might get later."

"But you said he killed a man?"

"That's right. Yuma Leslie was as wild as a mustang; just as wild as that brother of yores. And when Leslie killed a man I no longer needed, the rest was easy enough."

Mary Jane scarcely breathed. This man talked of death as though it meant nothing to him. Now his dark eyes were glowing with an inner excitement that held her spellbound while he talked. Talked like a man who has kept silent for many years, and seeks some avenue of escape from the repressions and loneliness of himself.

"My money bought the Circle L," he continued quietly. "I needed a place where I could carry out my plans. Leslie thinks he will pay off my notes when he gets his money next month," and he chuckled knowingly. "He won't live that long," he added softly.

"You did this terrible thing?" the girl asked with horror mirrored in her eyes. "To a boy not yet of age?"

Black Bart glanced at her coldly. "Why not?" he sneered. "I have hated Alamo Bowie ever since he refused to meet me more than ten years ago. I knew I could hurt him and his through you and yore brother. Now things have worked out better than I expected. I trained Yuma Leslie, and he came up here just to match guns with yore brother!"

The girl turned her eyes away to avoid the gloating expression on his thin weathered face. She had liked Yuma Leslie since their first meeting. There was something about him that was very much like Buddy and now she realized that he had been used as a pawn in the game Black Bart had devised. A game that was rapidly drawing to a climax, and would be finished before the sun went down.

The outlaw rolled a brownie and watched her lazily through the smoke. Mary Jane was thinking rapidly, trying to find some way out of the trap that threatened to destroy those she loved most. Alamo Bowie, who had fathered her when she and Buddy had been homeless orphans. Buddy, who had been her ideal until Yuma Leslie had entered her life. Yuma Leslie, who had brought something into her life she had never known before.

She remembered the kiss when he had taken his gun in the sheriff's office, and had given her his promise. A soft flush of colour mounted to the line of her blonde hair, and she glanced up to catch the look of understanding on the outlaw's face.

"I don't believe it," she burst out suddenly. "One man cannot do this thing to so many innocent people!"

"But one man has done it," the outlaw contradicted carelessly. "My only difficulty was in getting Alamo Bowie to face me after he made that promise to the Angel of Tombstone. You solved that little difficulty when you became impatient of waiting and decided to take a little ride this afternoon. That's the trouble with yearlings, they just can't wait."

The girl moaned softly and bit her lip. "He will come," she whispered, and then her blue eyes lighted up. "And he will kill you," she finished harshly, and glared into his sneering black eyes.

Black Bart came to his feet and ground the cigarette out under one high heel. Held out his right hand and spoke sharply when the girl stared at his long fingers.

"You are looking at the fastest gun-hand in all the world," he boasted arrogantly. "The hand that will kill Alamo Bowie. The same hand that will kill the survivor when Yuma Leslie and yore brother meet in a little game of draw-and-shoot!"

Mary Jane shrank away from the red gleam in his eyes, and from the savage promise in his deep vibrant voice. She knew that Alamo Bowie would come. Knew that neither Yuma Leslie nor her brother would give back a step. With this human vulture waiting while death lurked in his twisted mind, and looked out through his staring eyes.

"It can't happen," she heard herself saying. "I don't know why, but I feel it deep in my heart!"

Black Bart lowered his hand and laughed softly. "I could have killed Alamo Bowie several times," he almost whispered, and leaned forward until the shrinking girl met his eyes. "But that wouldn't have satisfied me. He claimed he was the fastest, and I knew I was!"

There it was in all its brutality. Gun-fighters' vanity, so often mistaken for pride. The answer could only come through death for one of two men, and each was willing and eager to pay that supreme price. Mary Jane realized then the force that had driven Alamo Bowie along the outlaw trails for so many gun-fighting years. The same force that had motivated all the actions of the mad killer facing her.

"And you laid your plans all these years," she murmured. "I don't understand how you have lived without going entirely mad."

"In prison," Black Bart muttered under his breath, "I practised every day to keep my muscles supple. Money means nothing to me. There never was a man so fast with a hand-gun as myself. There never will be. It is the only thing I have lived for!"

Mary Jane shuddered at the ferocious intensity in his deep voice. She felt the strange dominating power of his nature. Tried to tear her eyes away from his glittering gaze, and the outlaw smiled when she failed.

"My hand aches," he said soberly. "It aches with a pain that nothing can cure until I feel the kick of a gun against my fingers. And every time my gun kicks . . . *a man dies!*"

"I know," the girl heard herself saying. "Alamo feels the same way when someone speaks of a fast gun-fighter. Buddy feels the same way——" and the girl caught her breath sharply and stopped talking.

Black Bart smiled and nodded his head. "Whenever someone mentions Yuma Leslie," he finished for her. "And you are in love with Leslie. He feels the same way whenever he sees your brother!"

"Oh," and the girl moaned softly. "Something will happen to change them both!"

The outlaw shook his head. "Did anything happen to change me?" he asked soberly. "Did falling in love with Nellie Gray change Alamo Bowie?"

"Yes," the girl whispered. "I remember the night he refused to accept your challenge. The same night he made a promise to Mother Nellie. Something changed him that night!"

Black Bart growled under his breath. "You just thought it changed him," he sneered. "Right now that gun-fighting jigger is riding his spurs with the happiness of hell in his heart, Coming down here to bring me show-down, with his fingers twisting and hurting like raw nerves. Hurting so bad that he has no feeling any place else, and those fingers do most of his gun-fighting thinking for him. They never change!"

Mary Jane stared at his hate-distorted face and shuddered violently. She knew that he was right. Nothing could change a gun-fighter who had the salt of powder-smoke in his blood. And Black Bart read her thoughts and smiled mockingly.

"They owe me something," and his voice changed swiftly. "There never has been a woman in my life, but you are different. When the smoke has cleared away——?"

The girl jerked up her head and stared at his cruel face. All the conversation had been impersonal and away from herself. With the ambition of his life about to be satisfied, this human monster was making other plans. Plans to satisfy the other side of his nature.

"When the smoke has cleared away, it won't make any difference to you," she told him coldly. "I *know !*"

His dark face changed with incredible swiftness. "I take what I want," he grated harshly. "And now I find that I want you. Not right now," he added quickly. "Women don't mix with gun business, but it don't lack long until sun-down. After that we shall see."

"We shall see," the girl repeated as from a distance. "We shall see something that Gun Law won't change . . . for you!"

He turned away from her and rapped down for the gun on his long right leg. Drew swiftly and pouched the gleaming weapon without a pause. Several times he repeated the movements while the girl watched with fear clutching at her heart. She had seen Alamo Bowie do the same thing, and there seemed no difference in the speed of their hands.

Black Bart faced away from the sun and rippled his muscles until he was satisfied. Then he walked over to his horse and cut a latigo string from the saddle The girl watched him, scarcely daring to breathe when he came close to her.

"I've talked enough," he murmured softly. "More than I have talked to anyone in ten years. Now I will fasten your hands to this tree while I go down there to keep my promise."

Mary Jane bit her lips and remained silent. There was nothing for her to say. She had seen the same

inscrutable expression in the grey eyes of Alamo Bowie;
the same rugged set to his lean fighting jaw. The thong
drew her bound hands against the smooth trunk of the
tree, after which Black Bart straightened up and studied
her for a long moment.

His eyes rested on her smooth tanned face and dropped
hungrily to the curve of her rounded breasts. Mary
Jane tried to still the fear that made her heart pump
madly, and the outlaw smiled slowly and wet his thin lips.

"He should be here soon," he murmured. "When
the smoke has cleared away——"

He turned on his heel and walked across the clearing
without a backward glance. Tall and straight as a
pine; ruthless as a killing tiger. Then he parted the
brush and disappeared from her sight, and Mary Jane
closed her eyes while her lips moved slowly.

It might have been a prayer, or a softly muttered
wish. Alamo Bowie. Buddy and Yuma Leslie. The
three men she loved, each in a different way. Then
the tremble left her limbs when she opened her eyes
and found herself alone.

Black Bart was smiling when he stepped down into
the trail and continued to the big bend above the river.
The sun was at his back until he rounded the bend,
and he frowned at the advantage it gave him over his
enemy. The frown faded when he completed the
turn and found himself in cool shade. The Code
stipulated an even chance for all.

A big roan horse left the wide valley and swung down
into the river trail. Black Bart leaned forward to stare
intently. No other man he knew sat the saddle like
Alamo Bowie. Shoulders back and head held high. Like
the man-hunter of old, except for the left arm swinging
limply at his side. The long waiting would soon be
over.

The grey gun-fighter was staring straight ahead
and coming up fast. Black Bart could make out the

gleaming six-gun thonged low and toed-in for a fast draw. One gun where Alamo Bowie had formerly carried two. The famous twins.

The outlaw smiled grimly and twitched the handle of his own weapon to make sure against hang. While an eager smile of anticipation brightened his dark face and made his black eyes glitter like stars. Ten years was a long time to wait.

Alamo Bowie rode up to within twenty yards and caught the saddle-horn with his right hand. Swung down without a pause and dropped the reins to the ground. Waited until the roan and wandered into the trail-side brush to graze on the hardy browse. Grey eyes fastened upon the face of the man who had broken the peace of ten happy years.

Ten paces, the Code called for. Automatically he measured the distance with his eyes and stepped forward with stiff-legged stride. While Black Bart watched each move and nodded silent approval. Here was a master; one worthy of his steel. What was ten years compared to such a moment as this?

"I got yore message, Bart," and Alamo Bowie spread his boots for balance. His voice was low and steady; as steady as the right hand that raised slowly to hook into his broad gunbelt.

"Torio," the outlaw said quietly. "What of him?"

"I saved him a killing," Bowie answered in the same slow drawl. "He tried to knife me, and now he has two broken arms."

The black eyes changed swiftly. "He knew I had you marked for my own gun," he grated harshly. "You should have killed the dog!"

Alamo Bowie shook his head slowly. "I don't kill just to be killing," and the outlaw flushed at the reproof. "The Mexican will make a valuable witness when the proper time comes."

Black Bart smiled mockingly. "Against Yuma Leslie?" he murmured.

Alamo Bowie frowned. "You are mad, Bart," he answered sharply. "To do what you did to that boy, and him not man-grown!"

Black Bart raised his heavy brows. "He talk?"

Bowie shook his head. "He didn't have to do any talking. Any range-hand could read the sign. You poisoned his mind for three years, but he turned on you when he found out for sure what you were trying to do to him!"

"Still a lawman at heart, ain't you?" the outlaw taunted. "But I saw to it that Yuma Leslie rode on the other side of the law."

"I know," Bowie muttered. "But you over-played yore hand for one time. The man Yuma Leslie killed was an outlaw with a price on his head. Gun-bait for any man who cut his sign!"

Black Bart stared and thought rapidly. He also could read sign with the best, and he knew that the sheriff had received word from the law in Yuma. In spite of the fact that he, Black Bart, had robbed the stage and had stolen the first letters.

"I own the Circle L," he murmured mockingly. "What does that make Yuma Leslie?"

"It made him a special deputy when he volunteered to drive those rustled B Bar C steers back where they came from," Bowie answered softly.

He twitched the corners of his hard mouth into a smile when thunder swept over the outlaw's dark face. "I'll settle with him for that," Black Bart growled, and then he smiled slowly. "That yearling made a promise a long time ago," he continued. "And him prideful as any gun-hawk on the owl-hoot trail!"

Alamo Bowie stared for a moment. Then: "You mean Buddy?"

"Yeah; yo're Buddy. I told Leslie all about you. Told him that you were training yore chip to hunt down all the living kin of Three-Finger Jack. And then the young whelp falls in love with Mary Jane. It won't do him any good!"

Alamo Bowie leaned forward. "Before I kill you, Bart," he whispered. "Where is the girl?"

Black Bart laughed mockingly. "Waiting for me," he boasted. "In a place where you won't find her, and I've decided that I've lived alone long enough!"

He stiffened at the change which swept over Alamo Bowie. The grey gun-fighter was staring at him with an intensity that wiped the sneering smile from the cruel dark face like wind across high grass. Ridges of muscle framed Bowie's hard mouth and rippled across the livid scar on his jaw. His voice was a rumble of thunder when he spoke through tightly clenched teeth. Gave the go-ahead according to the Code.

"*Make yore pass!*"

Some strange psychological force had changed the balance, and Black Bart knew it. He had taunted with a smile. Alamo Bowie had reached to a steadfast purpose. And having given the signal the outlaw had waited for ten long years, the grey gun-fighter saw no reason to postpone the inevitable.

His right hand plunged down with Black Bart reflecting the move. Only that space of time separated them which marks the difference between a beam of light, and the flash that returns it from a polished mirror. Impossible to measure, but the difference between life . . . and death.

Both guns came out of moulded leather like one weapon. Alamo Bowie thumbed back and slipped the hammer without touching the filed trigger. Black

Bart eared back with fore-finger through the trigger-guard. Again the flash of burning powder was reflected to make the two shots blend with just the trace of an echo, and both men jerked under the impact of battering slugs.

Alamo Bowie's crippled arm flung out like a rag and settled limply against his side. Black Bart swayed forward with a bewildered expression of surprise on his dark face. He tried to bring his gun up again and lost his balance, and Alamo Bowie stared down at the polished boots rattling against the trail to dig little holes.

His right hand came up very slowly and pouched the smoking gun in his holster. His face was grey now to match the colour of his narrowed eyes. He tried to move his boots and found them fastened to the ground, and then he buckled his knees and coiled down like a worn rope. Caught himself momentarily with his right hand before a curtain of darkness sent him down with head resting on his arm.

He did not hear the roar of pounding hooves coming down the trail from the badlands. Hooves that slid to a stop to spill a hatless rider to the grass with gun spiking out from his hand. A tall dark cowboy who hunkered slowly down beside him and felt for a heart-beat with shaking hands.

"Alamo! You ain't dead, feller!"

Yuma Leslie bit his lip hard when he heard his own trembling voice. Shook his shoulders angrily when his heart betrayed him and ached with worry. Worry for the man who had killed his half-brother. Had fathered the tall young gun-fighter, and had sworn to kill every living kin of Three-Finger Jack!

He jerked to his feet and reached to the saddle-bag on his sweating horse. Brought out a flask and poured a few drops of whisky between the clenched teeth. Shook his head when he saw the soaked sleeve on the crippled left arm, and then the grey eyes opened slowly and stared up into his own.

"Alamo! *You* were the fastest!"

Alamo Bowie continued to stare. "Buddy," he whispered weakly. "He didn't take no vow to hunt you down, Yuma. Black Bart lied to make you help out his plans!"

Yuma Leslie jerked back with mouth open. "Is that God's truth?" he asked hoarsely. "On yore honour, Bowie?"

"On my honour," and then the grey eyes closed again while the pale lips moved very slowly. "Find Mary Jane. Somewhere close!"

Yuma Leslie jumped to his feet and stared at the body of Black Bart. Then with eyes to the ground, he backed-tracked the outlaw's steps and around the bend and up through the brush. A broken leaf here and there. A faint heel mark where the ground was soft. Straight to the clearing where he saw the two horses, and then he raced across and fell to his knees beside Mary Jane.

His arms went around her and held her tight, and he kissed her hungrily before he realized that her hands were tied. He fumbled for his stock knife and cut the rawhide while a flush of shame stained his dark face. And when her hands were free, the girl caught him with a little sob and held him close to her breast.

"Yuma," she pleaded. "Alamo?"

"He's alive, honey. He beat Black Bart to the gun!"

For a moment he held her close, and then straightened up to lift the girl to her feet. "He needs us, Mary Jane," and his voice was soft and low, and trembling with anxiety. "He's got to get well, Mary Jane!"

Taking her hand, he drew her across the clearing and

raced down the sloping bank to the river trail. Alamo Bowie was sitting up when they reached him, and he smiled at the girl in spite of his weakness and pain.

"Daddy Bowie! I nearly died when I heard the shot!"

"Shots," he corrected soberly. "We both cleared leather at the same time, but it don't matter. His slug got me in the same place as——"

He broke off suddenly and reached his hand toward Yuma Leslie. "Sorry, son," he murmured softly. "Yo're mother always was a good woman, and yore father was an upright man!"

Yuma Leslie gripped the wounded man's hand and nodded his head. "I know it now," he said slowly. "You think I can get things cleared up since you stopped me from taking the wrong fork of the trail?"

Wistfulness and hope in his husky voice while he stared at Alamo Bowie and waited for the answer. Mary Jane put an arm around his shoulders, and Bowie smiled and nodded his head.

"Sure of it, son," he answered quietly. "That feller you killed over in Yuma was an outlaw wanted in three States. There was a reward offered for him —dead or alive."

Yuma Leslie smiled then and turned to Mary Jane. "Something I wanted to say to you," and then a stricken look leaped to his dark eyes. "Reckon I can't say it now," he whispered.

"Yuma," and the girl tightened her arm on his shoulder. "What is it, Yuma?"

"I made a promise," he murmured, and refused to meet her eyes. "He's got it coming after what he done for me, and I won't——"

Alamo Bowie opened his eyes again. "Buddy," he said strongly. "You mean you promised to give Buddy show-down?"

Yuma Leslie stared straight ahead and refused to answer. Mary Jane locked eyes with Alamo and her lips moved mutely. Alamo Bowie started to speak, and closed his eyes before the words came. Then the cowboy stretched to his feet and pointed to the wounded man.

"We got to get him home right away, Mary Jane. He might bleed out with that arm, and right now nothing else matters!"

Chapter XV

ANOTHER PROMISE

THREE horses walked slowly up the long cottonwood lane and stopped near the porch of the rambling old B Bar G ranch-house. Yuma Leslie was supporting Alamo Bowie in the saddle, and the grey gun-fighter had his chin cradled on his chest. He raised his head when the horses stopped, and Mary Jane was out of the saddle helping him when Nellie ran down the steps.

Together the two women eased the wounded warrior from saddle-leather. Then the strong arms of Nellie Bowie held him upright while she looked deep into his grey eyes. Nodded at what she found there, and her voice was peaceful and soothing when she spoke.

"I was sure of it, Alamo. I knew that one so wicked as Black Bart could not triumph in a good world like this."

"He died like a man," Bowie barely whispered, and tried to keep his eyes open.

"Best to get him inside and call a doctor," Yuma Leslie suggested quietly. "He took a slug in the same arm, Ma'am."

"The doctor is coming now; will be here soon," Nellie Bowie answered, and her brown eyes held to the face of the tall boy who had changed all their lives.

A horse came racing up the lane, and Mary Jane turned swiftly. Sighed with relief when she saw a little grey man with a black satchel across his knees. The doctor nodded curtly and slid to the ground. Ran up the stairs to help with Alamo Bowie, and the two young people found themselves suddenly and silently alone.

Mary Jane crossed over and took Leslie's left hand and pressed it tightly. "Please go now, Yuma," she pleaded. "Before Buddy comes."

He shook his head stubbornly and slid from the saddle. "I can't," he murmured, and turned his face away. "He didn't know it, but Buddy came over to help me. Then Jim Golden was killed by the bullet intended for me. He's a square-shooter, is Buddy Bowie. He had to take care of his pard, and I made him a promise. Told him I would meet him here."

Mary Jane bit her lip and stared behind the big corrals at the mesa trail. Buddy would be coming that way, and then she remembered Bonnie Grant. If the tiny girl had worked as she herself had worked . . . ? With the only power that could change the stubborn hearts of fighting men. Men who had the salt of powder-smoke in their blood.

She knew what it did to them. Alamo Bowie seldom spoke of his past, but Joe Grant had told her of his battles against the lawless when the grey gun-fighter had carried the law for Wells Fargo. Of One-Shot Brady and Sonora Lopez in these same hills. When Alamo Bowie had worn the terrible twins in scabbard leather on his long legs.

Her mind raced back to her mother who had died in San Francisco. She remembered the long trip by train and stage. The day when outlaws had held up the Benson stage to kidnap Buddy and herself. The cold grey eyes of Alamo Bowie just before he had ridden out into the desert to meet Three-Fingered Jack.

Mary Jane caught her breath when Yuma Leslie moved restlessly. He was half-brother to the man

Alamo Bowie had killed that day. Sons of the same mother, and in the cattle country, blood is thick. If she could only get Yuma away before Buddy came down the trail. Again she raised her head and stared out over the barn.

And while she looked, two horses topped the rise and started down the sloping trail. A tall blond cowboy with the setting sun in his blue eyes. A tiny full-figured girl with the afterglow burnishing the copper in her brown curly hair. Riding side by side; silently and without haste.

Mary Jane did not speak when they rounded the horse corral and paced up to the porch. Buddy Bowie swung down stiffly. Fastened his eyes on the face of Yuma Leslie while his right hand moved swiftly to twitch the handle of his gun in careless passage. Measured the distance between himself and Leslie and nodded when he found it right. Ten paces.

Bonnie Grant came to the side of Mary Jane and circled the taller girl with her arm. Neither spoke. The sweethearts of fighting men who had made promises. "They also serve who only stand and wait."

"See you got there, Yuma," Buddy Bowie almost whispered, and his eyes swung to the saddle Alamo Bowie had wet with his blood.

For a moment the colour faded from his cheeks while he studied the gear and read the sign as surely as if he had seen the whole play. He knew Alamo's Snapper horse; knew that the grey gun-fighter had met his enemy and had ridden back home. Blood on Yuma Leslie's wool shirt and right arm, where the dark cowboy had supported the wounded man.

A trickle of blood leading up the steps and into the house. The doctor's horse ground-tied at the rail and lathered with foamy sweat. Mary Jane with an empty holster on the right leg of her Levis. Yuma Leslie waiting to keep the promise he had made.

Mary Jane studied the two faces and felt strangely at peace. The dark eyes of Yuma Leslie were steady and soft, entirely lacking the old glitter that always filled them when he saw Buddy Bowie. The blond cowboy had both big hands down at his sides, and the fingers of his right hand were not moving.

"I came," Yuma Leslie said at last. "What you waiting for?"

"Waiting for you to make the first move," and Buddy Bowie watched the dark face intently. "Call the turn, cowboy!"

Mary Jane opened her lips to speak and then held her breath. Yuma Leslie was making the first move. Walking slowly toward Buddy Bowie with his *right* hand stretched out. Offering his gun-hand to the man he had sworn to kill. To the man who had hated since the first time they had met.

"I can't draw a gun on you, Buddy," he said softly. "And I reckon you couldn't shoot a man who won't go for his gun. I talked to Alamo after he killed Black Bart. He told me the truth, and I remembered what he said several days ago."

Buddy Bowie stared at the hand, but did not offer his own. "What did he say?" he growled.

"Said that sometimes enemies made good friends," Leslie answered softly. "And he told me that Black Bart had made up all those lies. Alamo kept me from being an outlaw," and the cowboy lowered his dark eyes. "And I've been liking you in spite of myself," he finished huskily.

Buddy Bowie raised his head with a smile sweeping across his tanned face. His right hand swung out and smacked loudly against the offered palm of peace. Strong fingers clamped down and gripped tight, and then Buddy Bowie did a strange thing. Heavier than Yuma Leslie, and his left arm circled the broad shoulders with hand thumping the strong straight back.

"Damn yore soul, Yuma," he muttered thickly. "You rode in here and put the Indian sign on this whole outfit. Nellie and Alamo both liked you, not to mention Mary Jane. I kind a liked you myself the way you fought both sides including them rustling outlaws. Proud to touch skin with yuh, pard!"

"*Pard!*"

Yuma Leslie repeated the words with an expression of happiness making his dark face handsome and bright. Up came his arms to grip the man he had been trained to kill. Then he pushed Buddy away and held him at arm's length.

"Go to hell," he growled softly, and smiled like a girl when Buddy started to grin.

His face turned scarlet when he glanced at the porch and saw Nellie Bowie smiling down at him. Went to her when she beckoned, and tried to swallow a lump in his throat when the sweet-faced woman put her arms around him and held him close. Just like she often held Buddy.

"You are welcome here always, Yuma," she said softly. "And I am so happy that you and Buddy are friends. You will both make good friends," she added confidently.

"A man couldn't have a better pard than Buddy Bowie," Yuma said earnestly. "And I don't deserve all this."

"Looks like you do!" Nellie Bowie answered with a smile. "And now the sheriff wants to talk to you —alone!"

Leslie stiffened and glanced at Mary Jane. The girl smiled reassuringly, and Buddy nodded his head. Even little Bonnie Grant put in a word of encouragement.

"He's a square-shooter, Yuma. And he thinks a heap of his friends."

Yuma Leslie straightened his back and walked into

the house. Stopped at the door of the sheriff's room where he shifted his feet until a gruff voice bade him enter. Then he cuffed off his black Stetson and walked stiff-legged to the bed where Joe Grant was propped up against the pillows.

"Sit down, Leslie," the sheriff grunted. "Wanted to have a little talk with you about several things."

"I can think better on my feet," the cowboy muttered. "I'm still on parole, sheriff. Thought mebbe you had forgot."

"Yeah, that's what I wanted to remind you," Joe Grant answered dryly. "Black Bart is dead, Yuma. He had an incurable disease, and it killed him. He might have took the cure if he had started in time, but he was stubborn. Thought mebbe you had it there too for a while, but looks like you recovered."

Yuma Leslie raised his head and stared. "Meaning Buddy?" he asked quietly. "That what yo're getting at, sheriff?"

Joe Grant nodded. "We knew what brought you up here," he answered bluntly. "And we knew that you and Buddy would settle yore troubles sooner or later. You could have shot it out just now, the both of you. Even the women knew that. So we left you yearlings to read the sign and find out the answer for yoreselves."

Yuma Leslie shuffled his boots while his fingers turned the hat in ceaseless circles. "I couldn't gun-fight Buddy," he murmured at last. "Me and him edged at each other all this time, and he wouldn't take advantage. Me and him is pards now, sheriff."

Joe Grant smiled. "That makes you yore own man, son," he answered softly. "I'm releasing you from yore parole."

Yuma Leslie dropped his hat and stared at the Sheriff's weathered face. Then he cleared his throat and began to talk like a small boy. Freely and without repression.

"The Circle L was bought with stolen money, sheriff. I knew it all the time, but I thought I could figger a way out. I've got the money to pay off the notes, but I can't touch it until next month. I'll be of age, then. I like the Circle L layout," and then he shrugged wearily. "Reckon I'll have to let it go now."

"Looks like it will be my job to sell that spread again," the sheriff said carelessly. "It always has been hide-out country for rustlers; always will be until we get an honest man up there to connect with the J Bar G, and the B Bar G range. Course I know we can't get what Black Bart paid for it, because none of the ranchers will take it at any price."

Yuma Leslie dropped his shoulders and sat down on the edge of the bed. "Some feller will get a good buy," he muttered. "Reckon I'll be going now, sheriff. Thanking you for what you done for me."

"I figger forty thousand would be about right for the Circle L," the sheriff continued, as though he had not heard the interruption. "You reckon you could raise that much cash inside of ninety days, Yuma?"

Yuma Leslie jerked up and turned to stare at the sheriff's sober face. "You hoorawing me, Joe?" he whispered. "You hazing me just because I'm young and ain't rightly rubbed the velvet off my horns?"

Joe Grant shook his head slowly. "The court will sell at the appraised value," he answered earnestly. "That means forty per cent. of its value. The Circle L is yores for forty thousand cash if you want it."

Yuma Leslie choked up and turned his face away. He could take harsh words and abuse, and he could face blazing guns without a tremor. Silence in the room for a long time while he fought back the weakness that unmanned him, and his mind raced to catalogue the friends he had made in the Mimbres Valley.

Mary Jane and Little Bonnie. Alamo Bowie and Nellie. Even Buddy had called him pard, and now the sheriff exonerated him. Had offered him a chance to start life all over again with a going outfit, among neighbours who wanted him to stay.

"I've got the money my father left me, sheriff," and his voice was low and shaky. Then he gulped and cleared his throat. "Dammit, Mister," he growled hoarsely. "Can't you cuss a hand out for a change? You keep this up and I'm going to bust out crying!"

Joe Grant grinned and reached out his hand. "The cussin' comes with friendship, Yuma," he answered quietly. "First I want to thank you for saving my little gal, and after that mebbe so I can give you what you asked for."

His deep voice changed suddenly when the cowboy gripped his extended hand. For a long straight minute he swore heartily and with sincere pleasure. Cursed Yuma Leslie for his faults and virtues alike, with a laugh in his voice, and a bright twinkle in his blue eyes. And the Circle L owner stopped trembling and returned both the smile and the cussing until a soft voice called from the open door.

"Such language," Nellie Bowie scolded. "You both ought to be ashamed of yourselves for swearing like that at each other."

Yuma Leslie turned his back and refused to meet her eyes. She winked at the sheriff and came close to put her arms around the dark cowboy. Turned him slowly and kissed him on the cheek, and Yuma flushed and closed his eyes.

"It's all right, son," she told him softly. "Mary Jane told me the good news, and I saw her waiting out there in the horse barn. You better go to her before she takes a notion to go riding alone like she did before."

Yuma Leslie put on his hat and cuffed it cowboy fashion over his dark eyes. Squared his shoulders and started for the barn without speaking. Stopped when he saw Mary Jane waiting by the hay-mow. Then he moved swiftly and circled her with his strong young arms. Came right to the point with the directness of cattle country and its people.

"Reckon I can talk now, honey," and his deep voice vibrated like a distant bell. "I love you, Mary Jane. Loved you the first minute I saw you back there in Deming when the sheriff introduced us."

Mary Jane rested her blonde head against his chest and sighed happily. "Me, too," she whispered. "Please keep on talking, Yuma."

"I ain't much on the talk," he murmured. "I reckon you know most of the things I'd like to say if I was a good talker."

"You talk the kind of language I understand," the girl whispered proudly. "All of us up here are just cow-folks, and that's good enough for me."

"I just now bought the Circle L with my own money," he blurted boyishly. "And I'll be twenty-one next month. I got to thinking that mebbe my birthday would be a right good time, Mary Jane. I'm asking you to marry me and be the Big Augur on the old Circle L!"

Mary Jane began to tremble. He had said it at last. Her arms circled his neck and pulled his head down where she could reach it. Blue eyes wide and clear when she kissed him and nodded slowly.

"Three weeks is a long time to wait, Yuma," she whispered, and then she hid her face. "It sounds wonderful to me. Mrs. Yuma Leslie!"

Yuma Leslie tightened his arms and closed his eyes while the wonder of life dulled his senses and drugged him with happiness. His head jerked up suddenly when

voices came from behind the barn toward the mesa
trail. He could see Buddy head and shoulders above
the window sill. Bonnie's voice came softly through
the twilight, but the girl was hidden from sight. Yuma
shook Mary Jane gently for silence.

"You were wonderful, Buddy," Bonnie Grant said
softly. "My heart stood still when we first met Yuma.
I knew how fast you both were, and I knew that Yuma
would not draw against you. And then you read the
same thing in his face."

"I ain't never knowed Alamo or Nellie to read a
sign wrong," Buddy Bowie answered soberly. "Then
Yuma risked his life to save you, and all the time he
was working for the law to stop them rustlers. Reckon
I kinda liked him all the time. Only thing that came
between us was this here Gun Law. Now me and him
can do our fighting together. He's one of the squarest
gents I ever met!"

"I could see it in their faces," Bonnie whispered
softly. "When they looked at each other. It means
a wedding, Buddy."

Buddy's head disappeared below the window, but
his deep young voice came clearly through the shadows.
"You and me, Bonnie. I never told you before, but
I reckon we both knew it. Some day you and me
will do the same."

"Buddy," the tiny girl gasped. "You mean
you——?"

"Shore I do," Buddy growled. "Been loving you
now for a long time ever since you grew up. Must
be all of a year at the outside."

Silence for a moment. Then: "But we can wait,
Buddy," Bonnie whispered, but somehow her tone
was doubtful.

"Reckon we can, Little Bit," Buddy answered gruffly
"Only it's going to be a long time until you are eighteen."

"Six months," and now Bonnie's voice was happier. "Let's make it on my birthday!"

Yuma Leslie placed a finger on his lips and guided Mary Jane slowly across the barn. Back to the big house where the lamps were now burning. Through the front room to a door where voices were talking loudly. Nellie Bowie was standing at the foot of the bed where Alamo Bowie was propped against pillows arguing with the doctor.

"That arm ought to come off, Bowie," the doctor said bluntly. "I'll make arrangements at the hospital right away."

"You will play hell," the grey gun-fighter answered coldly. "I kept it before, and I'm keeping it now!"

Yuma Leslie pushed into the room and dropped a brown hand down to his gun. Cleared his throat until the doctor turned to face him.

"Alamo said not to bother," the cowboy rapped out. "And what Alamo says goes!"

The doctor stared at the gun-handle and rose to his feet. "Looks like," he grunted. "He will probably live in spite of all the laws of nature. And he won't ever be anything but a gun-fighter until he comes to the end of the trail!"

Alamo Bowie smiled when the little man walked huffily from the room with his black bag. Mary Jane sat down on the bed and took his hand, and Nellie Bowie came close to Yuma Leslie and put her arm around his lean waist.

"We have something to tell you and mother," Mary Jane began nervously, and glanced at Yuma for support.

"Yeah?" and Alamo Bowie winked at his wife. "You set the date yet?"

The girl turned to him with wonder in her blue eyes. "Who told you?" she whispered.

"Being an old hand that away, I just read the sign," and Alamo Bowie patted her hand affectionately. "Nellie and me are wishing you both as much happiness as we have had. You won't need any more."

Yuma Leslie squared his shoulders manfully. "Wanted to tell you and Mother Nellie before I married Mary Jane," he began slowly. "I knew Black Bart was a killer. He told me that you had sworn to kill every kin of Three-Finger Jack's. Said you was training Buddy to out-speed me, and I was fool enough to believe him."

"I know, son," Bowie murmured soberly. "I knew it when you and Buddy ruffled yore hackles at each other that day down in the saloon."

The cowboy flushed with shame. "I don't drink as a rule," he murmured. "But that day when you told me I couldn't come here to the B Bar G. Nothing seemed to matter much, and I went in there and tried to forget. I haven't had a drink since."

Alamo Bowie nodded. "I understand, feller," he answered slowly. "I've done the same thing many's the time. And I've been watching you close ever since."

"The Circle L was bought with stolen money," and Yuma Leslie stared down at his boots. "I knew that, too, but I figgered on paying off the notes when I got my own money. It wouldn't have mattered much if Buddy had called my hand."

"She'd have been a draw, Yuma," Alamo Bowie said gravely. "The both of you would have stopped doing what you was doing!"

"But now Buddy and me is pards," Yuma Leslie murmured, and his brown eyes were soft when he smiled.

"You see the sheriff?" Bowie asked carelessly.

Yuma Leslie looked up quickly. "I don't deserve it," he whispered huskily. "Joe Grant sold me the Circle L as it is for forty thousand. Gave me ninety days to raise the cash, and my birthday comes next month."

Nellie Bowie tightened her arm around him. "So you and our little girl have decided to get married on your birthday," she told him with a smile.

"Dog-gone," and the tall cowboy shook his head. "A feller don't dare to even think around this outfit. How'd you know?"

"I taught Nellie to read sign with the best," Alamo chuckled. Then he stared at the gun on Leslie's leg and squeezed Mary Jane's hand. "Better make him promise," he suggested.

Mary Jane nodded gravely and stood up. "What was good enough for Alamo and Nellie is good enough for me," she said soberly. "Will you promise never to use your gun again, Yuma? Unless somebody brings trouble to you?"

"I promise," the cowboy answered clearly. "Unless someone brings trouble . . . to us!"

Alamo Bowie nodded slowly and spoke softly. He said: "That's Gun Law!"

THE END

Charles M. Martin was born in Cincinnati, Ohio. In 1910 he worked for the California Land and Cattle Company. In 1915 he fought in Mexico as a mercenary soldier on the side of Pancho Villa. Later he worked on cattle ranches in various parts of the American West, sold paint products in Japan and China, was briefly a cowboy singer in vaudeville, and was a rodeo announcer in such places as Madison Square Garden in New York City and the Cow Palace in San Francisco. He began writing Western stories for pulp magazines in the early 1930s and continued to do so until the 1950s, something that in terms of his authentic background he was certainly capable of doing with a degree of verisimilitude. He published his first novel in 1936, *Left-Handed Law*, and followed it with *Law for Tombstone* (Greenberg, 1937). These novels introduced his character, Alamo Bowie, a Wells Fargo trouble-shooter and gunfighter. The character appealed to movie cowboy, Buck Jones, and both novels were made into motion pictures by Buck Jones Productions, *Left-handed Law* (Universal, 1937) and *Law for Tombstone* (Universal, 1937), with Buck Jones as Alamo Bowie. Martin was personally a brawling, hard-drinking individualist after the fashion of many of his fictional heroes. He carried on feuds with magazine and book editors as well as other writers. He worked so hard at his writing—at one time producing a million words a year for the magazine market—that on at least one occasion he suffered a nervous breakdown. In 1937 he began signing his name as Chuck Martin. He believed so passionately in the characters he was writing about that in the back yard of his home in southern California he created a graveyard for those who had died in his stories and by 1950 there were over 2,000 headstones in this private boothill. His stories always display great energy and continue to be read with pleasure for their adept pacing and colorful characters.

2. 12. 18